LAST STAND

Romeo shouted, "Sergeant, they're right here! Twenty meters!"

Small-arms fire pinged off the frontal armor as Neech strained to see anything in the GPS.

A head popped up from behind a fallen and snow-covered tree. Neech raked the tree with fire, caught the guy in the head, watched him jerk back, die.

"More, more, more!" yelled Romeo, wrenching his gun off to the far left and releasing another burst. "They're flanking us, Sergeant!"

Neech swung his turret around to spot another squad shuffling toward a stand of trees. He blanketed the area with fire while Romeo jammed down his own triggers.

"Troops to the front!" cried Choi from the driver's hole. "Troops to the front!"

Neech moved the turret once more to lay down some fire on the troops advancing ahead.

"Sergeant, we can't hold for much longer," Romeo warned.

"Yes we can," grunted Neech. "YES WE CAN!" And with that, he opened fire again, intent upon killing everything in sight . . .

ARMORED
CORPS

ENGAGE AND
DESTROY

PETE CALLAHAN

J
JOVE BOOKS, NEW YORK

THE BERKLEY PUBLISHING GROUP
Published by the Penguin Group
Penguin Group (USA) Inc.
375 Hudson Street, New York, New York 10014, USA
Penguin Group (Canada), 90 Eglinton Avenue East, Suite 700, Toronto, Ontario M4P 2Y3, Canada
(a division of Pearson Penguin Canada Inc.)
Penguin Books Ltd., 80 Strand, London WC2R 0RL, England
Penguin Group Ireland, 25 St. Stephen's Green, Dublin 2, Ireland (a division of Penguin Books Ltd.)
Penguin Group (Australia), 250 Camberwell Road, Camberwell, Victoria 3124, Australia
(a division of Pearson Australia Group Pty. Ltd.)
Penguin Books India Pvt. Ltd., 11 Community Centre, Panchsheel Park, New Delhi—110 017, India
Penguin Group (NZ), Cnr. Airborne and Rosedale Roads, Albany, Auckland 1310, New Zealand
(a division of Pearson New Zealand Ltd.)
Penguin Books (South Africa) (Pty.) Ltd., 24 Sturdee Avenue, Rosebank, Johannesburg 2196,
South Africa

Penguin Books Ltd., Registered Offices: 80 Strand, London WC2R 0RL, England

This is a work of fiction. Names, characters, places, and incidents either are the product of the author's imagination or are used fictitiously, and any resemblance to actual persons, living or dead, business establishments, events, or locales is entirely coincidental.

ARMORED CORPS: ENGAGE AND DESTROY

A Jove Book / published by arrangement with the author.

PRINTING HISTORY
Jove mass-market edition / October 2005

Copyright © 2005 by The Berkley Publishing Group.
Text design by Kristin del Rosario.

ISBN: 0-515-14016-3

JOVE®
Jove Books are published by The Berkley Publishing Group,
a division of Penguin Group (USA) Inc.,
375 Hudson Street, New York, New York 10014.
JOVE is a registered trademarks of Penguin Group (USA) Inc.
The "J" design is a trademark belonging to Penguin Group (USA) Inc.

PRINTED IN THE UNITED STATES OF AMERICA

10 9 8 7 6 5 4 3 2 1

ACKNOWLEDGMENTS

Major Mark Aitken played a key role in the development of this novel, and, in particular, helped me create the opening battle scene. Mark's expertise, willingness to read and design maps, and his uncanny ability to anticipate my questions were invaluable assets during the composing process. I'm honored to call him my friend.

Major William R. Reeves read and critiqued my chapters; spent many hours helping me to develop, describe, and map out the defensive operations on urban terrain; and provided his vast experience regarding mechanized infantry and fire support. Will taught me some incredible lessons in areas too many to list here, and I am deeply indebted to him for his extensive contributions to this book.

Shawn T. O. Priest, AKA "Black Six" (I'm known to him as "Bubba Six" since I reside in the South), once again read my outline and every chapter, advised me on technical aspects, and served as the primary inspiration for the climax of this novel. I knew I was doing well when he'd write: "All targets serviced with first-round kills! Standing by!"

Lieutenant Colonel Jack Sherman, AR, USAR, Operations Officer 5th Joint Task Force, once again read and commented upon the entire book. He kept me honest regarding military information processing and the psychological effects of war on the average soldier. He also mailed me a

Meal Ready to Eat so I could accurately describe the "cuisine" of the battlefield. His insights, great sense of humor, and incredible turnaround time helped me through some very long writing days.

Major Phil Corbo, CFC, C1 Plans Officer, Korea, is known by many who serve or served with him as an expert on both military operations in Korea and on fine cigars. I can attest to the former with great authority. Phil worked with me from outline to final draft, and his time, inspiration, ideas, and suggestions for revision are deeply appreciated.

Major Craig Walker, USAF, provided me with a plethora of information regarding Close Air Support in Korea. He answered many questions, made valuable contributions to my outline, and encouraged me to more closely consider the sky above my fictional battlefield.

Major Vince Carag reviewed my outline, offered detailed suggestions, and even proposed ideas for future missions. His enthusiasm and support are representative of all those who've worked tirelessly with me.

These folks offered technical assistance or helped me reach those who could:

Captain Keith W. Wilson
Lieutenant Colonel Tom O'Sullivan, US Army (Ret.)
Major Jeffery Price, S3, Support Squadron, 2ACR
Lieutenant Colonel Steven A. Boylan, Public Affairs, 8th
 US Army, Korea
Bruce E. Zielsdorf, dir., Army Public Affairs, NY Branch
Charlotte Bourgeois, managing editor, *Armor* magazine
David Manning, editor, *Armor* magazine.
Joseph S. Bermudez Jr., author of *Shield of the Great
 Leader, the Armed Forces of North Korea*
Nathaniel T. Robertson, regimental historian, 185th
 Armor Regiment, California Army National Guard

The listing of these individuals is my humble way to say thank you. None of them were paid. The fact that their names appear here does not constitute an "official" endorsement of this book by them or the United States Army.

CHAPTER
ONE

SECOND LIEUTENANT JACK Hansen felt a chill coil up his spine. Something was about to happen.

Something did.

Thirteen hundred meters ahead of his M1A1 Main Battle Tank flashes of light woke in twin rows beneath the bridge and cast fiery reflections over the river's still surface. The actual sound of the detonation didn't reach him for another four seconds, creating an eerie delay between his eyes and ears. "There it goes," he gasped.

"Would y'all look at that," sang Private First Class Victor Deacon from the loader's station, his North Carolina drawl turning somber as dozens of people began losing their lives.

"I'm looking at it, Deac," muttered Specialist Rick Gatch from the driver's station. "And I can't believe what I'm seeing."

Hansen sighed, shook his head, then glanced once more at the emerald images glowing in his tank commander's extension.

At approximately nine PM local time, a long train of vehicles carrying displaced persons had been crossing the ice-covered bridge over the Hantan River, a tributary of the larger Imjin River. The DPs had been heading south toward the South Korean town of Tongduch'on, better known as TDC. A stalled vehicle had caused traffic to slow, and little Daewoo cars, pickup trucks, and a few motorcycles had begun veering from their lanes.

Two seconds later, the cars, trucks, and bikes were plunging into the frigid water, along with massive stretches of asphalt and concrete that crumbled like saltines and sent six-foot-high breakers swelling in all directions.

Sitting warm and tight inside the turret, Hansen shuddered as he thought of those men, women, and children who had either died on impact, had drowned, or were now swimming toward the shoreline, soon to become victims of hypothermia. Still, lurking among those civilians were elements of a North Korean recon force, disguised as civilians so they could report back to their approaching 8th Infantry Division. Those enemy soldiers were equipped with small arms, RPGs, and maybe even shoulder-launched antitank missiles that could surely wreak havoc upon the defending American and Republic of Korea forces.

ROK officers had no doubt made the call, exactly as they had during the first Korean War when they had blown bridges across the river while ROK citizens were still on them. The problem was, this time representatives of the liberal international media were present and beaming live images across the world. Those reporters were immediately speculating that American military officers were responsible for sacrificing those civilians because, as Hansen understood it, America got blamed for everything—well, nearly everything. They may have instigated the war, but they had not started it.

Two days prior, the North Korean People's Army (NKPA) had launched a massive ground invasion during a

Christmas Eve blizzard. They had exploited the weather and the holiday by attacking swiftly and audaciously, breaching the DMZ along all three templated approaches. Hansen and the men of the Second Infantry Division, 1st Battalion, 72nd Armor, "First Tank"—the most forward deployed US armor unit in all of Korea—had shown their mettle by destroying a reinforced mechanized brigade that had been breaching a minefield and pushing south through the defile. However, a single victory still meant no rest for the weary. The war had just begun.

"Moving PCs," announced Sergeant Lee Yong Sung, Hansen's gunner. Though a Korean augmentee to the United States Army or KATUSA, Lee had grown quite comfortable in the unit and had earned the crew's utmost respect. Deac and Gatch liked to boast that Sergeant Lee had nerves made from the same depleted uranium armor that covered the tank and formed the sabot penetrators in the main-gun ammunition.

With the gunner's announcement still echoing in his ears, Hansen confirmed that the tracked infantry vehicles, BMPs to be precise, were rolling south, following a snow-covered route lying parallel to the road. "Near one first!" he ordered Lee.

With his gaze locked on his gunner's primary sight, and his hands firmly gripping his gunner's power control handle, Lee switched from 3X to 10X magnification and yelled, "Identified!"

Deac threw up the main gun's arming lever, sat in his loader's seat, clear of the path of recoil, and shouted, "Up!"

"Fire!" Hansen cried.

"On the way," answered Lee, squeezing the triggers on his control handle and sending a HEAT round hurtling toward the vehicle as the round's aft cap clanged across the turret floor.

A heartbeat later, an explosion enveloped the BMP,

balls of fire expanding in a slow-moving ballet of death as secondary explosions rose through the first like flaming curtains drawn to reveal the show. Surely none of the three crew members or eight infantrymen on board had survived.

"Target!" announced Hansen.

"Killed his ass!" cried Deac.

"Hooah!" added Gatch.

"Far BMP!" Hansen yelled over them.

Lee's response came a half second later: "Identified."

"Up," said Deac, arming the gun once more and slamming back into his seat.

Hansen's gaze narrowed on the target. "Fire!"

"On the way!"

The tank rocked back as the main gun spat a second HEAT round that thundered across the mountains and ripped through the wind. True, it was a little late to be exchanging holiday "gifts" with the North Koreans, but as Hansen's mother—and his instructors at Fort Knox had taught him—it is always better to give than receive.

That crew of the far BMP unknowingly accepted their present of fire and death, their vehicle heaving as the round struck, the fuel tank exploded, and fiery ribbons unfurled.

"Target!"

"Target is right," boomed Gatch. "Where are the rest of you assholes? You want a piece of us? Come on!"

Abbot, Neech, and Keyman, the other three tank commanders in Hansen's charge, had monitored his kill, but he still needed to report back to the CO, who was positioned well behind their battle position. Hansen grabbed the microphone and got on the company net. "Black Six, this is Red One, engaged and destroyed two BMPs, over."

Charlie Company's CO, Captain Mitchell Van Buren, responded, "This is Black Six, roger, engage and report, out."

That was the CO's habitual response to engagement reports, and that response always carried with it a reassuring tone and the implicit reminder to fight the battle first and report second. At the same time, First Lieutenant Randy Chase, the company XO, monitored the report and repeated it up to the battalion's Tactical Operations Center so that the S2 intelligence officer could update his "kill board," add the report to his running intelligence assessment, and further analyze the enemy commander's battle plan. Those BMPs were clearly part of divisional reconnaissance assets attempting to locate the US defensive belt.

During the OPORD with Captain Van Buren, Hansen had been told that because of the limited terrain, the enemy was only able to mass one battalion at a time, and they would be approaching the bridge in march formation, with supporting artillery moving up from behind. Hansen and his platoon, along with the rest of Task Forces 1-72 and 2-9, were conducting a defense in sector in order to destroy the enemy before he could cross the river and move down into TDC. In order to accomplish the mission and give the commander more flexibility on the battlefield, the 1-72 AR and the infantrymen nicknamed the "Manchus" of 2-9 IN (M) had formed two task forces. First Tank's Alpha and Bravo Companies had been sent to the Manchus, while the mechanized infantry's Alpha and Bravo Companies had been sent to First Tank.

The task forces had been further organized into company teams by cross-attaching platoons. Charlie Company sent Blue or 3rd Platoon, led by Hansen's former roommate, Second Lieutenant Gary Gutterson, to the Manchus' Alpha Company, while Charlie received 3rd Platoon (M), or Renegade Platoon, from the same company. This mechanized infantry platoon consisted of two squads of infantrymen and four Bradley Fighting Vehicles, all led by First Lieutenant James Ryback. Hansen had met Ryback during their first mission to defend the defile, and according to Gutterson, who had worked more closely with the man, Ryback was an outstanding officer who recognized the complexities and challenges associated with operating as a company team.

With armor and mechanized infantry working together, the enemy was in for one hell of a fight. However, those forces weren't the only ones in the NKPA's way. During their breach of the demilitarized zone between the countries, the North Koreans had relied upon the blizzard to keep US and ROK air support at bay, and while another front was approaching, during the past two days the skies had been clear, and the USAF, along with 2 ID's artillery, had been—in the words of 2 ID's leadership—"pounding the shit out of them with monotonous regularity."

Additionally, every time the NK artillery fired, the US and ROK network of Q-36 and Q-37 counterfire radars instantly pinpointed the artillery firing locations and either responded with massed MLRS fires or vectored ROK and US attack planes to the location to destroy the artillery before they could displace and hide in underground facilities or hardened artillery sites. The ROK and US counterfire team had practiced the scenario for years and were the fastest and most effective counterfire force in the world.

In the meantime, A-10 Warthogs and F-16 Fighting Falcons from the 51st Fighter Wing operating out of Osan flew multiple sorties, while more F-16s from the 8th Fighter Wing out of Kunsan joined the fight. The A-10s had been raging on the NKPA forces and serving as the primary Close Air Support platform, while the F-16s had been focusing on interdiction.

There were also other air assets close to Korea that were joining the party: F-15Cs from the island of Okinawa were flying counter air missions; F-16CJs (Block 50 HARM shooters) based at Misawa, Japan, were flying Suppression of Enemy Air Defenses missions; and F-15Cs, F-16s, and A-10s in Alaska were already en route to Korea and Japan. Additionally, B-2 bombers might begin flying missions against targets such as North Korean leadership and command and control. Each B-2 carried sixteen GBU-31 JDAMs, which were 2,000-pound GPS-guided bombs, or eighty GBU-30 JDAMs, which were 500-pound GPS-guided bombs. Within twenty-four hours just four B-2s could strike nearly three hundred and sixty targets, weather notwithstanding.

Rotary wing air support came from the 2 ID's Aviation Brigade, which provided the AH-64D Apache and the OH-58D Kiowa Warrior light helicopters, as well as from the 6th Cavalry Brigade, which offered more Apaches. Those pilots lived to destroy tanks and other armored formations and were eager to start firing some Hellfire missiles downrange.

And thanks to all those flyboys, the NKPA's 8th Infantry Division had already suffered 40 percent attrition. So many aircraft and so much artillery fire crisscrossed the sky above the approach to TDC that it was hard to imagine anyone co-ordinating all that traffic and deadly fire.

Oddly enough, part of Hansen hoped that the next storm front would arrive sooner because those flyboys were robbing him of more kills. Admittedly, they were doing a highly efficient job, but they could not decisively conduct certain tactical tasks such as fix, block, raid, seize, isolate, clear, and contain the way armor and mechanized infantry could.

Leaning back from his extension, Hansen rubbed his weary eyes and wondered about his girlfriend Karen. Had Staff Sergeant Owens picked her up and delivered her to the field house on Camp Casey? If all had gone as planned, one of the platoons from the 2nd Military Police Company would be escorting her and the other military dependents to Yongsan Garrison in Seoul, so they could be further evacuated to Daegu by an escort from one of the 8th MP Brigade Units. It was usually a four-hour drive from Seoul to Daegu, where they would reach Camp Walker or Henry. However, if the road became jammed with civilians or driving conditions became more treacherous than they already were, who knew how long it would take. He had tried repeatedly to call her on his cell phone, but he couldn't get through. The network was overloaded, and even text messages were temporarily unavailable.

The more Hansen thought about her, the more he ached. Ms. Karen Berlin, a petite brunette about his age, had worked at the American Language Institute, where she had taught English to Koreans in the travel and tourism industries. Although her contract was about to expire, she had decided to stay in Korea as long as he was there. She had chosen him over going back home. In fact, she had said that being with him was home. And that night, they had shared a perfect Christmas Eve. Sure, they had known each other for only three months, but Hansen was already seeing a future with her.

What future now? he thought grimly. He was torn between wanting to fight his war—which excited the hell out of him—and wanting to be with her.

Maybe it was Murphy's Law, but it seemed he couldn't have it both ways. He could only hope that she had made it out and was waiting for him. And he prayed he would make it home to her. That was all he could do. That . . . and feel guilty for falling in love, for luring her into a military life that would test their relationship in ways he could not even imagine.

Didn't she deserve better? Was there some way he could rationalize his leaving the service for her? Could he live with himself if he sacrificed his career? Still, Karen was a big girl and had made her own decision. She had sounded very sure of herself, and maybe . . . like him . . . was in love.

SERGEANT CLARK WEBBER had the dry heaves as he watched the civilians flailing in the water begin to grow still, their once warm bodies turning cold in his thermal sight. How cruel it was for such fantastic technology to show him people dying in such grim detail. It was also remarkable how quickly they froze, since water cooled the body something like five hundred times faster than air.

He leaned back from his primary sight and pursed his lips. Corporal Segwon "Smiley" Kim shifted in his loader's seat and raised his brows. "You okay, Webber?"

Webber glanced up to the tank commander's station, where Keyman was leaning into his extension, scanning intently for targets. With the coast clear, Webber shook his head, revealing the truth.

"What's wrong? You sick again?" Smiley offered him an empty MRE pouch in which to puke.

Putting a finger to his lips, Webber shivered and resumed his gaze through his sight.

During their last battle, his nerves had reached his stomach. And the contents of his stomach had found the turret floor. Yes, he had been drinking at the Christmas party, but that had nothing to do with it.

Before the war, Webber's life in the army had been a game whose rules could be bent, broken, reshaped, rewritten, and broken again. He had been a loan shark extraordinaire, a man who knew exactly how to exploit a young soldier's thirst for liquor and women. He had turned his secretive business into a highly profitable enterprise. And his success further supported the notion that Army life was just one big pastime filled with desperate people who could be played.

Then reality had trampled across his game board with the force of 100,000 NKPA infantrymen.

Death was all around him now, hanging in the air and on his breath. Maybe they had already died and just didn't know it yet. They were a ghost crew, sitting inside a tank and fighting a war across the hills and valleys of purgatory.

Could he be certain they weren't? Maybe God was punishing him for ripping off all of those guys and for not having a conscience.

To ease his fears, Webber had tried cutting a deal with the brigade commander in the sky, but since then he had begun to doubt he would get any help. God was still pissed.

So now he was on his own, back in the field with the crazed Staff Sergeant Timothy Key, the "Keyman" who had no keys, no answers, no desire to help Webber overcome this fucked-up feeling, this scary, jittery thing inside. That bald demon sat in his seat, chewing tobacco and thinking of ways to undermine Hansen's authority and illustrate to the CO that the lieutenant was incapable of leading Red Platoon. Yes, that was a full-time diversion for Keyman, who suffered from all kinds of psychological shit dumped on him by his father, an idiot who had always favored Keyman's brother over him. Before Hansen had come along, Keyman was regarded by all as the best tanker in Charlie Company, and he usually won the battalion's Top Tank honor during gunnery. Hansen had robbed him of that, the same way Keyman's brother had stolen all the glory and all of their father's love. And now Keyman, a fucked-up little boy in a Nomex combat vehicle crewman's uniform, was on a mission to ruin the young lieutenant from West Point.

The whole situation only added to Webber's nausea. All he wanted to do was find a nice, warm rack and go to sleep for, say, a few months, until all the bullshit blew over and North Korea had been leveled into a parking lot for a South Korean Wal-Mart.

"I want to shoot at something, God damn it," Keyman hollered. "Webber, can you find me a target or what?"

"I got nothing. No engineers. No recon. No joy. I think that maybe—"

"I don't care what you think, Sergeant. I care about what you see. And you ain't showing me the money, so show me a fucking target!"

Webber turned to Smiley, rolled his eyes, then went back to scanning. More dry heaves. More nerves.

"There's a guy running along the shoreline. Would you like to shove a HEAT round up his ass?" Webber asked in a half whisper.

Keyman booted Webber in the back of his CVC helmet. "Hey, Sergeant?" The TC leaned down from his station, widened his serial killer eyes, and spoke slowly, deliberately. "In two seconds I'm going to send you out there, armed with a fucking toothpick, do you understand?"

Webber sat there, suddenly winded.

"Are you listening to me?" Keyman demanded.

He breathed, but the air just wouldn't come.

"Sergeant Webber!"

The world grew dark around the edges, and a wave of dizziness passed through Webber before he looked up, realized he could breathe again. "Yeah, Key, whatever."

"Find me a target!"

STAFF SERGEANT RICHARD "Neech" Nelson wouldn't let them clean the blood stains from the inside of his turret. Neech's gunner, Sergeant Romeo Rodriguez, and his loader, Private First Class "Popeye" Choi Sang-ku, had not agreed with his decision.

Neech didn't give a shit.

That blood had come from Private First Class William Wayne, the nineteen-year-old kid who had driven the tank, the kid they had nicknamed "Batman," the kid whose mother was on her knees and crying her eyes out.

After they had thrown a track, Neech had dismounted, moved away from the tank, and gotten himself shot in the leg. Ignoring the danger to himself, Batman had darted across the snow and had carried Neech to cover. In doing so, the private had taken a bullet, one most definitely meant for Neech.

"Sarge? Sorry about getting high-centered. Sorry about throwing the track."

"Aw, shit. Don't worry about—"

Batman had died before Neech could finish his sentence. Now he wished he could tell the kid, "Thank you. Thank you for giving me my life . . ."

Neech dug fingernails into his palms and fought against the prickling feeling behind his eyes and the bridge of his nose. He was supposed to be scanning for targets since Romeo was now acting loader and Choi had become the tank's driver.

But what Neech really wanted to do was dismount, run across the snow, grab one of those fucking recon bastards in civilian clothes, and strangle the bastard right there. He wanted to feel that man's flesh in his fingers, listen to the gurgling sounds coming from his throat, hear the bones in his neck breaking, smell his last putrid breath. And then he would draw his knife and tap into some of that American Indian ancestry that coursed through his veins. He wanted to draw blood so badly that he was almost willing to cut himself.

They had told him that dealing with the loss of a crew member was always hard, but like everyone else, Neech had never thought it would happen to him. Not in a million years. In fact, war itself had never been a possibility in his little reality. He was a man who had joined the Army as a weight-loss program. And while he had become a dedicated tanker, his heart had always been elsewhere. Because of that, he had become vulnerable to what was happening. He knew it. He knew he had allowed the pain to seep inside—something you weren't supposed to do. If he were a real tanker, he would have suppressed Batman's loss and moved on. Years later, after he was discharged, he would make some therapist rich by finally dealing with the issue. Fact: you couldn't dwell on the dead in a combat situation. You had a job to do, a mission to accomplish. You couldn't blame it on yourself or feel guilty for surviving. And you couldn't take one man's death personally. At least not now. Not yet.

But Neech had done all of those things. And he didn't give a fuck anymore. He knew he was scaring the crew. They would have to deal with it or get the hell out of his turret. The guy who used to quote Nietzsche and warn his crew about becoming monsters on the battlefield had died with Batman. The guy who really cared about his mission and his men had been crushed beneath a weight far greater than a sixty-eight-ton tank. The guy who had fancied himself an armchair scholar and philosopher, the guy who wanted everyone to consider his M1A1 Abrams and its crew as "the think tank," was lying back in that defile, holding that kid in his arms, and realizing that he had made the biggest mistake of his life and that someone had died because of him.

"Neech, can we talk?" asked Romeo.

"We're in a battle position. They just blew the fucking bridge. Dismounts will move in. And Romeo wants to fucking talk. Okay. Nice weather we're having, huh? How was your fucking day?"

"Sergeant, please . . ."

Neech spoke through his teeth. "What the fuck?"

"Popeye and me? We're going to help you. But you have to keep it cool, you know?"

Neech looked at the scrawny, gaunt-faced kid whose acne looked more like a case of leprosy. Funny. Neech thought of him and Popeye as kids, though at twenty-four, he was barely older than them. But they just didn't get it the way he did. Consequently, they were just kids, stupid little children, followers who needed to understand that every godless, gutless bastard out there needed to die before sunrise.

"I'm going to say this once. And I'm going to say it very slowly," he began. "And I want you to listen to me real good. They killed a man whose name was Private First Class William Wayne."

"Neech, please . . ."

"THEY KILLED BATMAN! THEY KILLED MY DRIVER! THEY KILLED MY FUCKING DRIVER!"

"Jesus Christ. Calm down, please!"

Neech's cheeks had warmed and drool was leaking down his chin. He could barely feel anything, save for that pit in his stomach, the pit that wouldn't go away. At once, he lowered himself toward Romeo, seizing the sergeant by the collar. "No, I'm not going to calm down! We shouldn't be calm. Don't you get that? That's why we are here—to protect his sacred blood from those fucking animals out there. He gave his blood like Jesus so that we could be saved. Batman was like fucking God, man. And there ain't nothing that can come in the way of that. You understand?"

Romeo's jaw went slack.

"DO YOU UNDERSTAND?"

"Okay, I hear what you're saying."

"This ain't a fucking mission. This is bigger. Much bigger. . . ."

Romeo looked at him as though he were insane, and for a moment Neech softened. For a moment, he realized what he was doing, and he suddenly felt embarrassed and scared and unsure of what was happening. He released Romeo, took a deep breath. "Holy shit, man. I'm sorry."

"It's okay, Sarge. We've been through more shit in the last couple of days than I don't know what."

Neech looked at him, just breathing. He blinked hard, tired to focus.

The kid grinned weakly. "I guess everybody gets a little crazy around the holidays, huh?"

"Yeah, you're right." Neech returned to his station, the image of Batman's death flashing repeatedly in his mind's eye—an eye that was beginning to see things not as what they were but as what he wanted them to be.

He was losing it. He could feel it in his skin as tears rolled down his dirty cheeks.

SERGEANT FIRST CLASS Matthew Abbot was Red Platoon's old-timer, the platoon sergeant with the most experience and wisdom, the guy who had fought in the first Gulf War and in Operation Iraqi Freedom. He had the scars and war stories to prove it. As such, the men—including Lieutenant Hansen—looked to him for guidance and support. Hansen led the platoon, but Abbot ran it. He was a father figure among boys, once a boy himself who had realized over the years that you couldn't save the world and couldn't please everyone. He had learned that the unconditional love of a woman who respected you is more important than anything, especially when you were in the Army, where if you got hurt or otherwise became unfit for duty and were discharged, no one would care about you anymore. All you would have was your woman, which was why for the past forty-eight hours the cool, calm, and collected Platoon Sergeant Abbot, the guy some said resembled the Marlboro man from those really old television commercials, had been anything but. His wife Kim was evacuating with the rest of the military dependants, and he had been unable to verify whether or not she had left Camp Casey. He cursed himself for bringing her to Korea in the first place, but she had insisted upon coming. She still had relatives in Seoul and had wanted to visit. Damned Korean girl was more stubborn than a south Texas mule. But he loved everything about her, especially the Texas accent she had adopted. Sure, it sounded odd coming out of her, but he wouldn't have it any other way. Kim was the best. She loved him like no other woman ever had. She truly appreciated what he did, the sacrifices he made, and understood what drove him. She let him be a man. And if anything ever happened to her . . .

He had to stop worrying. She would be all right. Besides, he had a whole lot of other shit to worry about like fuel and ammo status for the tanks, technical problems with turrets or engine systems, and any other surprises that always came up. The damned worries went on and on like a general who liked to hear himself talk.

Abbot's primary concern rested squarely on Hansen, the twenty-three-year-old who was doing all right but who could slip or crack under the pressure. No, Abbot didn't resent having to babysit the lieutenant; men had done likewise for him. But it was even more difficult knowing that Hansen and Keyman were at each other's throats. Hansen was being distracted by Keyman's challenges to his authority, and while Abbot had repeatedly warned Keyman to stay the hell off the LT's back, Keyman had the selective hearing of old people and children. Abbot knew Keyman's type. He had been raised to become a bully. You couldn't change something like that overnight, and Abbot was left playing referee. They didn't pay him enough for this shit!

Staving off the thoughts, he returned to monitoring the company net, listening in to a report regarding the enemy's shift in position.

Just as the net fell silent, Abbot's loader, Specialist Jeff Paskowsky, blurted out, "They probably had apricots on board, you know that?"

Abbot snickered at the big-eared blond. "The Forward Support Battalion was nice enough to float us this tank, Paz, and all you've done is complain about it."

"These fucking float tanks are a jinx, Sergeant. I'm telling you! Everybody knows it!"

Abbot's last M1A1 had been struck in the ammo compartment, which had resulted in his ammo detonating. The resulting blast had severely damaged the turret, and no maintenance team could have repaired that tank in time. Abbot could have bet a million bucks on the fact that Paz would have a problem with their new track. The loader

would blame it on his family's curse or on any other super-
stition that crossed his mind. There was an old one, might
have dated back to WWII, about never bringing apricots
onboard a tank. Abbot wasn't sure where the hell that had
come from, but Paz had picked up on it. Even though
MREs did not contain the offensive fruit (the old c-rations
used to have apricots in small cans), he checked them anyway because you can never be too careful. And while loading or transferring ammo, he always taped each round
three times which, according to him, ensured that misfires,
jammed aft caps, or any other problems would not happen.
Abbot allowed Paz his eccentricities because, for the most
part, he was an outstanding crew member—when he
wasn't growing paranoid or bitching.

"Paz, we're not jinxed. If we were, we would already be
dead. Okay?"

"Not okay, Sergeant. I'm just really negative about this
whole thing right now. And the feeling's getting worse.
Something's going to happen."

Abbot chuckled under his breath. "Oh, yeah? What?"

Paz's lips grew tight. "Something bad."

CHAPTER
TWO

SERGEANT LEE YONG Sung's thoughts began to drift as he studied the cuts and pockets beneath the great shoulders of rock that lay beyond the Hantan River and the shattered bridge. Two enemy BMPs had moved forward for reconnaissance, but they had, at least for now, withdrawn back to their hide positions. Lee and everyone else expected that NKPA dismounts were closing in anyway and might even attempt to breach the river with ropes, but neither he nor anyone else, including the dismounts from Renegade Platoon who had assumed a position just east of Red's, saw anything yet. A bitter smile caught Lee's lips as he reminded himself that some of his relatives, men he would surely not remember but men whose blood he shared, might be out there, trying to kill him.

When Lee was eight years old, his parents, citizens of the Democratic People's Republic of North Korea, had tried to smuggle him into the south. Earlier in the month, he had shared the story with Deac and Gatch at a bar in TDC. He had told them that soldiers had caught his father and mother. He had said that he had been in a wagon, under a blanket, watching the whole scene, watching his father cry. Then he had closed his eyes and buried his head in his chest. Each shot had made him jolt, but he had not been discovered. The two other farmers had been allowed to pass, and they had delivered Lee to a group of young people, members of the underground network who had taken him across the DMZ and into the south.

Lee had been raised by his aunt, a woman who had also escaped and who had worked as a bar girl in Seoul. He had learned early on to be self-sufficient, and that discipline had served him well. By the time he had joined the Republic of Korea Army, he had become a strong, streetwise young man with an admirable work ethic. The men who had trained him often commented that he was unlike some of the other recruits who, like their American counterparts, were searching for order and discipline in their lives or running from their mistakes. Lee's whole life had prepared him for service. He was an excellent soldier who had advanced quickly. When he had been chosen for the KATUSA program, he felt fully prepared to accept the great honor. KATUSAs had a much better chance to live up to their potential than the average ROK soldier, who was beaten routinely for insubordination and whose opinion hardly mattered to his leaders. In contrast, KATUSAs were treated with the same respect as the American soldiers. They lived on US bases to the same standard of living and celebrated all American and South Korean national holidays.

While those prospects had excited Lee, he saw his two-year commitment as primarily a learning opportunity and a chance to further the reputation that the ROKs were more fierce and determined than the Americans. Failure for a US soldier just meant an After-Action Review and a chance to do it again. Failure for a ROK soldier meant a beating, a demotion, and a stigma that would be forever remembered by his superiors. ROK soldiers were trained to defend the homeland, which meant nothing less than fighting to the death.

With those models in mind, Lee quickly excelled in the KATUSA program. By the time he entered his second year, he was promoted and allowed to become a gunner. He was one of only two KATUSAs in Charlie Company who had earned that distinction. Abbot's gunner, Sergeant Park Kon-sang, was the other Korean, and the two had become fast friends and often shared their trials and tribulations. Yet there was one thing that Lee had never discussed with Park or anyone else.

He was beginning to resent the Americans.

Really resent them.

He understood why they were present. He agreed that the ROKA could use the help.

But Korea was his country, his people. And at the moment, the Americans had no problem destroying it, no problem referring to the North Koreans as "communist bastards," and "slanty-eyed motherfuckers," and "godless cocksuckers," which made Lee wonder what they said about him behind his back. He sometimes felt that they hated all Koreans and tolerated him because of political pressure. The Americans knew that the new generation of South Koreans had been heavily influenced by their liberal political professors and community leaders, who preached one message: Go home, Joe. Still, even Lee admitted that the South Korean people would always want American money, fashion, and hip-hop culture; they just didn't want to be occupied. Ironically, the Americans themselves didn't want to be in Korea because the newer generation did not appreciate what they had done for them since the first Korean War. The big picture wasn't very pretty.

However, on a much smaller scale, Lee's experiences inside the turret had been, for the most part, very positive. Lieutenant Hansen seemed genuinely grateful for his presence, had congratulated him many times during their gunnery and other training exercises, and had never once made a remark that could be construed as racially motivated. He was a good officer and tried very hard to make Lee feel welcome.

On the other hand, Deac and Gatch said anything they wanted, and almost always got away with it. They picked on other KATUSAs, though they always said they were joking, and when they went downrange into TDC, they treated the bar girls and *ajimas* with utter disrespect. Lee was getting tired of biting his tongue and watching them behave like dogs. As they chatted over the intercom, making more derogatory remarks about the enemy, he wanted to say, "Stop. Right now. They are men, just like us. If we were not enemies, we would drink with them because we are all warriors. Show your enemy more respect. Die with honor!"

But as always, Lee just sat there, listening to their crude remarks and to the LT shushing them. He was the robot they wanted because he had been ingrained with the cultural norm of hiding his emotions.

However, when a Korean like him reached a breaking point, the explosion was unequalled anywhere in the world.

Sadly, something told him that the pressure would continue to build. For now, he just ground his teeth and continued scanning.

THE FOUR UP-ARMORED HMMWVs of the 2nd MP Company were pulling out of Camp Casey, along with the three buses carrying Karen Berlin, Kim Abbot, and the rest of the dependant evacuees. Rounds of spontaneous applause rose from the vehicles, and Karen added her clapping and hollering to Kim's.

"Well, it's about time," said the Korean woman with the

Texas accent. "I don't know about you, but two days cooped up in that field house was enough for me."

Karen smiled and shivered. "Yeah, I hear that. But now we're on our way." She tugged up the collar on her woolen coat and repressed another shiver. Though the bus's windows were closed, there was no heat, and the condensation on the inside of those windows had turned to ice. Also, if she had a nose, she could no longer feel it. She cupped gloved hands over her face, breathed hard, and felt her eyes grow sore with tears. *No. No more crying.* She had stop it. *Right now.*

Kim shifted a little closer and threw her arm around Karen. "Don't worry, sweetheart. We'll all be nice and warm pretty soon." The Korean woman winked.

Karen rubbed her eyes. "When I got to the field house, I felt so lost. But then I saw you. Thanks."

"Well, Matt's told me what a great lieutenant Jack is, so I thought I'd be nice to the boss's girlfriend." Kim smiled. "It's all about war and politics, right?"

"If you're talking about my life right now, then I'd say you're right."

"But that's only temporary. This is going to end soon. And they'll come back to us. We have to be patient and believe that." Kim nodded, her eyes glimmering in the shadows. She believed. She really did.

Karen sighed deeply. "How do you do it?"

"What's that?"

"Stay so in love with him, even after all these years. Even after all the time spent apart. I told Jack I think I can do it, but you don't really know until you try."

"You're right. You don't know. And a lot of people can't do it."

"That's what I'm worried about."

"Yeah. Some even make their spouses choose between the Army and a relationship. That's not fair."

"People want to change each other. In the beginning, I wished Jack wasn't in the Army."

"I felt the same way with Matt. But then you realize what it means to them and how special they really are. Jack's going to be in armor until he retires, just like Matt. And if you want to be with him, then that's the sacrifice you make. Just remember . . . Jack's not being selfish. He's being who he is. And you have to let him be a man. If you can do that, he'll always come back to you, no matter how long he's deployed."

Karen sighed again and rubbed her nose. "I'm in for one hell of a ride."

"**TEAM COBRA, THIS** is Black Six," began Captain Van Buren over the company net. "Scouts report dismounted enemy recon elements moving northeast toward obstacle Charlie One-Three-Niner. Break.

"All Cobra elements will advance to the obstacle. Platoon leaders will meet up with me for a FRAGO. Black Six, out."

Hansen checked his map and overlay, identifying obstacle C139 as a low-water crossing—a key piece of terrain.

Before bridges had been built that could withstand the weight of a tank, Army engineers had found areas along the Hantan River where they could bring in tons of gravel to create low-water crossings that were only twelve inches deep and enabled the passage of tanks and other heavy armored vehicles. Like many other crossings, a narrow road led in and out of C139, and high embankments and vegetation provided cover for both defending and attacking dismounts.

With the bridge blown, C139 was now the enemy division commander's best avenue of approach, and he would pour everything he had into securing that area. He would first attempt to seize the high ground and crossing sites while determining the positions of US forces and ROKA bunker sites. Then he would attack—and it was up to Team Cobra to stop him.

"Driver, move out!"

Gatch rolled up the acceleration on his T-bar and took them up and out of their battle position.

"Hey, LT? If the TF commander knew the ROKs would blow the bridge, why didn't we go to the bypass in the first place?" asked Deac.

"Because if we did, then we'd be tipping our hand to the enemy."

"I get it. We drew them toward us, blew the bridge, then forced them into a chokepoint at the obstacle."

"That's right. We got that enemy commander to waste a lot of time there, and the flyboys took advantage of that. Now we need to hold that crossing. And believe you me, it's going to get hairy."

"How many dismounts?" Deac asked gravely.

"Not sure, really. Eight thousand? Ten? Maybe more?"

"Holy shit."

"Why are you surprised? You've heard this before."

"He's surprised because he don't listen to nothing they say," called Gatch from his hole. "Damned hillbilly thinks he'll live forever."

"Fuck you, Gatch!"

"All right, guys. Enough of the not-so-witty banter," said Hansen. "And that includes you, too, Sergeant Lee." Hansen grinned at the ever silent gunner, who just glanced strangely at him, then returned his gaze to his sight.

WITHIN FIFTEEN MINUTES they were nearing the low-water crossing and parked about fifteen hundred meters south along the reverse slope of a lazy string of hills draped in heavy snow.

Hansen, Ryback, and Second Lieutenant Dariel "D. T." Thomas, White Platoon's leader, dismounted and met with Van Buren to receive the FRAGO and overlays for their maps.

While the task force commander had assigned them to the obstacle, it was up to Van Buren to establish battle positions for each platoon so that all sectors around the low-water crossing would be covered. The captain's face looked drawn, his catalog-model good looks evaporated from lack of sleep, but his voice was hard and unwavering as he delivered their orders.

Basically, the company's mission was to delay the enemy for as long as possible to buy time for more evacuations of TDC and for reinforcements to arrive. To that end, Van Buren intended to exploit the terrain and position his platoons to best support the fight.

The river snaked its way from the northeast to the southwest, and Red Platoon's BP would lie on that southwest side, while the grunts of Renegade Platoon occupied two positions in the northeast. In one of those positions they would park their Bradleys on the high ground and their Forward Observer team would establish a Listening Post/Observation Post to scan the hilltops and ridgelines across the river for enemy scouts. That team would be equipped with a GPS, handheld laser rangefinders, a pair of secure radios, and a digital communications device. The platoon's second BP stood farther north and close to the river, where their dismounts would move up close and establish well dug-in positions with overhead cover. Northeast of them, White Platoon would establish their BPs in the higher ground overlooking the river to cover the enemy's northern flank as they pushed southeast.

Van Buren had picked out four target reference points, all on the west and northwest side of the river, and he had marked them on the overlays. TRP 01 was a sharp ridge lying directly west of Red's position. TRP 02 lay across from the breach point, while TRP 03 and TRP 04 were peaks along the northern slopes nearest the river. If you looked at them from above, the TRPs formed a jagged "Z" from 01 to 04 and allowed for each platoon to mass its fires on the center of the area marked by the TRP while also indicating the left and right limits of that area. As usual, Hansen would control his platoon fires by designating platoon TRPs to supplement those issued by Van Buren.

The captain went on to discuss in detail the fire support plan that he and Fire Support Officer Jason Yelas had devised. The priority of mortar fires would go to the dismounts/Forward Observers first, the Bradleys second, then White, and finally Red Platoon. Priority of artillery fires would go to Red since those artillery assets could put DPICM and HE fires on MSR 3 to disrupt the mounted assault/high-speed avenue of approach. However, Van Buren did warn them that the FA might be called upon to assist TF 2-9 as well, and they should anticipate such delays. Lastly, to supplement Renegade Platoon's defensive efforts, the company's platoon of engineers would place a command-detonated mine in the middle of the obstacle while the others were establishing their positions.

"Any questions?" he finally asked.

No one spoke up.

"Gentlemen, when they come down here, we're going to knock them into last week."

"Hooah," answered Hansen and Thomas in unison. Ryback offered his nod of assent.

Hansen shook hands with them all, then stole a quick look at the still and silent landscape. He imagined a long column of enemy APCs shifting down Main Supply Route 3, barely visible through the bone-white branches lining the embankments. He shivered and hustled off.

* * *

ONCE HE RETURNED to his tank, Hansen, along with Keyman, Abbot, and Neech, moved off to recon their BPs, while the TCs from White Platoon and LT Ryback from Renegade did likewise.

Leaving the platoon's loaders to establish forward and rearward security around their idling tanks, Hansen led the others over the slopes and down toward the river. They hit another incline, dropped to their elbows, M4 rifles in hand, then Hansen moved up alongside Keyman, who was already scanning the area with his night vision goggles.

"There go the sappers," the TC muttered, referring to the team of engineers who were emplacing the mine in the middle of the crossing, covered by one squad from Ryback's platoon. "Can't wait to see that go boom."

"Look at all those ridgelines," Hansen said, panning with his own goggles. "They'll have snipers all over the place. I'll keep an eye on them. We can shoot HEAT up there and take down some of the edges and expose them to more fire."

Keyman lowered his goggles and frowned. "Whatever you say, sir."

Hansen's eyes widened. "That's right. Whatever I say. But do *you* have something—"

"LT?" called Abbot. "This slope we're on looks good for us. Successive and alternate BPs can just work their way back in, say hundred- or two-hundred-meter increments."

"What do you think?" Hansen asked Keyman, waiting to hear something that would further stoke his fury.

The staff sergeant turned from his NVGs and cocked a brow. "I think that if we can't stop their dismounts from crossing, they're going to overrun this entire area. I think . . . this is going to get interesting." He spat a glob of tobacco, then returned to his goggles.

Abruptly, the thunder of A-10s broke over the landscape. The jets streaked by, their engines fading into the drumming of their bombs. The whole mountain chain rumbled.

"They can't kill 'em all," Abbot said gravely.

Hansen nodded slowly. "Neither can we. But no one will try harder, right?"

The platoon sergeant returned his own nod. "Hey, LT? You superstitious?"

"Not really. Why do you ask?"

"Ah, it's nothing. Just Paz trying to weird me out again. That's all."

Hansen put a hand on Abbot's shoulder, and for the first time since they had known each other, he called the platoon sergeant by his first name. "Matt, what is it? You worried about her?"

Abbott nodded. "And this. Something's not right."

"I don't feel that. I think we're good to go. Don't get negative on me. That's his job." Hansen raised his chin in Keyman's direction. "Anyway, they'll both be all right."

"Yeah, they will. Sorry, LT. It's just that . . . I don't know . . . taking on armor at long distances is one thing, but if they throw all those dismounts at us, there'll be a lot of infiltration."

That word made Hansen want to shiver. Infiltration was one of a tanker's greatest fears. "I'm up for the challenge," he said, half lying.

Abbot's eyes narrowed, then he released a long breath, as though freeing his demons. "Me, too."

Hansen happened to glance over at Neech, who was repeatedly lifting and lowering his NVGs and cursing under his breath. Hansen turned to Abbot and frowned.

"Hey, Neech, you all right?" Abbot asked in a hushed voice.

The TC continued his muttering.

"Hey, Sergeant Nelson?" Hansen called.

Neech finally craned his head, though the gloomy light hid his expression.

"You all right?" asked Abbot.

"No . . ." the sergeant answered slowly. "But I will be.

Soon . . ." For a moment, Neech's swollen and bloodshot eyes appeared and seemed to rise up from the plains of his face.

Keyman started laughing. "Wow, Neechy, I like your attitude. Hardcore."

"Fuck you, Keyman."

The staff sergeant looked confused because he'd been trying to compliment Neech, something Keyman rarely did. He raised an index finger. "You'd better watch that."

"He will," Hansen said, fixing Neech with a warning glance.

"LT, I'm just a little wired, that's all," Neech explained.

"I get that. Okay, everybody, let's finish up."

In the minutes that followed, Hansen planned his defense by establishing the platoon's target reference points, engagement and disengagement criteria, and by defining the engagement area. He discussed sectors of fire for each tank and went over the preplanned mortar and FA targets with them so they would all know their indirect fire plan and could call for fire if he or Abbot got taken out. Afterward, he addressed any questions. Remarkably, Keyman remained silent.

"That's it, then," Hansen said quickly. "Let's go. Neech, come here for a second." As the others began to slip off, Hansen studied the tank commander. "You look like shit."

"I'm okay."

"You'll tell me if you're not, won't you?"

"I won't let you down, sir."

"Don't let him down, either, okay? We'll keep making sure that he died for something."

"That's right, sir. We will."

Hansen gave the sergeant a quick nod, then gestured for him to fall in behind. During the quick jog back to their tanks, Hansen thought he heard Neech muttering to himself, but he couldn't be sure.

* * *

SPECIALIST RICK GATCH was walking on a beach with Jesus, and when he looked back, he saw just one set of footprints. "Lord, is that when you carried me?"

"No," said Jesus. "That's when you were drinking and whoring and you abandoned me."

"Oh. Oh, shit. Sorry about that, dude."

When Gatch looked back again, he saw tank tracks. "Jesus, does this mean you're with me inside the tank?"

"No," Jesus answered. "I am not a God of convenience."

"Then what do those tracks mean?"

Jesus smiled.

And Gatch shuddered from the thought as Hansen climbed onto the back deck, crossed the turret, swung open his hatch, and lowered himself into the tank.

"Okay, sports fans, let's roll."

After throwing the tank into gear, Gatch took them about two hundred meters toward the reverse side of a jagged slope where the LT said they would establish their battle and hide positions. The humming engine and heater were a source of comfort now, as was the clinking and clacking of the tracks. It was funny how he usually ignored that white noise, but when it was gone he felt naked and vulnerable.

Outside, the temperature was dropping so rapidly that water buffalos would soon freeze solid, dismounts who had not donned all of their heaviest cold weather gear would begin to get frostbite even as the water in their canteens froze, and some vehicles would need to remain running all night because come morning they would not crank up. Dismounted "roving guards" at each position would also frequently stop behind a tank that was idling to recharge its batteries so they could get warm in the hot engine exhaust.

When Gatch wrote to his buddies back home in Daytona Beach about the Korean winters, he told them that birds would die in midflight and just fall from the sky like ice cubes. Rubber got so cold that you could snap it off treads the way you'd snap off pieces of a frozen Snickers bar. Prostitutes were so frosty that you'd need to spend hours defrosting their privates (and their personalities) with your carefully held Zippo.

"You short guys are all the same," Deac had told him while reading an e-mail over his shoulder. "You always exaggerate." Gatch had punched the big loader and said, "Hey, motherfucker. I'm seven feet tall when standing on my charisma."

"Okay, right here," said the LT as they rose slightly up the mound.

Even as Gatch hit the brakes, the tank began sliding backward. "Fuckin' ice," he muttered, then kicked the M1A1 back into gear and turned left, veering off the patch of ice to find some rocky ground. The tank's tracks had rubber pads to protect the metal shoes and to prevent damage to the asphalt roadways. Gatch wished they had the authorization and the time to remove the damned things, which would give him much better traction, but the enemy had a way of squashing wishes and dreams.

Revving the engine, he drove once more up the slope, and the tank sank a little, stabilized, then remained in their hide position. Once the other three tanks reported that they were set, Hansen ordered them to shut down in unison and turn off their heaters. Everyone donned their ECWS gear, "bear suits" included, so they could survive the plunging temperatures.

Bundled up, the lieutenant and Deac dismounted to inspect the path up to their primary BP. Slipping again could prove fatal for them, for their wingman, or for anyone else in the company team, should they fail to fire because they were taking a sleigh ride back down the slope. You could just ask Neech, whose tank had slid down a hill and thrown a track during their battle in the defile. Neech and the rest of the crew had become pinned down by dismounts, and that's when Batman had been killed—all because of some ice.

"Hey, Lee, how you doing back there?" Gatch asked, feeling locked inside a meat locker and needing a little moral support.

"I am okay," answered the gunner.

"Dude, I'm just thinking about that night in TDC when you dropped Sergeant Shitface. Remember?"

"I remember."

Gatch, Deac, and Lee had been in a bar and had been harassed by a few guys from the 503rd Infantry Battalion. One guy, Shiffas, had passed a remark about Lee's parents—and that's when Lee had gone Bruce Lee on the guy . . .

"That was so cool. Man, did that guy go down hard or what? But you, man, you're so freakin' honorable. You still regret that?"

Lee hesitated, and his tone abruptly darkened. "Not anymore."

"Good for you."

"Gatch, is it okay not to talk?"

"Uh, yeah, I guess."

"Thank you."

Gatch shrugged, reached up, and tapped the "In memory of #3 Dale Earnhardt" bumper sticker on the inside of his hatch. The spirit of old Number Three would be looking out for them, as he always did.

Oh, Dale, as we wait now in the valley of the shadow of death for the signal to start, as we look forward to the checkered flag of victory, we want to say thank you for being in the driver's hole with us tonight.

So far everything looked okay. The tank's gauges all said, "Ready to kick ass."

But something deep inside told Gatch that while the machine was ready, the man was not.

He flashed back to that last battle and to the faces of

those men—those boys—he had mowed down with the tank. He kept giving them names, families, pets, hobbies, dreams . . .

Yet those bastards had been trying to kill him. Kill or be killed. It was stupid to feel guilty.

Then why was he being so stupid?

Man, it was just plain horrible to see them flinch, fall, and die and know that you weren't watching a movie or playing a video game. This was real. And you had caused it. You had paved the road with body parts.

Afterward, you could put on a macho front and matter-of-factly comment on how you had taken out a couple dozen of them, but in the days and weeks to come something got inside you, a pain you just couldn't wrestle off.

Deac was the more emotional of the duo, and the big oaf had started crying once they had returned to their Assembly Area. He was lucky. The guilt had hit him right away, and he'd already had time to deal with it before going out again. Gatch had been there to say don't worry about it. You get right with Jesus, and you'll be all right.

However, Jesus had taken his long board and gone off to surf, leaving Gatch standing there on the beach, looking back at those tank tracks. What the hell did they mean? Were they supposed to make him feel better? What?

A muffled rushing noise sounded close, followed by the dull thud of an artillery shell whose concussion shook the tank. "God damn it, that was close," he muttered. A cloud of smoke and tumbling debris lifted less than fifty meters ahead of their position. "Was that ours or theirs?"

Deac and the lieutenant abruptly completed their inspection of the BP, hustled back to the tank, and dropped into the turret, just as two more rounds exploded and Abbot's voice sounded on the company net. "Black Six, this is Red Four. Enemy artillery striking approximately five hundred meters northeast TRP One, over."

"Roger, Red Four. Stand by."

Gatch, like the rest of the crew, had been well briefed by Hansen, and he understood the platoon's mission as well as the company team's. He was also well aware of the team's fire support plan and always took a keen interest in how those boys could help prevent his butt from being blown off the mountain.

The first task for fires was to use mortars (a platoon of six guns) to kill any recon troops trying to get a look at the team's defensive preparations. The second task was to strike armored formations, and the third task was to target enemy antitank teams, considered the greatest dismounted threat to the company team, and hit with mortar fires immediately after they were spotted.

Fire from the Paladin howitzers of the Direct Support FA Battalion, task force mortars, and maybe even some Apache Hellfire missiles launched from choppers hovering from as far as eight kilometers behind the engagement area would do a real number on those enemy artillery assets and armor shifting from the bridge area. Also, those fires would be plotted to cover the low-water crossing itself, hammering the enemy once he attempted to breach.

If the commander wanted to obscure the enemy's vision, he could call for artillery and mortar smoke projectiles, and if he wanted to emplace a hasty minefield, he could request antipersonnel and antitank mines fired using the 155-mm guns, but that did tie up the tubes and prevent them from firing HE or dual purpose improved conventional munitions.

Were that not enough, suppressive fires would be placed on enemy mounted forces by using field artillery and on dismounted forces by using mortars. Field artillery would keep the mounted forces buttoned up, smash off their antennae, destroy their optics, and cause them to disperse to avoid presenting an area target. If just one 155-mm HE round hit on or near a tank, the damage would be akin to that tank running over a couple of AT mines. Final protective fires would occur in front of Renegade's dismounted position to prevent them from being overrun by an enemy attack. The task force's S4, considered to be a rather savvy officer, had positioned several HEMTT cargo trucks of ammunition with the mortars to ensure a large supply of ammo. Additionally, he had sent forward another truck loaded with $2' \times 4'$ steel plates precut to cover foxholes so the dismounts wouldn't have to fill as many sandbags to cover their holes.

To say that the commander's fire plan was a complex undertaking would be a true understatement, and Gatch had a lot of respect for Yelas and the rest of those "FISTers" who worked out of their M7 Bradley Fire Support Vehicle. That was a nice ride, loaded to the gills with radio gear, lasers, inertial navigation systems, computers, a twelve-disc CD changer, DVD player, and those fancy massage chairs you saw at The Sharper Image in the mall.

Well, those last few items were still on back order, but even without them those guys were much appreciated by Gatch when the battlefield got interesting.

For his part, Yelas had established a well-concealed OP on the west end of Red's battle position so he could observe movement as far up MSR 3 as possible with day optics and his Bradley Forward Looking Infrared Radar. He also had four radio nets, a laser rangefinder, GPS, and his two digital communications computers so he could plan for and coordinate all fires electronically. With him on the BFIST were his fire support sergeant, who doubled as the gunner, his fire support specialist, and his BFIST driver, a PFC. He was armed with a 25-mm chain gun and 7.62-mm coax, but they were for defense, even though Gatch suspected that when the situation got really hot, Van Buren would want to utilize Yelas and his crew as a direct fire asset, even though they could not coordinate fires and fight as "just another Bradley" at the same time. Gatch had listened to those arguments more than once, and he was mighty glad he was driving a more heavily armed and armored tank instead of a Bradley.

Yelas was also responsible for working with Close Air Support if it was available for the company team commander. After Operation Iraqi Freedom had begun, the chief of field artillery had mandated that all FISTers become "Universal Observers" and be certified to control any Army, Navy, Air Force, or Marine Corps aircraft or fire support asset available to the joint force commander. That meant that FISTers didn't have to rely on USAF Tactical Air Control Party personnel to control close air support, as they had in the past.

With that newfound operational capability in hand, Yelas could lase targets with his laser designator, so that A-10 pilots could pick them up with their Pave Penny pods. Those Warthogs could destroy tanks with their Maverick missiles and GAU-8 Gatling guns and sometimes drop GPS-guided bombs on key targets. Yelas would also provide terminal guidance for the Apaches' Hellfire missiles, once those elements entered the fight.

In truth, some tankers believed they needed only their M1A1s and some targets in their sights. Field artillery and mortars were an afterthought.

Then again, when the shooting started, many of those same hardasses would quickly call for fires from men who referred to artillery as the "King of Battle." Gatch had witnessed a kind of synergy on the battlefield between direct and indirect fires when they were well-planned and well-executed. You couldn't beat the one-two punch.

But more importantly, you had to appreciate those guys because they knew how to party with their armor brothers. You would frequently find Yelas and his crew in Cheers, the Starz Club, or in a few of the other places, hanging out with the tankers. The FSO had once bought the entire company rounds, and Gatch sure as shit wouldn't have paid that tab. The guy was all right in Gatch's book.

So long as he didn't make a mistake. As they say, friendly fire isn't.

Gatch breathed deeply, blinked hard, and continued scanning the area ahead, looking for signs of dismounts who may have somehow evaded detection to cross the river and launch a surprise attack on their position. On, yeah, the paranoia was settling in. And dismounts, were they to make it that far, wouldn't engage them. They would be calling back Red One's position to an antitank team, who would in turn launch their missiles. If those dismounts got even closer, they would fire off some RPG grenades at the top armor of the turret in an attempt to kill the crew, or try a shot at the rear engine grill doors to kill the engine.

Gatch flinched and cursed as another shell exploded dangerously close.

"Black Six, this is Renegade One," called Ryback on the company net.

"Go ahead, Renegade."

"Troops entering our sector, approximately five hundred meters north C-One-Three-Niner, to the north of TRP Two, over."

"Roger, One. Stand by, out."

Gatch gripped his T-bar more tightly, reflecting on those tank tracks Jesus had shown him, the ones coming to an abrupt halt were he stood.

CHAPTER
THREE

ALTHOUGH HIS TANK sat in a turret-down hide position, Hansen could still observe their sector by standing in his hatch and wearing his night vision goggles.

He knew he would have a hard time spotting dismounted enemy recon troops darting within the tree-lined slopes overlooking the riverbank; however, once they made their mad dash from the draws and valleys to the rear and headed for the steep embankments closer to the water, their movement and muzzle flashes would be easier to spot—that was until smoke filled the area. He figured some grunts would attempt to rappel down into the water from the tops of the ridges, especially the ones in Renegade's sector, though he felt confident that Ryback's platoon would make their calls for fire and address those rope climbers before they ever reached the ground.

Because Team Cobra was in the defense, and the enemy could approach from more avenues than the team could cover with available forces, a squad from the 102nd Military Intelligence Battalion had rolled in aboard an M113

Armored Personnel Carrier and had brought with them the AN/PPS-5B ground surveillance radar set and a collection of hand-emplaced seismic, magnetic, and infrared sensors known as the remotely emplaced battlefield area sensor system. Those MI guys had gone out across the river with a dismounted patrol to emplace the sensors in those areas that couldn't be observed from the south side of the river. Once the division's recon force moved into the area and tripped those sensors, the MI NCO, who was co-located with the Fire Support Team, would report the locations of the enemy movement to Yelas, who would in turn call for indirect fires.

The ground surveillance radar had been set up near the Fire Support Team as well so that the tripod-mounted dish could cover MSR 3 as well as monitor up the river, even after smoke or weather obscured everyone else's view. Better still, if one of the REMBASS sensors was tripped, the GSR could be cued to that sensor to help detect enemy movement.

Some tankers felt that GSR teams were magnets for fire, and they wanted those guys and their gear as far away as possible. Hansen had mixed feelings about that, especially after what had happened a few days prior. They had escorted another such GSR team into the defile to help detect the approach of the enemy's mounted recon force. That MI team had performed admirably—until an artillery shell had landed squarely on their M113 and killed the entire crew. The current GSR guys and FISTers were about two hundred meters south of the platoon, close enough for discomfort—but they still provided a vital early warning capability in areas the team could not observe or patrol.

A sudden gust of wind stung Hansen's cheeks, but he barely noticed. He was too damned excited, too damned scared, and ready to witness an amazing display of artillery fire that would rake the hills with death.

He panned down along both sides of the obstacle. Huge

chunks of ice floated lazily downstream between larger, snow-covered chunks that formed islands and continents glistening in the light of the rising moon. He could hardly imagine anyone wading into that water, let alone doing so while artillery blasted the place into a slushy nightmare.

But the North Korean People's Army wasn't just any army. The men conscripted to serve began their training in school or on the job by serving as members of the Red Youth Guard. They were recruits who would soon become soldiers—if they survived the physical and emotional abuse of their training. Most American commanders better defined their program as well-organized torture. When they weren't being beaten or deprived of food and sleep, the recruits studied the Fatherland Liberation War and the Anti-Japanese Partisan Struggle to learn from those experiences. They received, arguably, the most intense brainwashing available on the planet. They needed to become politically reliable in order to best serve the Dear Leader in Pyongyang.

With training complete, the survivors would go on to take the Soldier's Oath, receive their soldier's identification cards, and get assigned to their operational units, where they would be given further instruction.

Troops like those approaching the water crossing received unit training that stressed political education, unit cohesiveness, and operating in harsh conditions. Officers and NCOs were selected from the common soldiers and sent to training schools. Being an officer was a very prestigious job in North Korea and provided the only ticket out for men who came from rural or peasant backgrounds. Hansen had even heard that NKPA officers could choose from hordes of women eager to marry them.

Consequently, all of the NKPA's indoctrination and intense instruction produced warriors ready to die in a heartbeat for the Dear Leader's ideals. They might not be the six-foot, ten-inch muscle-bound action heroes of American cinema, but their strength was in their speed, agility, and numbers, and they could wreak havoc with incredible ferocity. When Hansen read accounts of the first Korean War, he noticed how in many of them the North Koreans were often referred to as the "fanatical foe." He had dismissed the phrase as a fancy writer's term—until he had experienced North Korean fanaticism firsthand on the battlefield.

Hansen glanced off to his left, where his wingman's tank lay just fifty meters away, in the far west position and closest to the FISTers and MI guys. Keyman stood inert in his hatch, goggles on and looking like a belligerent insect spitting chew. If there was anyone in the platoon as fanatical as those North Koreans, it was him. He was, in fact, so ill-humored and so intense that in the three months they had served together Hansen had yet to see the man fully smile. Sure, he had witnessed a hint here and there, but never a full-on, caught dead to rights, shit-eating grin. Webber reported in a deadpan that Keyman only smiled when he had orgasms or gas—and he certainly had not been smiling during the conversation they'd had in the Assembly Area after their battle in the defile:

"You don't think I can lead this platoon, do you?"

"I'll take the Fifth."

"I want to hear you say it."

"Okay. You can't lead this platoon. And do you know why? Because a good PL would've never put up with my bullshit. You've been stringing me along, cutting me slack the way you cut Webber slack. That's 'cause you're weak. You want to be our buddy, just a regular guy. But the weak get nothing but killed."

Hansen had tried to be a firm but fair platoon leader. He had shared in the grunt work and had told his men that he wanted to be a regular tanker, sleeves up, hands dirty, and ready to go to war.

Keyman called that weak.

What did the staff sergeant want? Was Hansen supposed to, like Keyman, bark orders and threaten his crew like an obsessed maniac?

No way. That was the kind of leadership style that in other wars got men "accidentally" killed.

At least not every member of Keyman's crew bowed to him as though he were a king wearing an olive drab crown. Webber, the platoon's recovering loan shark and resident wiseass, was unafraid to meet the bald man's gaze, meaning he had probably found a weakness beneath the TC's tough-guy facade. Hansen wished he knew what that was.

There must have been a time when Keyman was a tolerable guy. Assholes didn't get nicknames, at least not ones used around them. What was the man like when he had first come to Korea? Had he been as confident and arrogant? How quickly had he proven himself? Hansen should have learned more about his wingman's past, but he had been so wrapped up in training and in establishing relationships with the rest of the platoon that he had brushed the thought aside, only to have that oversight bite him in the ass when he had won Top Tank and basically blown the staff sergeant's mind.

As Hansen turned away, the air filled with those familiar and sometimes terrifying sounds: the whooshing of air followed by a millisecond of silence—then . . . BOOM!

Brilliant flashes lit the slopes like short-circuiting Christmas lights as the 120-mm mortar fires turned trees into kindling and kicked up showers of rock, mud, and ice. The NVGs gave Hansen a decent view of the fireworks, and his CVC helmet shielded his ears from some of the deafening roar. For a second, though, he flirted with the idea of removing the helmet and goggles to experience the mortar barrage with his bare senses—but the sudden report of gunfire from the opposite riverbank, just south of TRP 01, nixed that idea.

"Dismounts are on the move!" he shouted to his men.

Way up on the other side of MSR 3, Ryback and his mechanized infantry boys were still laying low and would remain so for as long as possible. They had positioned their Bradleys so that the crews could provide both supporting chain-gun and coax fires for them while still covering their sectors of the engagement area. The mechanized infantrymen always said that the dismounts did the real fighting and that the Bradleys should always give them supporting fire.

On the other side of the coin, tankers like Hansen always considered those Bradleys as "light tanks" whose crews should occupy a BP and help the entire team by fighting with their tube-launched, optically tracked, wire-guided missiles and chain guns. Consequently, those Bradley crews were constantly torn between watching out for their dismounts while servicing targets within their sectors. Bradley crews could lase those targets and calculate accurate grid coordinates for mortar and field artillery calls for fires. Commanders, known as a "BCs," was trained in how to call for fires and were in charge of a gunner and driver, very much like a tank commander. Some of the BCs were being directed to continually scan the ridgeline from TRPs 03 to 04, watching for enemy scouts and forward observers trying to steal a glimpse of Team Cobra's positions. The leftmost BC was scanning from TRP 03 to 01 for dismounted and mounted movement, as well as checking for scouts, observers, and engineer recon teams. Like the dismounts, those BCs would first rely upon mortar and field artillery fires so as not to reveal their positions.

To make his plan happen, Lieutenant Ryback had asked to use the first sergeant's M113A3, an armored personnel carrier with radios and a .50-caliber heavy machine gun. Since the vehicle would be positioned forward anyway to evacuate causalities under fire, and the Bradleys would need to remain in their BPs to help the company team mass its direct fires, Ryback figured he'd use the M113 to rapidly move his second infantry squad around the battlefield to counter major dismounted threats. Once the enemy was sighted and on the move, he could move his squad to the best possible position to ambush the enemy with rifles, carbines, SAWs, M203s, M240 MG fire reinforced with mortars and field artillery fires, and take advantage of the .50-caliber mounted on the M113, just like the days of Vietnam and the pre-Bradley Cold War Army.

Were those men to face mounted enemy forces, they had a deadly trick up their sleeves. Each squad in the platoon packed several Javelins, the "silver bullets" of the mechanized infantry that could be hiked anywhere around the battlefield and fired from the shoulder or pre-positioned to take out enemy armor. US Special Operations Forces in Afghanistan had killed dozens of Taliban tanks with those missiles when their dismounted positions had been attacked. In regard to direct fire and AT assets, the Javelin missile was the most lethal instrument in the dismounts' cache.

Meanwhile, Ryback's other squad along the river opposite TRP 03 was covering the site with claymore mines, surface-laid mines, and the Modular Pack Mine System, which contained a mix of 17 M78 AT and four M77 AP mines positioned on both sides of the river so that Van Buren could employ them on command to stop a mounted or dismounted attack in addition to the mine placed in the center of the obstacle by the engineers.

Once the enemy figured out where White, Red, and Renegade Platoons were situated, they'd begin firing smoke screens and artillery fires in front of the BPs in an attempt to soften up the team and keep everyone blind and buttoned up. However, task force observers, along with Renegade's dismounts, would be forward of the smoke screens and artillery and still able to make their own calls for fires.

With Ryback's people out there, serving as more eyes and ears and helping to stop those NK infantrymen and even take on some armor, Hansen knew that he and the others had a real fighting chance.

And the fight was about to happen. But would it go as planned? Never. No plan ever survived the first battle. Murphy's Law saw to that.

"How's it looking up there, LT?" asked Deac.

"They're putting a lot of fires on those hills. A hell of a lot of fires . . ."

"That's good. We can leave after the seventh inning and be home for a midnight snack."

"Come on, Deac. You don't want them to save a few for us? We didn't load all that ammo to let it sit in the rack."

"Uh, yeah, right."

Hansen dropped back into the turret and removed his goggles. He hoisted his brows at Deac. "You all right?"

"Yeah."

"I'm not convinced."

Deac shrugged. "Then I'll just have to show y'all when the time comes."

"You do that. How about you, Lee?"

The gunner sat back in his seat and folded his arms across his chest. "I am fine, sir."

"Something bothering you?"

"No, sir."

"You sure? You're not talking anymore."

Lee's gaze averted. "I am fine, sir."

"All right, boys. You don't need some bullshit pep talk from me, but you're looking a little strung out and depressed—and that goes for you, too, Gatch."

"I hear you, LT," the driver said from his station.

"All right, then. You know that rush you get? You know the one. If you can hang on to that energy, it'll carry you through. You know exactly what I mean. We've been here before. Enough said?"

"Yes, sir," answered Deac, followed by Lee and Gatch.

At the moment, Abbot was back on the company net, reporting the effects of the mortar fire to Van Buren and Yelas. The platoon sergeant from White Platoon was doing likewise, as was Ryback's FO team and the task force scouts. The latter had two up-armored HMMWVs equipped with .50-caliber machine guns and MK-19 40-mm grenade launchers that they had parked and concealed on the other side of the river.

Itching with the desire to tell his men to crank up their tanks and roll up into their battle positions, Hansen went back up top again, aiming his NVGs directly north toward the winding dark ribbon of MSR 3.

No sign of any vehicles or movement. While the enemy was moving northeast toward the bypass, that did not rule out elements of their supporting tank brigade, positioned northwest of the division, from utilizing those parts of the highway where obstacles had not been emplaced by the ROKs.

However, if Murphy went to sleep and the fire support plan unfolded as it should, then those formations would be delayed and disrupted by field artillery-delivered scatterable mines fired to create a FASCAM minefield. Also, a combination of antitank and antipersonnel mines would be fired on the road as more mounted forces were detected.

For the time being, though, the mortars kept falling, the time between detonations tightening, the smoke growing more dense. The stench of all the fire finally reached Hansen, but his nose was too cold to register the full effect.

A squad of soldiers dashed from an ice-covered thicket to another one about thirty meters away, but smoke quickly obscured Hansen's view. He inspected the steep embankments again, looking for any signs of ropes dropping over the edge.

Still nothing. The artillery banged on. The smoke grew more dense. The thumping of rotors resounded from somewhere far behind them.

"Oh, man, LT, it's getting so freakin' cold," said Gatch, his voice coming in a weird tremolo.

"What're you talking about?" asked Deac, incredulous. "You ain't got your hatch open! We do!"

"Thanks for the report, Gatch," Hansen said. "Now, unless your balls freeze off, shut up. We're not cranking up till the last second."

"Yes, sir," moaned Gatch.

A second burst of movement along the ridge caught his attention, and Hansen zoomed in on the area.

There they were, ropes dropping down over the side, darkly clad infantrymen getting ready to rappel to the riverbank. Hansen counted over a dozen positions where they were going to make the attempt, and he called up the FSO on the company net and conveyed the coordinates to put some mortar fire on them.

A minute passed. Those infantry began their descent, plunging like so many dark spiders in frozen attic rafters. Another minute. Then suddenly, a wall of North Koreans appeared through the smoke behind the rappelling men— literally hundreds and hundreds of them—so many, in fact, that the ropes swayed violently as they became overcrowded. The guys wailed war cries, while others, officers probably, shouted in Korean.

Three, two, one, and the mortar fires came in, blowing men off the embankments like specks of dust even as the explosions shredded others beyond recognition. Some men caught fire, dangled for a moment, then dropped, flames whipping until the muddy banks doused them.

Hansen stopped breathing. It was hard to process all that death. He wasn't sure if he should feel happy, sad, amazed, in awe, overjoyed, or what. He just held his breath as, in a matter of seconds, two, maybe three hundred grunts were put through the meat grinder, bodies piling up along the riverbank.

While he could no longer see anything north of TRP 02,

he listened in to the reports from the platoon sergeant over in White's position. Those guys were getting ready to move up into the BPs and mass fires on the infantry.

A unique aspect of the battle was the employment of a new round for the M1A1. The Army had been field testing the antipersonnel round for a while, having recognized the need for such ordnance in places like Korea, where massed infantry in limited terrain rendered the sabot and HEAT rounds inefficient against those widespread targets. The AP would rocket out to a set range, detonate, then launch flechette projectiles that would scatter and devastate a dismounted force. Each of Team Cobra's tank commanders had been issued one AP round, thus Hansen figured he would hold back the platoon until the last second, have them move up in unison, then have them mass their fires, utilizing the AP to take out as many infantry as possible.

Thomas had the same idea, but he beat Hansen to the punch. Four simultaneous thunderclaps echoed loudly from White Platoon's sector, and the ridgeline opposite them, still heavily draped in smoke, appeared in the sudden lightning of detonations. The wind carried shrieks of agony across the river as the platoon sergeant from White gasped unconsciously into the microphone, "Holy shit . . ."

Swinging around, Hansen kept his attention on TRP 01, shifting up and down the hills, then across the embankments once more, where new ropes were plunging over the sides as the next wave prepared to assault.

Tingling with a fresh rush of adrenaline, he ducked into the turret and got on the platoon net. "Red, this is Red One. Crank 'em up on my command. Three, two, one. Now!"

All four tanks started their engines in unison to conceal the number of vehicles in their position. Hansen then called for each TC to report that he was set. That done, he got on the net and said, "Red, infantry in our sector, south of TRP 01. Alpha and Bravo shoot AP. Stand by." Raising his brows at Deac, he asked, "Loader, are we battlecarrying AP?"

"Yes, sir. AP loaded. Loader ready!"

Hansen rose into his hatch for another look. He was glad he had, otherwise he might have missed them.

"WHAT THE HELL'S he waiting for now?" asked Keyman as he scrunched down into the turret. "Does he want them to say 'please' first? Jesus Christ . . ."

Webber just shrugged at the staff sergeant, then he shifted on his gunner's seat and wrung his gloved hands for the nth time. Nearby, Smiley, who was all bundled up, with arms folded over his chest, closed his eyes in ecstasy as the heater sent warm waves into the turret.

"Crew report!" Keyman ordered, even though he had just called for one only five minutes ago.

"Driver ready."

"AP loaded. Loader ready."

"Gunner ready."

"So, gentlemen, as you can see, we're as ready as it gets, but our faithful platoon leader is making us sit on our hands. I hear he's got a plan that'll get us all killed."

"Yeah, but at least we'll die warm," said Webber.

Specialist Anthony Morabito, who, at least in Webber's estimation, had been falling into a deep depression, spoke up from the driver's station, his tone the usual gloom and doom. "Sergeant, I think we might have a problem with the fuel gauge—wait, hang on a second. Okay, there it is. Must be the damned cold."

"Or your damned eyes," added Keyman.

Given the nickname "Morbid" by the staff sergeant, Morabito had been nearing the end of his tour in Korea when the war had started. He had told Webber, "Two more

months of that bald fucker. That's all I got. Then it's good-
bye Keyman, good-bye Korea, and good riddance to both."

Morbid had been "short," and sometimes bad things
happened to people nearing the end of their tours—like,
say, a war for starters. The thought of spending up to
another year with the infamous Keyman had turned poor
Morbid into a walking corpse—not that he hadn't already
been one before the war. He was just one of those "the
glass is half empty" dudes who saw the negative in everything. Webber usually ignored moaners and groaners like
him, but recently, he had been paying a lot more attention
because he feared he was becoming one himself.

"Red One, this is Red Two, over."

"Red Two, this is Red One, Stand by . . ."

Keyman bit back a curse and slammed down the mike.
"Hey, boys? Why don't we start the attack all by our lone-
some? Anybody up for a little insubordination?"

Webber tensed. "Stop fucking around, man."

"I'm not doing the fucking," Keyman corrected.

Shaking his head, Webber glanced away and started
thinking about the fight, about the targets, and about screw-
ing up. The goddamned glass was half empty.

"THIS IS NOT scary," Romeo was saying, just after
Popeye Choi had told Neech that he was scared. "Let me
tell you a story about being scared. Okay, senior year of
high school. Prom night. I got a hotel room booked. I got a
full box of condoms. I got wood even before I get to my
girlfriend's house. It's going to be great, right?"

"You got wood?" Choi asked, his expression hidden
since he was sitting in the driver's hole.

While Romeo went on to translate, Neech tuned out the
guy's voice and went up into his hatch.

He did a double take as he panned with his NVGs toward
the narrow defile just south of TRP 02.

Five BRDMs, those four-wheeled armored amphibious vehicles carrying crews of two, six troops, and machine guns or antitank missile systems, were shifting stealthily through the mountain pass opposite Renegade Platoon's mounted BP, heading toward the embankment running along the west side of MSR 3. Neech panted with the desire to move up and destroy them. He felt like a guy who had not eaten for a week, standing before a buffet table. He was a guy whose driver had been killed by those motherfuckers. He was a .guy who could not stand waiting any more.

"Red One, this is Red Three," he called over the net. "Five BRDMs moving through the defile, just south of TRP 02, over." He grit his teeth and trembled. "Let me kill them," he whispered. "Please . . ."

PLATOON SERGEANT ABBOT would give everything he had just to know that his wife had evacuated safely. He would give everything and then some if—right now—he could go to her, hold her hand, and assure her that he would be okay.

Damn, if he wasn't having trouble focusing on the mission. That wasn't like him, but the situation was unique. It was one thing to go into battle; it was another knowing that your wife was out there somewhere, possibly in danger. How was he supposed to cope?

And worse, he was supposed to be the old wise man, the guy with all answers who showed no signs of weakness, lest he undermine his authority and the crew's unfaltering belief in him. For Paz, Sparrow, and Park, he was the Army, and his failure would mean that the organization did not work.

So he had to fake it. Keep the exterior rough. Keep the emotions in check. That was easy for most men, right?

Trying to clear his thoughts, he took up the microphone

and conveyed the coordinates of the enemy BRDMs that Neech had reported and that he now observed. He figured that Ryback was having trouble seeing them through all the smoke, and that's why the lieutenant had not called in his own report. Didn't matter. Soon those BRDMs would be toasted by field artillery.

Even before that artillery struck, Hansen called over the platoon net for all four tanks to move up into battle positions: "Red, tophat! Tophat!"

"Driver, move up!" ordered Abbot.

Five seconds later, when all four tanks were idling in their BPs and set, Hansen gave the order. "Fire!"

AFTER NEARLY AN hour of being jostled in her seat as the bus hit pothole after pothole, Karen had grown so used to the ride that she was beginning to drift off. Abbot's wife sat beside her, hands folded neatly over her lap and staring absently though the dark window at more darkness beyond.

A sharp bang—as though the bus had suffered a blowout—wrenched Karen awake. She gasped, looked around.

Another bang sounded from somewhere ahead, and the bus driver jammed on the brakes.

But it was too late. They plowed directly into the bus ahead, metal crunching, plastic snapping, passengers thrown forward as bright light flashed across the windshield.

Reaching out, Karen gripped the seat in front, braced her fall, then chanced a look up. Flames spewed from the bus ahead. As their own bus's engine roared, bullets tore into a few windows near the front, glass flying.

One young woman who had been wearing a woolen cap and seated near those windows, slumped in her seat, her head hanging at an improbable angle.

Another woman—a girl really—maybe only seventeen

or eighteen, was clutching her neck and screaming as blood spewed from between her fingers.

More women, old men, and nine or ten kids began hollering and crowding the aisle, trying to squeeze their way toward the exit up front.

Amid the chaos, neither Karen nor Kim said a word. They just looked at each other then shoved themselves into the aisle, heading with the others toward the rear emergency door, which had just been opened by a dark-haired woman chanting, "Oh my god . . . oh my god . . ."

"Stay in the bus! Stay in the bus!" yelled one of the MPs from an HMMWV behind them. The soldier worked a big machine gun, bearing his teeth as he sent automatic fire into the woods on the east side of the road.

The dark-haired woman started back, just as more gunfire raked across the side of the bus and stitched up, across the rear windows, shattering them. People collapsed, and one little girl fell at Karen's feet, her face stained by blood.

Her jaw falling open, Karen reached down toward the girl, but Kim was pulling her away, back toward the exit. "No, we have to stay in the bus!" she told Abbot's wife.

"We have to leave!" the woman shouted back, then hopped down onto the icy dirt road, dragging Karen with her. They slipped and fell to their knees.

Which saved their lives because out near the woods, rockets whistled, drew closer and, a breath later, one struck the bus while the other blasted into the HMMWV behind. An MP let out a strangled cry as the explosion echoed and flames whipped over the shattered vehicle. The soldiers in the far HMMWV began shooting wildly, one weapon thumping loudly, the others rattling.

Flaming debris that had blown off the bus clanged to the ground all around them as thick, black smoke began to fan down, and the hollering of the MPs, that terrible hollering, continued.

Back in the woods, tiny lights flashed, and if Karen didn't

know better, she would describe them as pretty. The popping, banging, shouting, and screaming continued as yet another terrific boom resounded from the front of the convoy. One of the other HMMWVs must have been hit.

"We have to go," Kim said between her teeth.

Karen shivered, saw one of the MPs sprawled out in the road, his body ablaze, a sickly sweet stench carrying on the wind. She wanted to gag. Couldn't.

"We have to go!"

More bullets pinged and punched into the bus behind her. She smelled gasoline, looked down, saw the flood beneath the tires and a stream pouring down from the fuel tank.

A heavyset woman with short, brown hair reached the emergency door, looked out, was about to scream, then jerked her head sideways and fell. Karen frowned. Then it dawned on her. The woman had just been shot in the head.

How could this be happening? Her name was Karen Berlin. She was just an English teacher for God's sake. She had come to Korea to help people. She wasn't a threat.

"We have to go!" Kim screamed, then dragged Karen to her feet and toward the edge of the road.

Off to their left, Koreans wearing civilian clothes but carrying rifles were charging from the woods toward the burning busses and HMMWVs. Some fell as gunfire from the front of the convoy tore through them, but another line of men took their place. A pair of powerful explosions rose from inside the woods, sending fireballs into the treetops.

She and Kim reached the edge of the road and jumped into a ditch. There, they hunkered down as sporadic gunfire echoed once more.

Karen trembled so hard that it hurt. And she was about to cry—but Kim grabbed her hands. "We're going to run again. Are you ready?"

"I can't."

"You can. NOW!"

She wasn't sure what it was—the woman's tone, her expression, something—but the courage to move was suddenly there. She turned, glanced up along the embankment, and dashed off, just behind Kim.

Between the uneven ground and the ice and snow, it was all she could do to remain on her feet. She hunched over and kept on as the fires from behind grew smaller. Ahead lay more woods, more darkness, and either safety or enemy soldiers. There was no way to know.

"Just keep going," came a voice from the rear.

It was one of the MPs running behind her, the black man's face half covered in blood from a series of gashes along his forehead and cheek. He had a rifle in his hand and waved with the other. "Don't stop!"

Like her boyfriend, Karen knew how to obey orders, especially those that might keep her alive.

Kim reached a stand of trees and vanished behind them. Karen followed up to find the woman squatting behind one tree and fighting for breath. The MP charged up and paused with them, his eyes wild as he got on his haunches.

"We'll stay here for a minute," he said, his own breath ragged. "But then we have to keep moving. They sent a patrol this way."

"Who did?" asked Karen.

"Ma'am, are you kidding me?"

"I saw Koreans, but they weren't soldiers. I mean they had guns but they weren't dressed like soldiers."

"SOF guys."

"SOF?"

"Special Operations Forces. Bad guys. The baddest kind. Okay, let's go."

"Wait a minute," said Kim. "Go where?"

"We have to swing back and keep heading south toward Uijongbu. If they've penetrated this far, then that's our only shot. We can't go back to TDC or Casey anyway. There's a division heading there. With all due respect, ma'am, we are in enemy territory right now, and I suggest you listen to me."

"Y'all got a name?" Kim asked, turning up her Texas accent to catch the MP off guard.

"Uh, yeah. I'm Corporal James Reese, Second Military Police Company, United States Army. You?"

"I'm Kim Abbot. This is Karen Berlin."

"Kim and Karen. That's going to get confusing."

Kim smirked. "I think you can handle it." She took in a long breath before regarding Karen. "Are you ready?"

Karen hesitated, then a shout from nearby sent her springing to her feet.

Reese cocked a thumb over his shoulder. "Follow me."

CHAPTER
FOUR

DENSE CLOUDS OF smoke from the mortar and artillery fires spared Hansen from some of the carnage wrought by the platoon's AP rounds. Still, what he could see through his extension left him feeling achy and hollow.

All along the ridges, cuts, and smaller hogbacks beside and below TRP 01, men blew apart like rag dolls stuffed with firecrackers, all of it playing out in the thermal sight, as though Hansen were watching in his living room as he listened to the reality show's narrator talk about how lucky producers were to have obtained such graphic war footage. But be warned, the narrator would add, you may find some of these images deeply disturbing.

Thankfully, the crew kept their mouths shut, perhaps watching the slaughter unfold with the same awful fascination. Hansen had even forgotten to yell, "Target!" after the round had detonated, releasing its deadly confetti on those insanely determined troops.

As a volley of mortar fires dropped, catapulting an entire squad off the ridge, Hansen became more torn. In one breath he wanted to drum his fists on his chest and curse the enemy. In the next, he wanted to say he was sorry for what they had done because there wasn't much glory in conducting a mass slaughter. He told himself: This is my job. Do it.

On a more positive note, the commander's fire plan was—quite remarkably—going off without a hitch, and the A-10s were rumbling overhead, adding their ordnance to the fray. Van Buren was once again working closely with FSO Yelas to ensure that Team Cobra was well supported. Artillery now pounded the hell out of TRP 03 to protect the dismounts near the river, while more fires were put on MSR 3 as the GSR team reported that mounted forces were moving south down the road. Those BRDMs that Neech had spotted were already history, but Hansen was keeping a close eye on the defile, figuring another company would push through and dismount their AT teams.

Even as he took another look at the mountain pass, Lee called out, "Two BRDMs."

Hansen stared hard through his extension, saw the vehicles as they were lost in the smoke, then emerged again. "Near one first."

Lee scanned for the target but remained silent.

"Near one first!" Hansen repeated.

"Target obscured! Can't get a good lase."

"Try one more time. You got him?"

"Yes! Identified."

"Up!"

"Fire!"

"On the way!"

"Red One, this is Red Two. Troops have entered the water directly west my sector," reported Keyman. "We have swimmers in the water. Engaging, over."

"Target!" Hansen yelled as the BRDM exploded into superheated scrap metal. "Far one!"

Lee once again paused.

"Come on, Lee. Lase that fucker!"

"He's obscured. Wait, there he is. Identified!"

"Up!"

"Fire!"

"On the way!"

"Red One, this is Red Three! I have more swimmers in the water, over," called Neech.

Continuing to ignore both TCs—though he knew he should be fighting his platoon and not just his own tank—Hansen waited until the second BRDM exploded in a wide conflagration. "Target!"

While Deac and Gatch issued their usual victory cries, Hansen keyed his mike. "Red, this is Red One," he began, panning with his extension to see dozens of men entering the icy water directly south of Keyman's position. They dragged across ropes that would be used to guide the rest of the infantry. Hansen went up top, pulled on his NVGs, and picked out more NKPA grunts farther up the river, opposite Neech's BP. "Check your ranges and continue engaging those dismounts, out!"

The TCs acknowledged and got to work, as did Hansen. It was time to rely more on the M1's coax and the commander's and loader's machine guns. The coax could effectively engage area or point targets out to 900 meters. Any farther, and the tracers would burn out. The maximum effective range of Hansen's M2 .50 caliber was 1,800 meters, while Deac's M240 didn't have any sights and was only used to engage area or aerial targets. Some loaders weren't very adept at firing the weapon because they didn't get enough training with it. Deac was no exception—though he would never admit that. His primary job was to load the main gun; however, Hansen would put him behind the 240 if the situation got out of hand.

From inside his hatch, Hansen sighted the nearest targets and announced, "Caliber fifty!"

That was Deac's cue to move up into his hatch and

assume Hansen's job of primary target acquisition (ground and air). He might also assist in adjusting Hansen's machine-gun fire, watching as the tracers streaked across the landscape.

Although Hansen could lay the weapon for deflection and simply estimate the range, he called out, "Lee, can you lase them—or is there too much smoke?"

"I'll try." The gunner lased the targets. "Range one-two hundred. Looks correct."

Once he was set, Hansen opened fire. His first fifteen-round burst carried three tracers that slashed a phosphorescent red line across the foothills, the riverbank, and the patches of ice floating along the river. His bead terminated on a small group of heads bobbing hear the southern bank.

As he squeezed off his second salvo, Deac yelled, "Right!" to adjust his fire, and Hansen shifted the weapon.

"That's good!" said Deac. "Now back left! Left!"

The big fifty caliber nicknamed "Ma Deuce" (it was really "Mod" for model, yet the "Ma" had stuck) had been designed by John Browning. Though one of the oldest, the M2 was widely considered the most reliable machine gun in the US Army. Were one of Hansen's bullets to hit a man standing on the snow, he would cartwheel through the air, hit the ground, and never get up again. The Army had yet to find a better replacement.

And so, with decades of history and tradition in his hands, Hansen continued to deliver bloody lightning into the water, but now there were so many troops that he was hardly putting a dent in their advance. "Lee, get ready, man. The second they come into your range, you coax the bastards, you hear me?"

"I will coax the troops, sir," the gunner said rigidly.

EVEN THOUGH AN ammo truck had been co-located with the company team trains and could come forward within moments of the XO or first sergeant's call, that still didn't make Webber feel better about going through rounds like toilet paper. He figured that even if they repeatedly resupplied, they would probably run out of ammunition long before the NKPA ran out of men—but no one else seemed to acknowledge that. They would live and die in denial. He wanted to tell Keyman to take it easy on the fifty, conserve ammo, and ask Abbot or Hansen to call in more mortar fires.

Sure, he wanted to do that, but he knew it'd be a waste of time. Keyman wanted to be superman in the turret and single-handedly take out every infantryman crossing the river. He needed to show his father that he was number one. He needed to show his brother that he was worth something. And most of all, he needed to prove to himself that he wasn't and would never be second best.

Unfortunately, he hadn't done the math.

They carried 10,000 rounds of 7.62-mm ammunition for Webber's coax, 1,400 rounds of 7.62-mm for Smiley's M240, and 1,000 rounds of .50-caliber ammunition for the bald man's weapon. Webber estimated that Keyman had already used up about 40 percent of his cache, but the TC forged on, muttering, "Got that motherfucker," between squeezing off killing bursts and taking cues from Smiley to adjust his fire.

Moreover, anything could happen to that ammo truck as it moved forward. Anything at all . . .

Since the troops were still out of his coax's range, Webber sat there, a bag of nerves bolted to his station, his gaze never leaving his gunner's primary sight and the troops displayed as white-hot images by the thermal imaging system. While the TIS could see through all the dust and smoke, the laser rangefinder was often degraded and reporting incorrect ranges—even though Webber could plainly see the troops in the water. Of course, they had trained on visual range estimation using the TIS image and on manually indexing the range in the computer.

But what they hadn't anticipated was how taking on a battalion-size force of dismounts would scare the living shit out of them. Or was Webber the only one freaking out? No, he couldn't be. They had been told that the division had suffered 40 percent attrition. So where were all those guys coming from? When asked, Keyman had snorted and said, "Someone left the gate open in Hell. And it's our job to ship 'em back."

Four explosions from either enemy artillery or mortars repeatedly rocked the mountainside behind them, the booming growing louder, nearer, then another four shells struck a little farther west, closer to the BFIST and the GSR team's M113. "Of course those fucking guys are drawing fire," Keyman groaned, then he cut loose another burst of .50 caliber.

At the same time, more mortars dropped like hammers from heaven, blasting up fountains of water, fire, and ice as they beat paths of death along the north side of the river. Platoon Sergeant Abbot was no doubt on the company net, acting as forward observer and as Webber's temporary savior since Keyman was now well beyond calling for assistance. Finally, the tank's glorious commander silenced his gun, leaned back in his seat, and flexed his gloved hands. "Hey, gunner? You ready?"

Webber glanced away from his GPS. "Yeah."

"You don't sound it. And I bet you look scared. You look like maybe you're going to fuck up. Don't. 'Cause they're still coming." He leaned forward to peer through his extension. "Jesus Christ, they're still coming."

Oh, no. It can't be.

Webber had never heard that tone come from Keyman's mouth, a tone that clearly and definitively indicated that he was, excuse me, scared?

No way. It isn't possible.

Returning his gaze to his sight, Webber took in a quick

breath and muttered, "Oh, man. It's company after company. They're coming out of the fucking woodwork—literally."

"At least we lived through Christmas," groaned Morbid over the intercom.

Webber shifted back in his seat, felt light-headed, a little dizzy, a lot dizzy. He turned, glanced up at Keyman, who gave him the strangest look.

Then Webber fell out of his seat, listening to the thud of his own collapse as darkness smothered him.

NORTH KOREAN PCS and armor were now being engaged along MSR 3 by field artillery and by TOW missiles from the Bradleys. Once those ready TOWs were expended, the Bradleys would rely upon their chain-gun fire to take out the remaining PCs, leaving the armor to the tanks of White Platoon, who were flanking the enemy's avenue of approach. This division of labor to service targets allowed each platoon to fight at its maximum potential. Moreover, those chain-gun fires could devastate dismounts at greater ranges than machine-gun fire could, so the Bradleys would be called upon to hit those area targets as well.

While Abbot needed to keep well abreast of that engagement, his primary concern remained with those hordes of NKPA infantry and dismounts who were more afraid of their own superiors than they were of the enemy. You wouldn't find too many of them going AWOL.

Another wave of the maniacal bastards suddenly reached the northern riverbank and swarmed like camouflage-colored roaches toward the low-water crossing, where they would only sink up to their shins. Abbot and Neech began cutting them down with their machine guns.

But then an RPG whistled out of nowhere to explode against Abbot's forward hull. The hissing and reverberation passed through the turret like a freight train and was gone as quickly.

Abbot ceased fire, went up into his hatch, took a quick look at the flames still flickering over the tank. "Where is that bastard?" He called to Paz for an extinguisher, quickly doused the flames, then asked for a crew report.

"Looks good down here, Sergeant," said Sparrow. "Driver, ready."

"HEAT loaded, loader ready."

"Gunner ready."

Back on the company net, Abbot requested that more FA fires be placed upon the southern riverbank across from TRP 01. He conveyed the grid coordinates, but as usual, the request for that support was just that—a request—and he wasn't sure whether those guys could remain in the fight for much longer before TF 2-9 called upon their services. Time would tell.

Reports from Yelas and the GSR team's NCO suddenly burst over the net. Infantry forces had crossed the river and multiple squads were closing in on their positions along the reverse slopes. The FISTers and GSR guys were taking both small-arms and occasional RPG fire.

Abbot relayed the report to Hansen, who said that Keyman and himself would shift southwest to provide suppressive fires for those teams while Abbot and Neech continued to cover their sectors. Yelas had already requested that mortars be placed along the river opposite his position.

Ryback got on the net to say that he and his second infantry squad were already moving into position west of Red's BP to ambush those forces attacking the FISTers and GSR guys. However, they wouldn't turn down any tank support.

"Red Three, this is Red Four, over," Abbot called Neech, who had been breathing dragon fire with his .50 for the past few minutes. After a few seconds' delay, he repeated the call.

"Go ahead, Four," Neech finally responded.

"Are you watching your ammo, over?"

"Yes, I am, over."

"Just make 'em count, out."

Such reminders were hardly necessary, but Neech required careful watching now. Hearing his voice come steadily and clearly over the platoon net put Abbot at ease, though just a little. If he didn't keep close tabs on the man, Neech would become the proverbial and cliché loose cannon, so bent on payback that he might sacrifice the rest of his crew. Abbot had seen it happen more than once, and while the quest for revenge sometimes enabled you to commit extraordinary (and brutal) acts, playing cards with the devil was never wise. Never wise at all.

Abruptly, the platoon net cracked to life: "Red One, this is Red Two," Keyman called to Hansen.

"Go ahead, Two."

"Shifting position southwest, but I'm operating with a three-man crew, over."

"Do you have a casualty, over?" Hansen demanded.

"Negative, negative. Red Two Golf had a fuckin' panic attack or something, and he passed out, over."

Static filled the net for a few seconds, and Abbot could only imagine what Hansen was thinking. The LT eventually answered, "Well, try to revive him, out."

Webber is unconscious? Abbot still couldn't believe it. He would have never thought a guy like Webber—a schemer, practical joker, and fast-talker who had already proven himself on the battlefield—would have a meltdown. At the moment, he expected such a collapse from Neech.

And worse, how was Keyman reacting to the situation? He was probably getting ready to throw the unconscious gunner out of the turret and leave him lying in the snow.

What else can go wrong?

* * *

HANSEN BRACED HIMSELF in his TC's seat as they clanked up and over a slight hill, continuing southwest to assist the FISTers and GSR team.

He kept drawing back his head in surprise as Keyman's words repeated in his head. Webber had passed out. *Passed out? What the hell was that?* It just didn't make sense. Webber wasn't the type, hadn't exhibited any signs or symptoms of a problem. Or maybe Hansen hadn't been scrutinizing his platoon as closely as he should.

Knowing that he couldn't let his failure and Webber's shake his confidence, he steeled himself, shouted to the crew, "All right, guys, we're going in there to protect those FISTers and GSR guys, and we're going to show them and these North Korean sons of bitches how we do business."

"Hooah!" Deac and Gatch cried.

"Lee, are you with me?"

The gunner nodded shyly. "I'm with you, LT." His voice came much too thinly.

"Hey, man, you'll be all right. We're badasses. Bad to the bone. We can do this. You know we can."

"Yes, LT."

Drawing in a huge breath, Hansen went up into his hatch and, wearing his NVGs, directed Gatch toward the top of a rocky hill that overlooked the river.

Off to their left, Keyman's tank was already rolling toward the same hill and turning to ascend the slope. The BFIST and M113 lay about fifty meters farther west, tucked deeply into a slope and well out of sight from even Hansen's NVGs. However, grunts must have come over the hill to identify and engage those vehicles, and Hansen and Keyman would need to focus their initial hunt on those suspected and potential enemy positions while keeping in close contact with both teams and with Ryback's squad.

As they neared the crest, Hansen ordered Gatch to slow down, then come to a full stop. A glance at the river and valley below stole his breath and began sapping away his courage.

It was a sight he would remember for the rest of his life, an image that appeared almost biblical, borrowed from some old Cecil B. DeMille film.

Perhaps two thousand men were in the river, guiding themselves across via ropes spanned between the riverbanks. Another four or five hundred had already hit the opposite shore and were advancing toward the higher ground. Still more troops were rappelling down the ridges, while others who had just hit the bank were now rushing toward the water. All of this went on as fierce winds began blowing the valley clear of smoke to reveal that the enemy was literally everywhere.

And the artillery fires had gone silent.

"**ROMEO, GET ON** your two-forty," Neech ordered as several squads of enemy grunts working along the southern side of the low-water crossing reached the shoreline and dropped to their bellies. "They're coming in range. I'm getting on the coax."

Neech was almost out of ammo for the .50 cal, but they still had a full cache for the loader's M240 and the coax—not to mention a whole lot of ammo for the main gun. Too bad they didn't have, say, twenty more AP rounds. Those grunts near the water would be hating life for a half second before they became cushions for shrapnel.

"Sarge, how the fuck are we supposed to stop all these troops?" Romeo asked. The gunner/loader wasn't scared. In fact, he sounded pissed off—but not at Neech. He was angry at the Army for putting them in such a shithole. But you couldn't blame the Army. You couldn't blame anyone but yourself.

Neech had become an expert at that.

"If we can't shoot 'em all, Romeo, we'll run them over. And if we can't do that, then we'll get out and club those motherfuckers to death. And if we can't do that, then we'll—"

"Incoming!" cried Romeo as he slammed himself down in the hatch just as a mortar shell ripped a chunk from the hill below the tank and booted it up at them.

"Stay up there, God damn it," Neech boomed. "They're coming in! Take the guys on the left. I got right!"

Ryback's people at the low-water crossing were blowing their claymores and engaging the enemy from the flank, causing them to disperse, which was quite all right with Neech, since many of them were running directly toward the tank—and into his coax, just as he opened fire.

The task force scouts had already crossed the river and pulled out in their HMMWVs, but one vehicle had become stuck in a ditch just below the Bradleys' BP. While a Bradley crew provided covering chain-gun fire, troops from the stuck HMMWV dashed to the other one, about twenty meters away. Not three seconds after they left the disabled BFV, it exploded under wire-guided missile fire. Neech flinched as two of the fleeing scouts were cut down by hurtling debris.

Then another rocket streaked in and took out the second HMMWV, killing the rest of those scouts. The guys running from the stuck vehicle would have been killed anyway.

Up top, Romeo had adjusted his stand so that he could use the chest-hold technique to steady his machine gun while firing. He grasped the handles of the M240 mount, held them closely against his chest for steadiness and control, and fired the weapon in twenty- to thirty-round bursts, adjusting tracer impact on his targets. His gun spoke violently to the enemy, sending tremors through the top of the turret, while he added his own voice to the racket, cursing in Spanish like Ricky Ricardo on cocaine.

Down below, Neech was in the gunner's seat and had just lased another group of grunts. He immediately dumped the lead by quickly releasing then reengaging the palm switches. He did that based upon the slow ballistic characteristics of the 7.62-mm round that caused the ballistic computer to induce a large lead angle. You didn't want such an angle when you were firing killing bursts and sweeping in the Z-pattern technique. He opened fire, dropped a half dozen, watched the rest hit the deck, then swept them once more.

"Motherfucker!" Romeo suddenly shouted in English. "Sergeant, they're right here! Twenty meters!"

· Small-arms fire pinged off the frontal armor as Neech strained to see anything in the GPS.

A head popped up from behind a fallen and snow-covered tree. Neech raked the tree with fire, caught the guy in the head, watched him jerk back, die.

"More, more, more!" yelled Romeo, wrenching his gun off to the far left and releasing another burst. "They're flanking us, Sergeant!"

Neech swung the turret around to spot another squad shuffling toward a stand of trees to their north. He blanketed the area with fire while Romeo jammed down his own triggers.

"Troops to the front!" cried Popeye Choi from the driver's hole. "Troops to the front!"

Neech moved the turret once more to lay down some fire on the troops advancing ahead.

"Sergeant, we can't hold here for much longer," warned Romeo.

"Yes we can," grunted Neech. "YES WE FUCKING CAN!" And with that verbal explosion, Neech fired again, intent upon killing everything in sight and wishing he could also murder that other version of himself dressed all in black, that guy who kept whispering in his ear, *"Batman died for you. But you didn't deserve it. You know that."*

"**BLACK SIX, THIS** is Red One," Hansen called to Captain Van Buren. "Unless we can put more fires here, the enemy will overrun positions south of TRP 01, over."

"Red One, this is Black Six, be advised tubes have been diverted to support TF 2-9. Disengagement criteria is a company-size force through the breech. Hold your position as long as possible, then fall back to successive BPs, out."

"Well, there it is," Hansen said, hanging up the mike. "I didn't expect anything less. We stand and fight and delay them for as long as possible."

"Delay all of them?" Deac asked, his eyes pleading. "LT, begging ya'll's pardon, but we're fucked!"

"Not yet." Hansen winked at the loader, then climbed up into his hatch. He surveyed the river once more, then spotted a group of infantry ascending a hill, coming toward them: range about a thousand meters.

Dropping back hard into the turret, he manned his .50 and took aim. "Caliber fifty!"

The rounds punched blistering red holes in the troops as puffs of snow and shattered rock rose near and around his tracers. He suddenly ceased fire, went up into the hatch, then ducked hard as small-arms fire ricocheted all over the turret. "God damn it! Lee, where are they?"

"Troops to the left," the gunner reported evenly. "They're in my range."

"Well, coax the fuckers right now, God damn it! What are you waiting for?"

"Kill 'em, Lee!" cried Deac.

The gunner opened up with the coax, leveling the attacking troops, then Hansen shouted, "Target! More troops—right!"

* * *

WEBBER AWOKE TO the sensation of a fist in his sternum and to the rattling of the tank's coaxial machine gun.

His eyes focused. Okay, there was Smiley hovering over him with that dumbass grin plastered like pink icing across his face. The KATUSA was using the old trick of rubbing the sternum to revive someone from unconsciousness. Webber used the old trick of punching the asshole away.

But hey, at least the KATUSA hadn't gone for those ammonia capsules in the first aid kit. Those things were nasty.

"Ouch! You fucker!"

"Get off of me!"

"Okay, good, Webber. You back from Las Vegas. Sergeant, he awake!"

"Webber, take over on this fuckin' coax!" yelled Keyman. "Smiley, get on your gun."

The loader proffered his hand and helped Webber to his feet. Then he went up into his hatch to man his weapon, while Webber assumed the gunner's seat and Keyman went up into his hatch, now brandishing his M4 rifle. "Morbid, you'd better be ready to move," hollered the TC.

"I can't be any more ready—unless I put on a condom," said the driver.

"Well, get it on, because in two minutes we're doing the dickey dance!"

Webber rubbed his eyes, leaned into his sight.

Then he lost his breath.

Oh, God. He couldn't believe what he was seeing. It was like an NKPA military parade through downtown Pyongyang, and Red Platoon had been invited so they could take one in the ass for the Dear Leader.

"Get me the fuck out of here," he muttered.

Smiley cursed in Korean as he fired at the grunts to the left, while Webber turned his arms to steel and began firing at those to the right. In the meantime, Keyman's M4 cracked from up top.

Holy shit. It dawned on Webber that the TC had exhausted the ammo for his .50—and then it dawned on him that, oh my God, he had passed out! Gooseflesh worked into every part of his body. He had let down the crew, the platoon, his country.

In the next breath he told himself to stop being so dramatic. He was under a lot of stress. Shit happened. He had to deal with it. And he would. With his coax.

Was his confidence back? *Maybe. Ah, no.* It wasn't. But he had to do something.

"Troops to the rear!" screamed Smiley.

"Troops to the front!" Morbid added.

"Oh, well," Keyman said, his tone almost casual. "We're surrounded."

CHAPTER
FIVE

SOMETHING'S GOING TO *happen. Something bad . . .*

Abbot glared at Paz, who sat ready at his station.

"What?" the loader asked.

"Nothing." Abbot wanted to curse the guy for making him paranoid, but an admission like that would make Paz go even more nuts —and Abbot no longer had the patience to listen to his ranting and raving.

The loader's expression softened. "You look mad."

"Not mad," Abbot groaned. "Just frustrated."

"Don't worry. I'm sure she's all right."

Abbot nodded, though he felt otherwise. He didn't believe in ESP or any of that other paranormal crap, but he and Kim had developed a shorthand and a sense about each other that was hard to explain. Sometimes he could just tell when she needed him, even if she was half a world away. He turned back to his extension and squinted.

So many explosions tore up MSR 3 that he could barely discern the road, let alone anything else within the defile between TRP 02 and TRP 03. Unlike the much smaller mountain pass lying just south of TRP 02, where those BRDMs had attempted to advance, this corridor was about eight hundred meters wide, heavily wooded, and frozen into timelessness by what forecasters were calling the harshest winter in Korea's history.

According to reports from Ryback's people, a company of BMPs and VTTs—comprised of ten or twelve of the armored personnel carriers—was rolling down the road and being led in by three T-54 tanks whose drivers navigated through the wreckage of their fallen brothers. They were heading directly for the low-water crossing.

At the moment, one section of White Platoon was still transferring main-gun ammo, while the other employed their machine guns to place suppressive fires on the enemy grunts moving east of TRP 03 as they closed in on Ryback's squad.

Concurrently, one section of Bradleys was busy putting long-range TOW fire on the tank brigade's follow-on forces. They had displaced to reinforce Red's sector and to get a clean shot up the road. To the west, Keyman and Hansen were busy covering the FISTers and GSR team, who were moving back into their successive battle positions behind Red Platoon, while Ryback scooped up his dismounts with the first sergeant's APC and headed back for his Bradleys.

So, the way Abbot saw it, he and Neech needed to destroy those personnel carriers and tanks, and they needed to do so yesterday. "Red One, this is Red Four, over."

Abbot tapped his boot. "Come on, come on . . . Red One, this is Red Four, over."

"Go ahead, Four," Hansen answered.

"Enemy armor and PCs heading south MSR 3, vicinity TRP 02, over."

"Roger that. Engage those bastards and we'll join you after we kill these two thousand motherfuckers, out."

That woke Abbot's grin. The kid was learning the lingo

and fully appreciating the irony of the battlefield. "Red Three, you hear that, over?"

Nothing.

"Neech, you hear that, over?"

SOMEONE WAS TALKING over the platoon net. Was it Abbot? Neech didn't have time to chat like a couple of high school kids on cell phones. There was a fucking war going on. And his .50 cal had just run dry. He ducked into the turret, went over to the coax, and worked it for a moment while Romeo got religious with his 7.62, dropping more of the godless bastards while using the Lord's name in vain—in both Spanish and English.

"Hey, Sergeant," the kid called. "Abbot wants you. We gotta engage armor and PCs coming down the fucking road up there!"

"Yeah, how—with all these fucking grunts crawling through the hills?"

"I don't know. But we have to!"

"Sergeant, please. Listen to Romeo," said Popeye Choi from the driver's station.

They were begging him. His crew was literally begging him. How had it come to that? Was Neech so far gone that he couldn't obey orders? *No.* He had to help out his brothers. He fought for them. No-one else.

What the fuck? He was crying. He backhanded away the tears and cleared his throat. "All right, Romeo. Arm the gun. Stay on the coax till I need you to load another round. Let's go hunting."

"You got it, Sergeant!"

WEBBER FELT LIKE a fly trapped in a soda can targeted by a troop of belligerent Boy Scouts armed with BB guns.

But those scouts weren't packing toy guns, and if they saw an old lady who needed help crossing the street, they would shoot her and her little dog, arrest her children and sentence them to work camps, then indoctrinate her grandchildren into the Red Youth Guard.

The streets of North Korea were a dangerous place.

But not quite as dangerous as one particular low-water crossing along the Hantan River.

As the small-arms fire kept raking the tank, forcing Keyman and Smiley down into the turret, Webber thought he heard shouts, footfalls, and more gunfire above the ticking heater and idling engine. Had he? Even with his CVC helmet on?

Maybe. The walls of the turret were moving in on him. He thought he had grown used to the narrow space, but this was different.

The gunfire tapered off, and the turret grew still.

Webber held his breath, his gaze slowly lifting to the ceiling. Out there, somewhere, those lanky little maniacs were about to jump on the tank and attempt to drop grenades or other deadly surprises into their open hatches.

He flinched as a metallic clang hit the turret floor. Three, two, one, and the explosion tore off his right arm and leg and threw him back against the turret wall. He lay there, bleeding out, as Keyman leaned over him, shaking his head in disgust . . .

But there was no grenade, no explosion—only a tank gunner who had forgotten how to breathe.

Then he gasped, willed himself back to the moment. Another scan through his sight turned up nothing.

Where were they now? Still out there. Waiting. Regrouping. Reassessing. Getting ready to fire Sagger wire-guided missiles that might cause catastrophic damage to the tank, not to mention what it might do to their pathetic bags of flesh and blood. Webber's hands were trembling.

Something thumped on the turret from behind. "I think they're in the bustle rack," he said in a broken voice.

"There's a guy coming up the hull," yelled Morbid.

Keyman rose into his hatch, shot the bastard, dropped down and adjusted the boom mike closer to his lips. "Red One, this is Red Two."

"Oh my God, they're all over us," screamed Webber, as six or seven more guys took flying leaps onto the hull.

"Go ahead, Two," responded Hansen.

"Scratch my back!" Keyman cried. "Scratch my back!"

"GATCH, BACK UP!" Hansen ordered as he grabbed the TC override and brought the turret around to face Keyman's track.

Infantrymen crawled over the tank like maggots on roadkill.

"Gunner, coax troops!" he ordered.

Lee looked confused for a second, then abruptly checked his sight and cut loose with the coax, firing directly at Keyman's track, rounds glancing and sparking off armor, tracers caroming to flash like crimson sparklers.

Deep down, in a sick little part of Hansen's psyche, he almost wished those rounds could penetrate armor, do real damage to Keyman's track, and take the man out of the fight. Not kill him, of course, though Hansen's thoughts had occasionally strayed to that dark place. He definitely had developed a love-hate relationship with the guy, loving the way he fought like the meanest bastard on the battlefield, hating the way he conducted himself as a human being. What a relief it would be to see him leave. No more thorn in Hansen's side. No more albatross. No one second-guessing him anymore. *Wouldn't that be nice?* Damn, he shouldn't be thinking like that about his wingman, but he was.

* * *

WEBBER STILL FELT like a fly in a soda can, only now the can was receiving hits from a 7.62-mm coaxially mounted machine gun. The guy firing that weapon, Sergeant Lee, a KATUSA who would've made a brilliant Boy Scout, was getting ready to earn his merit badge. While their extra cold weather clothing, personal items, and other field gear stored on the outside of the tank would be shredded by the friendly fire, it was worth the price, and they could get new gear in the next resupply run.

The fire rattled on, the enemy soldiers falling across the hull and rolling onto the snow. Morbid was already backing up out of their BP, while Webber spun the turret in a full circle at maximum speed, usually a routine way of warming up the turret hydraulics, now a method to fling guys from the tank.

"Grease those fuckers!" cried Keyman.

Morbid "pivot steered" over the enemy grunts on the ground, greasing the treads of their tank just like Patton had said in an address to his troops.

Keyman, his M4 tight in his grip, the business end pointed up through his open hatch, yelled, "I don't think so!" and fired. Though Webber couldn't see what had happened, Keyman whooped and filled in the crew: "Blew his fuckin' head off!"

Another burst of coax fire ripped across the turret from front to back. A second one hammered in the reverse direction, and when the firing stopped, Keyman went back up for a look. "All right! All right!" He grabbed the mike. "I'm clean! I'm clean!"

"Roger," said Hansen. "Ceasing fire."

The lieutenant went on to report that FSO Yelas and the NCO from the GSR team had checked in and were heading southeast toward their successive BP behind Red's position, with Yelas covering the GSR team with his BFIST's coax and chain gun. Hansen and Keyman would remain in place to cover them for a few minutes more, then shift directly east to join Neech and Abbot.

Webber clutched his control handle much too tightly and caught himself. He was losing his breath again. What the hell was wrong with his body? Energy leaked from him like oil from his old Trans Am, only he couldn't stop the leak by simply replacing a worn gasket. Was he going to pass out again? *Dear God, no.*

"Dude, you should see this," said Keyman, standing in his hatch as they bounced across the hill. "Those rude heathens from the north bled all over my tank. What a fucking mess!"

Ironically, the only subjects that seemed to awaken Keyman's sense of humor were killing and death. Was he making wisecracks to compensate for the horror? No doubt he was. Did he think he was funny? He had once compared himself to the immortal Rodney Dangerfield. Webber had burst his bubble by comparing him to the immortal—and very bald—Don Rickles. While Morbid and Smiley had cracked up, Webber had found himself on his knees, his ear twisted in Keyman's grip.

Those were the days, the days when Webber had been the expert at covering up his feelings with wisecracks. Why couldn't he marvel in all the grotesqueness, wipe the enemy's blood on his face, howl at the moon and laugh? Why did he feel so utterly terrified?

"Yeah, the least those fuckers could've done was die neatly," said Morbid. "And I thought they were as easy to train as bar girls."

"What do you think, Smiley?" Keyman began. "Should we wash off this blood or leave it there like a fucking badge of honor? Or maybe we can go psycho like Neech and demand that it stay on because we're hardcore? Yeah, I say we leave it on."

"Whatever you say, Sergeant. You the boss!" Smiley

knew how to play the game. He winked at Webber, then gave Keyman the finger when the TC wasn't looking.

Webber grimaced and checked his sight.

There he was, a grunt perched atop a small mound of snow with an RPG resting squarely on his shoulder as a few of his bestest buddies fanned out around him.

Why hadn't Keyman spotted them?

And why wasn't Webber immediately alerting the crew? Would he let the guy fire?

Let the guy kill Keyman?

After all, no one would miss the arrogant asshole, right?

"Troops!" the TC hollered.

Webber did the "right" thing, firing at the guy and his buddies. Mr. RPG's chest turned into lean ground beef, and his buddies took rounds and tumbled back like stuntmen hanging from wires in some cheesy martial arts film.

Keyman banged a fist on the turret wall, then shot up into his hatch. "You want more of that, you fucks! Let's do it! Let's do it right now!"

"I COME WITH sixty-eight tons of baggage, and that's only the tank I'm talking about. There's the people I'm responsible for, the moves, the deployments . . ."

"So you've said. I've thought about everything. And I've made up my mind. So now, can we get out of this cold?"

There it was again, the cold. Even when Karen tried to purge it from her mind, tried to reflect on her relationship with Jack, the cold found a way in.

She wondered if she were more frightened or more cold. She couldn't decide because, well, she was too frightened *and* too cold. Maybe the cold outweighed the fear? Did it really matter?

Why was she trying to make such a useless calculation? To keep her thoughts away from the moment? To forget about the fact that at any second, any second at all, she could die? Well that was a no-brainer . . .

So now, can we get out of this cold?

Shut up, Karen.

Where are you now. Jack, I need you to keep me warm . . .

Corporal Reese was leading them along a mountainside that was damned steep, maybe a forty-five-degree angle. The snow came up to their knees at times, and Karen could only go twenty yards or so before stopping to catch her breath and feel the fire in her legs begin to cool.

Kim, who was probably fifteen years older, was really pissing off Karen because she easily kept up with Reese. Where the hell did that woman find the energy? And how could she remain so calm and determined? If they got a moment, Karen wanted to ask.

At the next cluster of four or five trees, Reese hunkered down and waited for them. Kim tucked herself below a tree, put her hands to her face, and breathed deeply to warm her nose and cheeks as Karen came up, wanting to collapse right there. "Oh, God," she said, struggling for breath.

"Get down," ordered Reese, scanning the mountain ahead with some kind of goggles. "Do you actually want to get us killed?"

Kim snorted. "I'm sorry we're not performing to your standards, but, excuse me, we're civilians."

"Just do what I say."

Wincing, Karen squatted down and tried warming her own nose and cheeks without much success. "We're going to get frostbite out here."

"Sorry for the inconvenience," Reese snapped.

"Hey, Corporal, we don't need that," said Kim.

Reese frowned. "All right, ma'am. Just the nerves getting to me, that's all." His bright eyes turned up toward the mountainside, the trees in silhouette and positioned like sentries monitoring their escape. "Did you hear that?"

The wind blew hard through the branches, then as they grew quiet, something cracked.

"There!" Reese said in a stage whisper, pointing toward the stand of trees they had last used for a pit stop. "Get around the other side!"

Kim grabbed Karen's wrist and pulled her to the back side of the trees as Reese plunged to his elbows and aimed his rifle. "Don't move," he said.

Lowering her head, Karen held hands tightly with Kim, and they sat there, inert, in the snow, in the middle of a war.

Why her? Had she done something to offend God or the universe? Was she such a bad person that she needed to be punished? Had she asked for too much when she had decided to be with Jack? Was it her fault for being greedy?

No. And she wasn't a bad person. She was someone who helped people, a teacher for crying out loud. Did bad things always have to happen to good people?

Karen couldn't take anymore. Her nerves had been stretched so thinly that the faintest breeze would blow them—and her grip on reality—away. She tried to stifle the tears, the gasps, but they kept coming.

Kim quietly shushed her and slid an arm around her shoulder—as a shot rang out!

Karen jolted back as Kim fell face forward into the snow. Mouth open but words failing, Karen grabbed the woman by the shoulders, rolled her onto her side and saw the gaping gunshot wound in her head. There was blood— so much blood—everywhere. Something finally came out of Karen's mouth, a hollow little scream that faded to silence as every part of her body grew rigid in horror.

Suddenly, Reese was there, seizing her wrist. "Come on," he barked, dragging her from the snow as two more shots struck the trees, shards of bark tumbling onto her.

She was on her feet now, running through the snow beside him as three or four more rounds struck another cluster of trees to their right.

"They killed her," Karen said between breaths.

"They'll kill us too. Faster!"

"I can't," she said, the image of Kim's bloody head flashing like a camera bulb.

"Right up there," Reese said, pointing to a little mound. "Right over the top and down."

She could barely keep up with him.

But then, as Kim's face completely filled her mind's eye, Karen reached into a place deep inside, one she never knew existed. There, waiting for her, was a river of fresh anger. She reached down, cupped the water in her hand, and took a sip. Her eyes widened.

They had killed Kim. She couldn't let those bastards win. She had to be strong now. For Kim. For herself. She worked her legs harder, raced up and over the mound with Reese at her side. They dropped down, got on their hands and knees for a moment as he put a finger to his lips.

Karen glanced down, realizing only then that Kim's blood had splattered all over her woolen coat, her jeans. She reached up, felt her cheek. More blood. At once she retched as Reese rose slowly to peer over the mound.

It was all coming out of her. All of the fear and anger. Because it couldn't stay inside anymore. Her stomach heaved.

"We have to get higher. Let 'em walk on by," he whispered, sliding back down.

"I'm okay," she said sarcastically. "It's all right."

"What're you—her now?"

Karen faced him, drool dripping from her chin. "She's dead."

"Look, I'm sorry—"

"Just shut up and get us out of here."

* * *

AS HANSEN DIRECTED Gatch into a battle position to help take on the PCs and armor nearing TRP 02, he wondered how many more infantrymen had pushed on into the valley. He would get his answer in four, three, two—

"Dale, you seeing this!" hollered Gatch. "If you're with us now, then you know we need your help!"

At the same time, voices burst over the company net. Thomas from White Platoon and Ryback were requesting artillery support that was still being delayed. Yelas was probably screaming to his boss, the task force FSO, that they needed fires, but even he was just a liaison officer with no command authority to bring the tubes back into the fight. Ryback reported that his dismounted forces at the crossing could only hold their successive position for a few more minutes. He believed the North Koreans were preparing to make a major assault across the river. Moreover, the Bradleys were beginning to run low on 25-mm and coax ammo, and each vehicle's crew had already launched the pair of TOW missiles they kept ready in their launchers. Reloading the missiles without dismounts onboard to help was not something done easily or quickly in a hot fight. Doing so required the Bradley's gunner or loader to jump in the back, and during the procedure the turret would be paralyzed.

"Red, this is Red One. Alpha section is back in the fight! Let's give them pause, out."

"PC," said Lee as he targeted the moving vehicle, a VTT. To the right lay the smoldering ruin of a T-54 tank that either Abbot or Neech had destroyed. That VTT and its crew were about to join their unlucky comrades.

"Up!"

"Fire!"

"On the way."

A brilliant mushroom cloud of smoke and fire enveloped

the vehicle, yet right behind it came a BMP that Hansen announced.

"Identified," answered Lee.

The "Up!", "Fire!", and "On the way!" came so swiftly that to the uninitiated observer, they would have sounded like one word.

BMP? History. World kept free from communist aggression? Hardly. They were about to get their asses whooped by dismounts if they didn't destroy that armor and disengage. Enemy forces were amassing on both sides of the low-water crossing, and Hansen was a heartbeat away from notifying Black Six that he should call the engineers and press the button on his command-detonated mine, if the CO hadn't done so already.

Keyman's tank boomed, and another PC lost its game of chicken with a HEAT round.

Hansen made the call to Van Buren, as Lee picked up another VTT, identified it, then, with Deac's report and Hansen's command, blew it off the battlefield.

The stench of cordite and a thick cloud of dust filled the turret, and Hansen wanted to do his Robert Duvall impression and say that he loved the smell of cordite in the evening—it smelled like victory—but they weren't going to win this one. Hopefully they had delayed the enemy long enough, and that was the best they could do for now.

Suddenly, the mine positioned in the center of the low-water crossing exploded like a depth charge in a farm pond, ice water and body parts jetting in all directions as perhaps a hundred men succumbed to the blast. However, the explosion was like a battle horn, summoning the others into the breach like rabid dogs chasing rabbits.

Perhaps it was the surreal nature of the moment, Hansen wasn't sure, but he realized even then that what he observed was historic, that should he survive, he would remember this night for the rest of his life the way the men of the first Korean War never forget their battles or their brothers in arms. The thought lasted for only a few seconds, but it was so powerful, so chilling, that he whispered aloud, "I won't forget."

As yet another pair of BMPs steamrolled behind the infantry, and Hansen was about to call out those targets, Lee opened fire with the coax a second before he cried, "Troops!"

About thirty grunts came up and over the slope to the their left flank. They charged on, seemingly oblivious to the tank before them. They broke ranks, and two dropped to their knees to take aim with their RPGs. The turret came immediately alive with their small-arms fire.

"Coax troops!" Hansen ordered.

But Lee was already a second ahead of him, hosing down the troops with deft, practiced hands. Even as the first group of men got punched back over the slope, and the others began to drop to their bellies, Hansen was yelling for Lee to get the bastards with the RPGs. The gunner adjusted his fire.

But the tank shook as an explosion sounded from the left hull.

"Lee, kill the fucker that did that to us!" shouted Deac. "Kill his fucking ass!"

"Come on, Lee, get him, get him, get him!" added Gatch.

"Where is he?" Lee asked.

Hansen picked up the guy—and his buddy—who still hadn't launched. He worked his .50 caliber, ending the threat and adding more blood to the snow. Then Lee finished coaxing the rest of the troops, though probably a half dozen or more had retreated back over the hill.

"They're still out there," reminded Gatch.

"So is that armor," Hansen said, using his override to swing the turret around and put them back on MSR 3. He began scanning aggressively, found two VTTs that had veered off the road and were creeping slowly past TRP 02. "Two PCs," he said. "Near one first."

Again, the announcements from Lee and Deac echoed and foretold of the massive boom to come. It did. And as the aft cap rattled to the floor, the near VTT shed metal like a tumbling Indy car.

"Target!"

As Hansen was about to call out the far VTT, a Javelin missile struck the vehicle, warming its once frozen passengers before separating them from their heads and limbs.

Grimacing in disappointment, he muttered, "Renegade got the second one. Keep scanning."

HIS MEN DESERVED better; Neech knew that. And at the moment, knowledge was poison. He glanced down at Romeo, who was shoving another HEAT round into the breach. He and that young sergeant were a good team, destroying PCs and tanks with machinelike efficiency, but they would be even better if Neech's head was clear, if his heart was in it, if, if, if . . .

He didn't belong here. He felt as though he needed to kill them all, die trying, or just give up and run. And even then he wasn't sure whether doing any of those would really make him feel better. Batman's ghost would still be hovering, and the guilt would continue tearing apart his head and heart. Maybe there was no escape. If he resigned himself to that, then he might as well just put a bullet in his head and quit fucking around.

And then he looked again at Romeo, knew the guy needed him, knew that KATUSA in the driver's hole needed him, too. And that knowledge wasn't poison; it was a fact, one he could almost not bear. But he had to do the right thing. Be selfless, not selfish. He had to remember that it wasn't about him and his problems. It was about them. *The crew. The platoon. The company team.*

Why is it so damned easy to forget?

With his gut still twisting and turning, he scanned the

narrow defile south of TRP 02, where the enemy had just put up another smoke screen. The thermals did a good job of seeing through it, but the laser rangefinder was fast becoming a high-tech piece of shit. Neech would compensate.

A PC, probably a BRDM with attached missile launcher, reached the crest of a jagged hill, and the second Neech spotted it, something flashed atop its turret.

If that wasn't a wire-guided antitank missile rocketing toward them, then Neech would eat his CVC helmet.

"Driver, back up!" he cried.

The tank lurched and began rolling down the reverse slope. Neech took in a breath just as the missile made impact with a string of rocks along the slope and detonated, casting debris all over their hull and turret.

"Red Three, this is Red Four," called Abbot over the net. "Are you all right!"

"Yeah, just kill that bastard," Neech answered. "Driver, go right to the other side of those rocks, then move up."

"Yes, Sergeant," answered Popeye Choi.

Out of nowhere, Neech began crying again, and he caught Romeo staring at him as the tank jerked up, tossing them out of their seats.

"Sergeant . . ."

"I'm just getting tired, Romeo. That's all."

The kid bit his lip. "Okay. We're cool. So . . . that was fucking close, huh?"

Neech groaned through a sigh. "It won't get any easier."

"I think you're right." Romeo used the heels of his hands to rub his weary-looking eyes.

"Okay, Choi, right there, move up now," Neech said, observing the course ahead.

The tank dug deeply into the snow, pushing harder and harder up the slope until they neared the top and came to a halt in a hull-down position.

Off to their left, Abbot's main gun resounded, and out

within the defile, a second BRDM lit up next to the first the platoon sergeant had serviced.

"Red Three, this is Red Four!" Abbot suddenly called. "I think we got some AT teams setting up along the riverbank, just south of the crossing, over."

Neech confirmed the same. "I see them. Let's get ready to rumble."

Those enemy grunts were setting up the MCLOS AT-3 man-portable antitank missile carried in a suitcase. The missile had a 3,000-meter range, a wire command link, an armor penetration estimated in excess of 400 meters. It was the most widely deployed antitank guided missile system in North Korea. The Russians called it Malyutka, which meant little baby. Most tankers just called it trouble.

The section of Bradleys began laying down some coax fire to help out as Abbot and Neech joined the fray. Tracers flitted and crisscrossed near the riverbank, marking an impenetrable gauntlet of fire. Still, the storm could not last forever.

"Red, this is Red One," called Hansen. "Black Six reports more PC's and armor moving down MSR 3 and into the defile near TRP 02. Shift back to successive BPs and report when set, out."

Neech grinned crookedly.

He wasn't shifting back anywhere until they killed those antitank bastards. He leaned harder on the control handle.

And then . . . a break. Angels of death in the form of mortar shells descended from the heavens to blast the living shit out of everyone and everything along the frozen banks south of the low-water crossing.

Allowing himself the barest of sighs, Neech ceased fire and ordered Choi to move back to their next battle position.

His timing could not have been more fortuitous.

A pinprick of light shone against the smoke screen of mortar fires. The light grew brighter, brighter.

"Faster, Choi!"

Neech shuddered as he realized one of those bastards had miraculously still survived to launch his antitank missile.

And worse, as they backed down the slope, Romeo, who was peering through the vision blocks of his loader's hatch, spotted movement to their right flank. "Oh, shit. Sergeant! Troops. And we're backing right into them!"

"Fuck 'em! Run them over."

"Got a guy with an RPG!" cried Romeo.

Neech strained his eyes. "Where is he?"

"Right there!"

"Where?"

"He's going for a shot at our grill!"

Neech drew the 9-mm pistol from his Blackhawk thigh holster, stood in his hatch, and, in the dark, swung around and aimed at the shifting silhouettes of infantrymen moving toward the tank.

CHAPTER
SIX

NORTH KOREAN GRUNTS advanced silently from tree to leafless tree like the ghosts of those who had fought on the same hill over half a century ago.

But they weren't ghosts.

They were men who would bleed.

Neech fired at figure after figure, working in a slow pan along the tree line. His hand was a rock, his finger working fluidly on the trigger, his aim seemingly true.

He laughed in disbelief as he ducked back into the turret. He must have hit the RPG bastard, because other than a few rounds of small-arms fire, nothing of the rocket-propelled variety came hurtling toward them.

Romeo had assumed the gunner's seat and was already swinging the turret around, bringing the coax to bear on the rest of these dismounts as Choi turned the tank parallel with the hill so they wouldn't have to fire over the rear deck. The driver continued his turn, while Romeo kept traversing the turret as he got off his first burst.

With the tank now facing the enemy, Neech gave the

order to move out. The tank jumped as the gears engaged, and when Choi hit the gas, the turbine whined like a gigantic hair dryer. They started toward the woods, the thermals revealing dozens of troops scattering from their positions as once more Romeo let them have it with the coax.

"Fuckin' guys are everywhere!" the young sergeant cried over the drone of the machine gun. "Everywhere!"

"Get up on your gun," Neech said. "I'll take over there."

"This is insane, man!" Romeo slid out of the gunner's seat and went up into the loader's hatch. He shouted something, probably in Spanish, then let the rounds fly.

Neech swept the fleeing grunts with the coax, dropping a few, then, as the tank came between a stand of trees, the ground dropped away at about a thirty-degree incline. "Choi, slow down! Slow down!"

They had to be careful around trees because if the gun tube was sticking out to the side too far it could hit a tree, which could easily strip the turret motor gears and dent up the gun tube thermal jacket.

With a grinding, creaking noise, the tank tipped forward and began rolling much too quickly down the slope, smashing into and leveling several thin trees while Choi applied the brakes.

Just as they came charging onto level ground, aircraft engines rose in a timpani drumroll across the sky, followed by the most intense onslaught of mortar and artillery fire Neech had heard all evening. The dismounts from Renegade were probably firing their final protective fires while mortars created a continuous ring of steel around their position.

Neech went up into his hatch, put on his NVGs, and furtively searched the area for more enemy troops.

About a hundred meters to his left he spotted Abbot's tank churning up snow and ice as it turned around a few trees. Off to Neech's right, slighter hills rolled out toward a broad plain of shadows, where MSR 3 wandered like a black snake through the defile, heading toward an even more immense darkness. Neech wondered how many grunts hid among the hundreds of trees out there. He wondered which guy would get off that lucky shot with his RPG. He, Romeo, and Choi might have only minutes left to live. What should they do with that precious time?

Should they pretend that the danger did not exist, that Batman had not died, and that they truly believed in what they were doing?

Neech didn't know anymore.

GATCH REMINDED HIMSELF that they still had plenty of main-gun ammunition left and the lieutenant had every intention of firing most if not all of those rounds.

Man, that sucked. A lot had happened already, and the adrenaline rush left him feeling more spent than he did after a weekend at *ajima's* whorehouse. He was all about getting back to an Assembly Area, taking a load off, and having a nice cup of coffee or hot cocoa. He had enough war stories to tell about their first battle on Christmas Day. He had grown two feet taller based upon his acts of courage on the battlefield. He was as Dale Earnhardt as you could get behind the T-bar of a sixty-eight-ton tank.

And if you believed that, then the beers were on you, because for the past thirty minutes, Gatch was nothing but scared shitless.

It happened to even the best of them.

Would he get his wish? *Nope.* Falling back to an AA wasn't an option yet. According to the LT, more PCs and armor were coming down the road, and those enemy vehicles had a much better chance of breaching the river because they had so many dismounts to support them. And worse, more PCs had moved into the defile south of TRP 02, although the A-10s and some Apaches were supposed to be addressing that threat while also targeting armor from the next enemy battalion heading toward the engagement area. However, when the shit hit the fan, you couldn't count on everyone to be where they were supposed to be, especially the enemy . . .

Gatch settled them into their successive BP, which was about two hundred meters south of their first one and about fifty meters higher up the ridge. They would have had a better view of the river, but a thick layer of smoke had unfurled all the way from TRP 01 to TRP 03, and clouds had moved in to obscure the moon.

As Gatch sat there, waiting to hear the LT or Lee announce a target, he kept seeing things in his vision blocks:

A North Korean soldier hung from a cross and bled all over the snow.

Then, Dale Earnhardt's race car came charging across the hill, with more North Koreans hanging from the windows and firing their AK-47s. They mowed down the crucified guy, then tossed a grenade that rolled across the hull and into Gatch's open hatch.

The explosion shook him hard—but no, that was Lee firing the main gun.

"Target!" the lieutenant reported. "Far tank!"

"Identified."

"Up!"

"Fire!"

"On the way!"

They were servicing targets, one after the other, but the damned enemy armor kept coming.

Gatch imagined that as those enemy tank crews advanced down the road, passing dozens of metal carcasses and literally hundreds of dead comrades, they pissed in their pants and shook in their boots. If they weren't—if they were growing more enraged at what they saw—then the good ole boy from Daytona Beach might be the one sitting in the puddle and applauding with his knees.

Two more sabots left the gun tube before the turret grew

calm. Lee thought he saw a VTT, and Hansen ordered Deac to battlecarry a HEAT round.

After another quick check of his gauges, Gatch gave a cursory glance through his vision blocks.

And holy shit, there he was, a grunt hoisting himself onto the tank's hull. "There's a little fucker on the hull!" he screamed. "Cocksucker's on the hull!"

He clutched his T-bar as though it were the trigger on a big machine gun. For a second he considered popping his own hatch, but that would be way too reckless. The LT or Lee needed to handle the guy.

Gunfire cracked from up top, and the grunt writhed as he threw up an arm and tumbled back off the hull.

But then, seemingly out of nowhere, several squads of men, maybe more, clutched their rifles and charged like an army of hunchbacks over the slope. They came from the front, from the flanks . . . from everywhere.

FLASHBACKS OF YOUR war experiences were supposed to happen some time after you left the battlefield.

Webber bet that nearly all vets had some form of post-traumatic stress disorder—but did they have flashbacks while their damned battles were still in progress?

Dismounts had already stormed the tank and had been climbing all over their turret and hull. The lieutenant had cleaned them off with his coax.

But now it was happening again, and not just to them but to every tank in the platoon.

"Red One, this is Red Four. We got beaucoup infiltration!"

"This is Three! Fuckin' guys are coming," said Neech, his coax thundering in the background. "There's too many of them!"

"This is Two," said Keyman. "Ditto over here! We need to move! Now!"

The enemy infantry had coordinated a simultaneous attack, and they knew exactly what they were doing.

While those grunts running around outside kept the crews occupied, other bad guys would set up their Saggers or move up with their RPGs to deliver the final destructive blows. Evidently, the North Koreans didn't care if their own guys were crawling all over a tank before they blew it up. Those men serving as the diversionary force regarded their sacrifice as a great honor, even if they were killed by their comrades. Still, they probably wanted to take as many of the enemy with them.

How were you supposed to fight against guys that committed?

Damn it. Keyman was right. They needed to get out of there.

But for the moment, Smiley and Keyman were up top, the loader working his gun while Keyman spouted his usual rant at the enemy and fired his pistol. Webber opened fire with the coax, striking two grunts nearly point-blank. Those rounds cut through their bodies and took out another pair of grunts jogging straight for the hull.

It was sick, really sick out there, a total bloodbath that would make the most callous, dark-hearted soldier want to puke. They bore witness to an incredible display of men turned into zombies blind to the horror shoved in their faces. They just kept coming, kept bleeding, kept dying.

"Morbid! Let's roll!"

"Incoming!" screamed Smiley.

ABBOT SLAPPED A fresh clip into his pistol then rose back into his hatch.

He addressed each man in an even voice before he fired. He knew they couldn't hear him over the metallic chinking of the coax and the deeper thudding of the 240, but he did not care. Speaking to them organized his thoughts, kept him calm.

A guy pulled himself up into the bustle rack. "Son, you don't belong on my tank." *Boom!*

Two grunts crawled alongside the right track, probably getting ready to stuff a grenade in the sprocket. "You guys checking for loose wedgebolts or what?" *Boom! Boom!*

Then Abbot began singing under his breath, "I . . . want to rock 'n' roll all night . . . and party every day. I . . . want to rock 'n' roll all night . . . and party every day." He loved that old Kiss song and had been a fan since the band's very first album. He kept firing, kept singing the chorus, until he saw a break. "Sparrow?" he cried to the boy from the hood, better known as "the boy from the hull" who would be America's next president. "Move back!"

Sparrow got them in gear, got them out of there, just as the next horde charged mindlessly over the hill.

SERGEANT LEE WASN'T sure which was worse: the dreadful onslaught of men who rushed the tank and died by the dozens—or the cursing and screaming from Gatch and Deac.

It was bad enough having to engage in and watch so much killing. The last thing he needed in the world was a running commentary by two spoiled Americans who knew nothing of true sacrifice. It was almost too much to bear.

A grenade bounced off the hull, failed to explode, then dropped over the side as another volley of small-arms fire sewed wildly across the turret. The lieutenant had been driven back inside by grunts who had taken up positions along their left flank. Those troops lay on their bellies, issuing a steady stream that would keep the LT buttoned up until Lee could put some fire on them.

He shifted his aim as Deac and Gatch kept screaming

for him to hurry up and "whack the beady-eyed fuckers." As usual, Hansen shushed them, but the LT always managed to throw that punch too late, after the damage had already been done.

Nevertheless, Lee serviced the area target with several killing bursts and quickly eliminated the threat. Such threats should be described in that manner, not only out of respect for the soldiers but as way to detach emotions from the task. He had not "whacked the beady-eyed fuckers." He burned with the desire to correct Deac and Gatch, but doing so would shock them and the lieutenant and would just waste his time. His thoughts must remained focused on the enemy.

But who was the true enemy? The North Koreans? The Americans? His own fear? The war itself? The distinction grew more vague by the minute. Something was happening to him. Something frightening.

"Troops to the left!" Hansen shouted. "Driver, back up!"

As Lee coaxed the soldiers, Gatch took them down the reverse slope toward the base of another hill. Then, as the lieutenant instructed, Gatch turned them completely around. With a tingling feeling running up his neck, Lee sighted a grunt waiting for them atop a hill about fifty meters out, his RPG jutting from his shoulder not unlike a knight's lance. The weapon flashed before Lee had a chance to squeeze his triggers.

"Holy fuck! He fired!" yelled Gatch.

Lee's heart sank as he replied with the coax. He was going to die with these Americans.

WEBBER WASN'T SURE what had just happened, but somehow he had been knocked to the floor and was groping to get back into his chair.

"Motherfucker!" shouted Keyman. The staff sergeant burst up into his hatch, firing his pistol and shouting "Fuck you!" after each discharge. For the time being, Webber had no problem with Keyman's venting, which seemingly kept them all alive. Webber checked his sight, saw flames coming from the left side of the hull where an RPG must have struck.

Smiley already had the extinguisher in hand. He went up into his hatch and began spraying down the tank, while Morbid continued pushing them back toward the next row of trees. They were either doing an excellent job of falling back from the enemy infantry or heading directly into their hands, depending upon how many grunts had managed to circle behind them.

And depending upon how much sympathy the good Lord had for one hyperventilating loan shark who begged for a little help and swore to repent.

THERE WASN'T ANY time to brace himself before the grenade exploded over the forward hull, but Hansen managed to take a breath and think, *Shit!*

The last time his tank had taken RPG fire, his loader's weapon had been trashed, one of his vision blocks had somehow been shattered, and he had received a nice gash in his head. Sure, the M1A1 could sustain a fair number of hits—providing the North Koreans' aim remained haphazard. "These Orientals all shoot as bad as they drive," Gatch had said earlier, proving that he would never serve as an American ambassador to an Asian country or be noted for his cultural sensitivity.

Great shots or not, the grunts only needed one carefully placed grenade to take out the tank's engine, fuel tanks, or ignite the ammo stored in the bustle rack, while another to the front might cause damage to the machine guns and maybe even the gun tube. An RPG fired down at them could punch through with ease because the armor on an M1 was thinnest on the top—only about an inch. You weren't invulnerable while inside a tank. Guys who thought they were died first. Simple as that.

Lee had already killed the shooter and had not missed a beat, even as the grenade had rung their bells. Deac was up in his hatch, putting out the fire, while Hansen swung his NVGs right and left, looking for more attackers along the rockier ridges and near the trees.

The enemy grunts had tied up the entire platoon, and Hansen knew the North Korean PCs and armor were now pushing on toward the low-water crossing. The order for Team Cobra to disengage had to be only minutes away, and Hansen felt solely responsible for that. But what could he have done to avoid those grunts?

He sighed heavily in disgust. Abbot had called this one, all right. There was a whole lot of infiltration. An unbelievable amount.

"Red, this is Red One," he called over the platoon net. "Fall back to supplemental BPs and report when set, out."

Those supplemental battle positions lay on the east side of MSR 3, adjacent to the Bradleys' BP. Hansen didn't believe they would engage any PCs or armor from that area before the order to saddle up came in. Given the sheer number of grunts combing the hills, it was better to anticipate that order and begin to evacuate than attempt to pit one tank against, say, a thousand dismounts. You could leave your scientific calculator at home and still reach that conclusion.

Unless, of course, your name was Keyman. Hansen half expected the TC to challenge the order to move back, calling it cowardly or something akin.

Surprisingly, that pain in Hansen's ass was keeping right on them, rolling off to their right flank and coming up hard. Hansen stole another look back at the TC, then swung around as the tank dipped hard. The engine revved, and the tracks creaked in protest as Gatch pulled them out of a slight depression and toward a cluster of trees whose limbs created a thick canopy of gnarled, icy branches.

They rolled up and passed into the tunnel of limbs, snow shaking off some of the closest branches. It was like being squeezed in a cold, wooden fist, and as they neared the edge, the canopy descended so low that Hansen could reach up and snap off a few twigs.

A flurry of snowflakes blew past his left shoulder. As he turned slightly, about to look up, a dull thud, barely discernable were it not for its accompanying vibration, struck behind him.

He tugged down his goggles, whipped around to find a North Korean grunt lying on the turret just behind the hatch. The red-nosed solider who couldn't be more than eighteen years old had jumped from the limbs and was grimacing in pain as he raised a pistol in one hand and clutched his ankle with the other.

Hansen reached for his own pistol—thought better of it. *No time!*

He lunged for the Korean's wrist, seized it.

The gun went off, splintering overhead branches and knocking down more snow.

As Hansen fought against the kid's grip, the tank hit a rut, threw both of them back, arms still straining against each other.

Hansen grunted, pouring all of his energy into his hand while reaching around with the other, fumbling for his pistol and beginning to panic, really panic.

At once the kid jerked away so hard that Hansen's boots left the floor as he was pulled partly out of his hatch. The kid hollered something in Korean and kept pulling.

Abandoning the thought of going for his sidearm, Hansen slapped that free hand on the grunt's wrist.

Bang! The kid fired once more, the shot missing Hansen's shoulder by inches.

"LT!" Deac shouted, appearing in his hatch.

Shifting his grip, Hansen took the barrel of the pistol in one hand then slammed the kid's arm across the hatch's rim. The pistol came free.

The kid's mouth fell open, pure horror flooding his eyes. *"Soo-jee-ma!"* he yelled, and that much Hansen understood: Don't shoot!

Was there really a choice?

Hansen already knew the answer. He had been taught that in the heat of battle you were all about action and reaction. You could not hesitate to weigh options. You could not believe you ever had a choice between sparing a kid's life and shooting him.

So even as the kid begged for mercy, Hansen grimaced and squeezed the trigger.

The round struck just beneath the grunt's helmet, in the side of his forehead, his head twisting in an unnatural angle. Blood sprayed across the turret as the kid went limp.

With the shot still blaring in his ears, Hansen shoved the grunt over the side, watching him fall beside the rattling tracks.

Deac, waving his own pistol, glanced worriedly up at the trees. "I hate this fucking place, LT. I hate it. I hate it!"

Hansen dropped into his hatch and glanced down at the kid's weapon. It was a very compact Makarov 9-mm, with an external hammer and safety lever on the side. It held eight rounds.

As he further examined the pistol, the tremors continued working into his hands. He felt like Superman holding a piece of kryptonite. He wondered if he should keep the weapon or throw it away. Yes, the Makarov would make a fine souvenir and fetch a hefty price from a collector on eBay, so even if he didn't want it, he could still sell it.

Or he could keep the gun around, put it in a display case in his future home office, brag about how he had wrestled it away from a North Korean and had killed the soldier.

Brag? Maybe that wasn't the right word.

In fact, Hansen already had a feeling that the weapon, like the memory, would be stored in a trunk of war mementos that would sit patiently in his attic, waiting for him to return when—and only when—he was ready to deal with the pain.

"IT'S SNOWING AGAIN," said Keyman as they moved up toward their supplemental battle position. "The storm's coming."

"Just what we need," groaned Webber.

Keyman breathed deeply through his nose, then came down into the turret and booted Webber in the shoulder. "Yes, sir, the storm's coming. Can you smell it?"

"Not really."

"Well, you'd best learn to engage your senses because they will keep you alive."

"I can smell you."

"And you know what I smell like? Like war, motherfucker. Shit. What will you do when I'm gone?"

"Where you going? Vacation?"

"Hey, asshole, they'll put you in command of my tank, you know that? What're you going to do? Pass out?"

Webber smirked but maintained a watchful eye through his sight. "Weren't you supposed to live forever? Guys like you don't get killed."

"Guys like me?"

"Don't make me go there."

"Fuck you, Webber. And FYI: I'll be lucky to make it through the night."

"Thanks. That makes me feel better. Makes me not want to pass out."

"What's up with you, man? This ain't you."

Webber bit his lip. "I know."

"Don't be afraid to die. Just don't."

"If I knew where I was going, I wouldn't be. And don't tell me you're not."

Keyman muttered something under his breath and went up through his hatch.

"What did you say?"

"Nothing, man. Hey, Morbid, right there. Pull us right up that slope."

"Okay, Sergeant. But I don't like it."

"You don't like the order? Too fucking bad!"

"I'm just saying the grade doesn't look—"

Morbid broke off as sporadic gunfire pelted the turret, coming in from the crest of the hill. He eased off the throttle as a second salvo came in.

The muzzle flashes shone brilliantly in Webber's sight, and he was already firing as Keyman called out the targets.

At the same time, Hansen's voice came over the platoon net. The order to disengage had come in, and they were heading back about five kilometers to Assembly Area Crusader for refitting and resupply.

"Driver, keep moving up!" Keyman hollered, then he was on the platoon net. "Red One, this is Red Two. Troops in my BP, over."

"Roger, I can see you," replied Hansen. "I can get 'em from the flank."

Coax fire tore in from the east, raking the crest of the slope and silencing every gun up there.

As Hansen's gunner ceased fire, so did Webber.

He waited three, four, five seconds, and then, finally, Keyman gave the order for them to pull away and roll out behind Hansen.

"The lieutenant did a good job," Webber remarked.

"No, Lee did."

"C'mon, you have to give him some credit."

"Webber, don't talk anymore . . ."

"Fine."

In the minutes that followed, Webber brooded, but then

his thoughts turned back to the moment, and he became more nervous than he had been during the entire night.

Guys did four tours in Vietnam, came home, and got hit by busses while crossing the street.

Guys got shot up all to hell in the first Iraqi war, came home, slipped in the bathtub, died.

Guys watched half their squads get killed in shithole towns in Afghanistan and Iraq during the war on terrorism, only to die in chopper crashes during the ride back to camp.

Some guys said that when it was your time, there wasn't a damned thing you could do.

But it always seemed more dangerous when you knew you were heading back. If you allowed yourself a sigh of relief and bought into the idea that you had made it—then you'd be killed.

So Webber's seat became an electric chair, and the current coursed through him, alerting him to every bump in the turret, every hot spot in his thermal sight.

CHAPTER
SEVEN

KAREN COULD BARELY keep her eyes open as she and Corporal Reese hid beneath the ridge where a tree had fallen just above a narrow depression. Reese had helped her settle into the meager hiding spot, then he had spent several minutes scanning the terrain with those goggles that made him look like a bug. He finally joined her, and they sat there, listening, waiting, as soldiers searched the hills below.

"Here," he whispered, pushing a pistol into her hand, his eyes growing heavy.

The gun felt heavier than it looked. She imagined herself firing it, killing someone. But she couldn't forget that she had never believed in war, even though she had fallen in love with a warrior. Now she was being asked to become just like him, but that was not her. She shook her head, reached out to return the weapon, but he blocked her hand.

"Take it."

"I don't know how," she argued, her voice cracking then finally coming in her own whisper.

"Aim and shoot."

"Please . . ."

He turned his head slowly, his breath coming in little gasps. "You can do it. Fifteen rounds in a mag. The release button is here." He showed her what to do, but she was barely paying attention. She kept staring at a tree, its limbs shivering in the wind and making her feel even colder. "Your range is only about fifty meters, okay? And here's another magazine." He handed her the cartridge.

"How much longer?" she asked.

"They should be passing us by now. Couple more minutes. Then you'll have to move."

"Me?"

"Yeah, you."

"You're kidding."

"Nope." A stern look came over the corporal's face, though it seemed undercut by a trace of sadness.

"You're not coming with me?"

With a slight moan he rolled over to one side and lifted his jacket, revealing a large, dark stain across the lower back of his shirt. "They got me when we were running, but I didn't think it was too bad."

"Oh my God. Why didn't you say something?"

"Doesn't matter. I can't go with you.

"But you . . . you can't—"

Reese pressed a finger to her lips. "I'll draw you a map of where I think we are. My buddy has my GPS, otherwise I would've given it to you. But hell, it don't matter." He reached into a pocket, produced a pen, then he dug out his wallet, withdrew a business card, and began sketching a little map on the back. "As you get close to Uijongbu, you might run into some scouts or maybe some of my bros from the Second MP. Then you can send back help."

"No, you have to come," Karen said, pleading with her eyes, her mouth, with everything she had. "There's no way in hell I'm going alone."

"Who's your husband?"

"My husband? I don't have one."

"You're not a dependant?"

"My boyfriend's a lieutenant with First Tank. He called in a favor to get me out."

"You want to see him again?"

"More than anything."

"Then you'll do this. Make sure the road is always on your left, then you'll know you're heading south." He shoved the card into her hand, then fished out his cell phone. "God damn it, my battery is almost dead. You gotta love that." He sighed, then his gaze went distant. "Shit, you know what? I forgot to zeroize the SINCGARS back in the Hummer when I bailed out. Damn it. Pray that thing burned."

Reese was talking gibberish now, but Karen clearly understood what he was asking of her—and it was way too much. "Corporal, I can't go. I'm just a fucking English teacher."

"Those assholes down there? They don't know the difference." Reese pulled off one glove, fished out something from a breast pocket. He lifted his hand to his ear, then struggled a moment before lowering the hand to reveal a silver hoop earring dangling from his left lobe. "Like it?"

Her jaw went slack.

"The Army doesn't let us wear earrings," he went on, "but if a brother's going to die out here, a brother will do it looking cool."

Karen couldn't speak. The enormity of the moment had wrapped its fingers around her throat.

"Ma'am, I'm sorry I got my dumb ass shot. But I got you this far. You can do the rest. Now here, take my night vision goggles, too."

He handed over the goggles and gave her a rushed

lesson in how to use them. When he was finished, he said, "Get out of here and get me some help." He shoved her. Hard.

Losing her breath, Karen crawled a few feet away from the furrow, then hesitated, her heart beginning to race. "Reese, I can stay here with you. It's all right." Damn, her teeth were chattering.

"Listen to me. You have to keep moving. Either way, you might get frostbite, hypothermia. Shit, you might even break a nail."

"Don't fuck with me."

He gasped, flinched in pain, then his eyes widened as the agony seemed to pass. "Look. You have to get me help. You can do it. Please."

Words came from her mouth, but she could scarcely believe what she said: "All right. I'll be right back, Corporal. I'll be right back."

"I know you will."

WHILE HANSEN AND the men of TF 1-72 had successfully disrupted and delayed elements of the enemy division assaulting through the low-water crossing, follow-on forces had ultimately seized control of that key piece of terrain and would continue to advance toward the vicinity of Camp Castle and the Dong An train station in North TDC as they continued their push on toward Seoul.

As Hansen understood it, American forces did not mind trading space for time, thus pulling back to an Assembly Area to refit and resupply before heading off on the next mission was not only supported by conventional wisdom but by history itself. American forces had backed all the way down to the Pusan perimeter before counterattacking during the first Korean War.

However, while moves like that and their current withdrawal seemed like sound doctrinal decisions to Hansen and the others, ROK tactical commanders were trained and conditioned to never move their units southward/rearward; instead they were to only move northward/forward, as in the attack. They even did all of their field exercises that way, always moving toward or defending facing the north. They would fight to the last man to hold all of their terrain. Interestingly, when writing in English, the ROKs refused to capitalize the "n" in North Korea, writing "nK" to ensure that those from the north were never placed on an equal level with them.

Consequently, the ROK leadership no doubt regarded the withdrawal from "nK" forces as either an act of cowardice or a tactical error, and there had to be growing friction between ROK and US commanders.

Even so, according to Captain Van Buren, American forces north of TDC had not completely pulled out of the fight. While the armor battalions were beginning to rearm, resupply, and reorganize, the Division Cavalry Squadron was setting up a screen line with their tanks and M3 Cavalry Fighting Vehicles, along with their OH-58D Kiowa Warrior light helicopters whose pilots would help to delay the enemy and provide early warning. Setting up a screen line was a common security mission for cavalry troops and company teams, and it often allowed them to conduct the counter recon fight. The cavalry's air and ground units would be reporting intelligence on enemy forces to division, who would send that info down the line. Eventually Captain Van Buren would receive it in the form of an intel dump from the battalion S2.

Additionally, task force scouts were putting out their own screen line, and the TF mortars were being used to cover them. Those scouts reported directly to the S2, who would periodically put out an intel update over the battalion net. The direct support field artillery battalion commander had already provided a dedicated Paladin battery to shoot in support of the TF scouts, should they become engaged with enemy recon and with infiltrators. Artillery was never in reserve, and that was their most basic absolute doctrine. They were ready 24/7.

At the further urging of the artillery battalion commander, the FIST teams were taking turns rearming and refitting, after which they would move forward to help with the screen and to assist with indirect fires. They, like the commander's guns, were prohibited from being in reserve.

As those teams prepared themselves, men from the 102nd Military Intelligence Battalion were repositioning the GSR and REMBASS to cover likely avenues of approach and buy time for defensive forces to react to the enemy's advance. The GSR and REMBASS would once again act as all-weather "electronic eyes" for the battalion and complement the CAV and scout platoon assets/capabilities.

Finally, attack aviation and Close Air Support had already been given free reign to engage targets in "free fire areas" designated forward of the newly formed Forward Edge of the Battle Area.

No, sir. The Americans had not abandoned the fight.

But tell that to the liberal anti-US media whose embedded reporters were no doubt declaring that the "mighty American forces were heavily outnumbered and now on the run." Video coverage would most likely show US forces moving rearward, with close-ups of burning US tanks and other vehicles. Hansen didn't need to overhear or see those reports to know what was in them. Those clowns would imply that the Americans weren't really interested in defending South Korea because of strong anti-American sentiments across the peninsula. Some of the more vicious embeds would start rumors about how the

American leadership was engaged in a cover-up regarding their "failure" at the low-water crossing. Even worse, a flood of negative reports could eventually weaken the United States' credibility with the international community and cause allied forces to withdraw their promises of military support to the conflict.

And it was all because you couldn't tell the media everything, lest you endanger your mission and your men.

So while the rumors and misinterpretations flew as rapidly as the A-10s, and the cavalry forces, scouts, and others worked diligently to prepare their screen lines, Hansen stood in the Assembly Area, helping Deac and Gatch load main-gun and small-arms ammo onto the tank. It was nearly three AM. The wind had picked up, and the edge of a major storm front was creeping across the valley, promising to dump a trillion wheelbarrows full of snow. Pretty soon some aircraft would be grounded.

Deac and Gatch, who usually liked to joke around during the arduous task of lugging heavy ammunition, kept strangely to themselves, their senses of humor gone to ice, along with everything else. Hansen didn't bother luring them into a conversation. He simply worked with them, just breathing in the cold air, the exhaust fumes from nearby HMMWVs, and the stench of fuel. Sergeant Lee was inside the turret, taking care of his prep to fire checks and doing computer and laser rangefinder self-tests. Never much of a conversationalist, he, too, was keeping very much to himself.

Perhaps the crew's reticence wasn't strange after all. They were all dead tired—which was still better than being just dead. Hansen wanted to remind them of that and congratulate them once again for a job well done, but the thrill of it all was just . . . gone.

After hopping down from the tank, Deac paused, leaned back near one of the ballistic skirts, and covered his face in his hands. Gatch went over and began tugging at his arms. "Leave me!" the loader screamed.

"It's all right," Hansen told Gatch. "I got this."

The driver threw up his hands, made a face, then got back to work as Hansen leaned in close to Deac. "Hey, man. What's going on?"

"Just taking a little breather is all."

"Gatch and I'll finish up. Go get some coffee, then get back inside and warm up for a few minutes, okay?"

Deac blinked hard, nodded, then pushed off the tank. "Hey, Lieutenant? Did you think it'd be like this?"

"What do you mean? Going to war?"

"I mean killing so many guys. I never seen anything like that. It's just crazy."

"Yeah. But you know, those guys are just like us— willing to die for their country."

"I wouldn't be willing to die for that prison they call a country."

"Me neither. But they are. And we shouldn't feel bad about it."

After a moment's introspection, Deac blurted out, "I hate those fucking bastards. But after seeing so many of 'em die, it's like . . . oh my God. And it gets you thinking, hey, that's somebody son or somebody's dad you just killed. You see little kids running around, crying for their daddies."

"Oh, man, don't go there."

"I know. I don't like to think about that stuff. But I can't get it out of my head. I don't know what to do, sir. And I feel like no matter how many times we say we're doing our duty and fighting for our country and that it's okay to kill people, we're just fooling ourselves. And then another part of me asks, so why did you join the Army, asshole? I guess I never thought it'd come to this."

Hansen pursed his lips, unsure how to respond.

Deac heaved a sigh, rubbed his eyes again. "I'll go get that coffee." He hustled off.

Shit. Which was worse: having technical problems with the tank or emotional problems with the crew? *Didn't matter. Both sucked.*

Hansen swore aloud over his hesitation. He should have counseled Deac right then, saying that you can't think of the enemy as human. You shouldn't attach names, faces, or families to them. They were all nondescript combatants, *Star Trek* red shirts fated to die at the hands of TF 1-72. And the more of them you killed, the more bragging rights you had.

But it was hard to say that with any conviction when you had the blood of a young man splattered across your turret, a young man whose breath you had felt on your face and whose cry for mercy you had ignored.

It was hard to say anything.

Gatch trudged up, snow collecting on his shoulders as he backhanded snot from his nose. "Deac's just worried about going to hell, LT. I told him he should stop worrying. We're both doomed anyway, so we should have some fun while we're here, right?"

"I thought this was hell."

The driver grinned. "Too cold. Or you can say it's so cold that it burns."

"You're right. This isn't hell. Just another day at the office—"

"Yeah, with a hundred thousand backstabbing middle managers breathing down our necks."

Hansen smiled weakly. "I hate when that happens."

"Still beats a real job."

"You got that right. So what about you, Gatch? You worried about going to hell?"

"Funny you should ask, LT." With that, the driver pulled himself up into the bustle rack.

Before Hansen could pry further, Abbot came hurrying over. "Hey, LT?"

"What's up, Sergeant?"

Abbot held up his cell phone. "Just wondering if you had any luck getting through."

Hansen shook his head. "Network's still jammed."

"Yeah, but I've been sending some text messages, and I'm pretty sure they got through."

"I sent one myself, but I haven't had any luck. Maybe they're still down. Here. Wait a minute." Hansen dug through his pocket and produced his phone. He scrolled through to create a message, selected a template that he had used before, and thumbed in a request for Karen to text him back. "Okay, I'll let you know."

"Thanks, LT. And, uh, little heads-up. You might want to have a word with Neech. I know he could use some encouragement from you."

"Okay. But what do you think?"

"I think he's getting real quiet on us now. And that's a little scary—if you know what I mean."

Hansen nodded.

Abbot started to leave, but then Hansen called after him. The platoon sergeant lifted his chin, and Hansen waved him in closer. "Matt, I . . . I don't know what to tell him. I don't know what to tell any of them."

The platoon sergeant's expression softened.

"It was a fucking bloodbath out there," Hansen went on. "I went hand-to-hand with this guy on top of my turret. Blew his brains out."

"Better his than yours."

"Yeah, I mean, I'll get through that. But these guys. I thought I knew what to say, but it's just getting worse and worse. I can see it in their eyes."

Abbot held up a palm. "Don't stress out. Sometimes all you have to do is listen. But when they get real quiet, you have to get them talking. One thing I can tell you—don't lie or try to quote anything. Not now. They can see through that shit."

"But what if I—"

"Hey, if you don't know what to say, then just tell them that. Then they know they're not the only ones who're feeling all screwed up." Abbot lowered his voice. "But make no mistake—you have to assure them that you're in command and that as a team we're going to get through this."

"Yeah, I know. Because if I don't, Keyman will be right there, ready to fucking gloat."

"No doubt. Just be yourself."

"I'll do that. Thanks, man."

"Anytime, sir."

Thank God for the platoon sergeant. Hansen wasn't sure what he would do without the man's carefully measured advice and reassurances. Abbot was the rock upon which the entire platoon rested, and no matter how difficult the situation became, his voice of reason would rise above the chaos. Hansen knew that the sergeant had already spent a lot of time trying to defuse the situation with Keyman, and Hansen had already thanked Abbot for that, but the sergeant had just shrugged it off and told him not to worry about it.

After helping Gatch finish loading and securing the ammo, Hansen moved down the row of tanks to Neech's track, where Popeye Choi was standing at the end of the main gun tube, staring into the bright red peep sight of the boresight device and doing a little dance that resembled a three-year-old trying to tell his parents that he needed to use the potty. That was Choi's way of battling the cold. Romeo was inside the turret, being guided by the KATUSA's hand signals to the prearranged point on the panel.

Meanwhile, Neech sat on the rear deck, sipping some coffee, and staring off into the darkness. He failed to acknowledge Hansen's approach.

"Hey, Neech. How you doing, brother?"

Neech frowned, took another sip of his coffee, then finally said, "Excuse me, Lieutenant?"

Hansen sat beside the man and thought a moment before answering. "Just came by to see how you're doing."

"Sir, we are rearmed, refueled, and resupplied. We're boresighting right now. No technical problems to report, sir."

"C'mon, Neech. I wasn't talking about the tank."

The TC turned slowly to face Hansen, his eyes swollen, his unshaven face looking more gaunt than usual. "Somebody starting rumors?"

"No, no, just relax, man. And hey, when was the last time you ate something?"

"I don't remember."

"Get something, okay? MRE stands for meals you should remember to eat."

"Yes, sir."

Hansen took a long breath and began to feel even more awkward. "It was pretty brutal out there."

"Yes, sir."

"Can I ask you something?"

"You're the lieutenant. Fire away."

"Why don't you get that blood out of your turret? Get clean, you know?"

Neech sat there, frozen, breath jetting from his nose.

"Well, I think they'll send us back to TDC," Hansen continued. "MOUT fight. Some real shit. Worst ever. And all of us will be depending on you."

"Yes, sir."

"Batman was my guy, too, Neech. Yeah, you knew him better than me. He saved your life. And you're hurtin' worse than any of us. I guess I realize now that there's nothing I can say to make it better. But I just want you to know that we're here, man. We're your brothers. You're *not* alone."

"I want to believe that, sir. But the truth is, we're born alone, we die alone. And the Army doesn't give a shit about that . . . or us."

"Neech, come on, man, you know—"

"I'm sorry, sir. I just don't want to talk anymore, if that's all right?"

Hansen tensed. "Yeah, okay."

KEYMAN SNORTED, THEN spit some chew. "Look at the motherfucker over there."

Webber had already seen the LT walk over to Neech's track, so he didn't bother looking. He just continued to warm himself on the tank while working on his second cup of hot chocolate. "I wonder if you'd still hate him as much if he didn't go to West Point and he didn't win Top Tank."

"He thinks he can help Neech?" asked Keyman, totally ignoring Webber. "Bullshit. That guy will have a serious meltdown. You mark my words. He doesn't belong in the turret."

"I don't know about that."

"Was I asking for your opinion? You, especially. Shit. I thought I had you all figured out, but you're one of these strange fuckups who train like hardcore motherfuckers and never give you trouble. Then you take them out into the real shit, and they faint like fat ladies."

Webber lost his breath.

No, he wasn't going to pass out.

A sharp crack resounded in his head, and within a second he had the gloved fingers of his left hand wrapped around Keyman's throat.

Unaware of everything save for his own rage, Webber reared back with his right hand and delivered a round-house, just as he released the TC.

Keyman's head snapped back as the fist connected with

his cheek. His arms flailed as he staggered a few steps, slipped, and fell onto his rump, a hand going immediately to his face.

"Holy shit," Webber muttered, shivering through the words as he gaped at the most improbable sight he had ever seen:

The mighty Staff Sergeant Timothy Key on ass, struck down as though by lightning.

What Keyman had not realized, and what Webber had not considered until that very moment, was that Webber's fear had distilled to pure anger sealed in a vacuum. Keyman had unknowingly pushed the release button.

Yet Keyman had about twenty of his own buttons —all labeled anger—and Webber had pushed them all. "How dare you strike me, you cocksucker!" Keyman got onto his hands and knees, then bolted up and charged Webber, sacking him so hard that Webber literally saw stars.

Then Keyman rolled him over, climbed on top, ripped off his own glove, and drew back a bare fist.

Webber blocked the incoming knuckle sandwich, then drove up his knees, throwing off Keyman. With the TC's next attack already playing out in his mind's eye, Webber rolled onto his gut, got onto his knees as Keyman scrambled to face him.

"You think I'm a coward? You think I'm a fuckup?" Webber screamed. "Let's go, you bald piece of shit! Right here! Right now! We finish this! You're going to be second best again! Do you hear me, Sergeant!"

Webber had banged a fist solidly upon the crimson surface of Keyman's biggest button of all, the one labeled *childhood issues,* the one that informed his very identity and drove him to be the best in everything he did but also caused him the greatest pain and insecurity.

Oops.

The TC's eyes turned coal black, like a shark's, and

spittle leaked from his lips as he panted, chest heaving, cheek growing red.

And then he came at Webber with a guttural war cry that rose above the drone of idling engines.

He didn't make it two feet before Neech came around behind him, wrapping big arms around his chest.

Suddenly, arms slammed across Webber's chest, and the lieutenant was screaming in his ear, "What the fuck is this shit!"

Keyman wrenched against Neech's grip, but the big TC was just too powerful. "Let go of me!"

Then, to Webber's utter surprise, Neech did, in fact, obey Keyman's order, yet the second Keyman started forward, Neech tripped the TC, grabbed him by the back of the neck, and shoved him down into the snow. "You don't like that, motherfucker, do you?" Neech growled. "You think you're the baddest ass in the platoon. You don't know anything. THEY DIDN'T KILL YOUR DRIVER! THEY KILLED MINE! Maybe you need to learn what it's like to suffer!"

The lieutenant screamed for Neech to stop.

But the possessed TC repeatedly shoved Keyman's face into the snow, as though he were trying to drown him in a toilet.

Then Abbot came charging over, dropped to his knees, and tore Neech away from Keyman. "Jesus Christ, what's going on here?" hollered the platoon sergeant.

Keyman sat up, wiping muck from his eyes and blood from his mouth. Even with his ass kicked, the staff sergeant did not miss a beat of sarcasm: "Uh, Sergeant Abbot, we wanted to see what the lieutenant would do if we pretended to have a fight."

"Shut the fuck up," Hansen snapped, then he let go of Webber and shoved him forward. "All of you, listen up. We're strung out. Tempers are flaring."

"You got something less obvious you want to say," Keyman began, continuing with his sarcastic singsong, "because you're already boring me."

Webber's eyes bugged out as he watched the lieutenant's hands clench into fists. Was he going to strike Keyman?

"One more word," Abbot said, raising an index finger. "One more word . . ."

Keyman hocked a big loogie, let it hurl.

"That's right," Hansen said "Another word out of you, and you'll be watching this war from the sidelines. Do you understand?"

Keyman thrust out his lips like a drunk realizing his bottle was empty. "Yes, sir."

"Lieutenant, it was my fault, sir," said Webber. "I threw the first punch."

"Webber, I don't give a shit right now. All I know is, we're the best platoon in the company—and this is an embarrassment to me, to yourselves, and to the unit. This will never, ever happen again. Because if it does, someone will not survive it."

"Yes, sir," they all answered.

"DO YOU UNDERSTAND?"

"YES, SIR!"

"Keyman, you get somebody to look at that lip. Webber? You come with me." The lieutenant's eyes ignited.

KAREN'S CELL PHONE suddenly beeped, notifying her that she had just received a text message. She was at once overjoyed and frightened. She ran to the next tree and kept low, wondering if any of those Special Operation Forces had heard the sound. She put on the goggles, took a look, and listened for footfalls or anything else that might betray them. Nothing.

Satisfied that she had a moment, she removed the NVGs,

then thumbed the phone's arrow key. The tiny screen lit with Jack's text message. He had finally gotten through! However, judging from his vague request to contact him, she wasn't sure if he had received any of the messages she had sent him earlier, before their bus had been attacked.

With cold and shaking hands she began to write him a reply, utilizing the phone's predictive text feature that allowed her to quickly type words with fewer keystrokes.

Even so, she wanted to pour out her guts but knew she had to stick to the most important facts: her bus had been attacked, Kim Abbot had been killed, and she was somewhere in the mountains along MSR 3, heading south toward Uijongbu. Could he send help?

Although the act might be useless, she extended her arm toward the sky and pressed the send button. *Please, God. Let this get through . . .*

Okay. She had to keep moving. She couldn't think about what she had seen back there.

If she focused on getting help for Reese, she would be all right. She had a purpose, a mission, just like Jack. She couldn't be some scared idiot. She had to find the strength inside to save herself and him.

It was the only way she would ever return to Jack.

But it was damned hard pushing through the snow, the air like the inside of a meat locker, her legs like toothpicks trying to remain upright on wet ice. She had the pistol in hand as she crunched toward the next group of trees.

Distant gunfire rattled across the mountain. *Rat-tat-tat . . . rat-tat-tat . . .* then . . . just the wind.

She stopped again, kept low, tried to feel her toes within her sneakers and heavy tube socks.

Maybe she had felt something. Her lips were chapped and cracking. Licking them made it worse. Maybe she could keep mentally strong, but her damned body was turning against her.

She sank onto her rump, leaned her head against a tree, and tried to keep her eyes open.

Oh, just a minute was all she needed. One minute. Her lids came down, and suddenly . . . she was out.

"**IT'S NEVER HAPPENED** before, and it won't happen again, sir," Webber was telling Hansen as they watched Ryback's people working hard to rearm their Bradleys.

"If you can, just think of this as another gunnery," Hansen suggested. "You guys have been Top Tank before. So . . . be the best out there, all right?"

"No problem, sir."

Hansen offered his hand and gave the gunner a hearty shake. "And, uh, just between you and me, how much is he hating me today?"

Webber cringed. "I think the usual amount, sir."

"No more kicking his ass, all right?" Hansen winked.

Webber wriggled his brows. "Not without your permission, sir."

"Careful there, Sergeant. Where's the love?"

"That's what I want to know, sir."

They shared a grin, then Hansen left the gunner and headed back to his tank. As he neared good old *Crimson Death*, his cell phone beeped with an incoming text message. He nearly jumped a few feet in the air as he fished out the phone and frantically hit the buttons to read it.

The screen glowed a pale blue in the darkness, and Hansen had to read the message three times before he could fully comprehend its meaning.

And then it struck him so hard that his eyes welled up and his breath simply vanished.

"Yo, LT, I took another look at those wedgebolts like you asked," Gatch called. "We're looking good over here. Really good!"

Karen was out there in the mountains and on the run.

Kim Abbot was dead. *What do fucking wedgebolts have to do with that?*

"Hey, LT, you hear me?"

"Just shut up, Gatch! SHUT UP!"

The driver shrank away behind the tank as Hansen read the message yet gain, his hand growing tighter around the phone until he almost crushed it.

CHAPTER
EIGHT

THE MILITARY INFORMATION processing system worked very much like a straw, sucking up things from the bottom, but it wasn't very good at taking them in from the sides (which was also known as "stovepiped" information).

In situations where someone who was not a traditional source of information got something of value and inserted it into the information collection chain, that intelligence would receive action or would be ignored based upon who that person had told. Wars and fights were run by operations people and supported by personnel, supply, and intelligence people. Operators attempted to unconsciously manage their information flow so they could stay sane. They were only human, and after a few twenty-hour days, they would burn out and run on autopilot.

All of which was to say that Hansen did not want the news regarding the ambush and Karen's escape to be lost or ignored. He knew that if he sent a spot report up his chain of command, it would probably be acted upon in a year or two. He figured that if he asked Captain Van Buren to get the message to the task force or brigade commander, Karen would have a much better chance at being found. Of course, that wasn't going "by the book," but he was damned near ready to take the book, stomp on it, set it on fire, then fling it at the enemy.

Unfortunately, by the time he reached the captain, the poor man was being pulled in ten directions by ten different people. Moreover, he was about to take off with the FSO and the company's senior KATUSA to receive their operations order.

Still, Hansen managed to gain the CO's attention and give him a capsule summary of what had happened. Hearing the news, Van Buren scratched the stubble on his chin, waved off the people at his sides, and gestured Hansen to the hood of his HMMWV.

"Jesus, Lieutenant, I'm sorry to hear that. You can count on me to send up word, but I have to remind you, that's some rough terrain out there, and another storm is on the way."

"I know. That's why this can't get blown off. If somebody can get to her in time—"

"Somebody's going to have to—because the mountains are crawling with special forces now. They probably ambushed the convoy in the first place."

Hansen's expression grew even more pained, and seeing that, Van Buren quickly asked, "Tell me, Lieutenant, was she any more specific about her location? Does she have GPS on her? That would really help out."

"She's an English teacher. She might have a grammar book, but no GPS."

"Yeah, I guess it wouldn't be that easy."

"Sir, all I know is, she's just out there in the mountains along MSR 3. If we could find out where those busses were attacked, then she couldn't be too far from there."

"Gotcha. I bet someone can get through to the 2nd MP Company. They must know something by now."

"Thank you, sir. And sir, what about my platoon sergeant? I, uh, I'm not sure—"

"Abbot's a good man. One of the best. I'll send over the chaplain to meet you, but I think he should hear it from you."

Hansen took a long breath.

Van Buren tightened his gaze and placed a hand on Hansen's shoulder. He gave a solid squeeze, then lowered his voice. "Lieutenant, you can do it."

"Yes, sir."

The captain's expression grew long. "I'm sure you and Abbot aren't the only ones affected by that ambush. I'll be joining you soon, telling guys that the worst has happened. God, I don't even want to think about it." The captain breathed a huge sigh. "Anyway, I'm off to get the OPORD and pass on that word. I'll meet up with you and other TCs when I get back. Get with the XO if you need anything."

"All right, sir."

As Hansen shuffled away, the Assembly Area transformed into a blur of silhouettes and shadows, as though someone had thrown a thin, dark curtain over the entire valley. Voices grew strangely pitched, dreamlike, and the wind and cold no longer gnawed at him.

That's right. He was dreaming. He had stayed up late to watch an old war film and had transported himself into the role of the young lieutenant who was forced to tell a man he deeply respected and trusted, a man who had become almost a father to him, that his wife had been killed.

Were that only the case.

He stopped. Closed his eyes tightly. Opened them. The AA was back, with all the sights and sounds and smells.

Shit.

What would he say? How would Abbot react?

Hansen needed to believe that the platoon sergeant would, of course, be devastated, but as a career NCO fully aware of his responsibilities, he would somehow manage to drive on and do his duty. Maybe he would perform even more seriously.

In fact, Hansen would hate to be on the receiving end of the most experienced NCO in the platoon after he'd heard of his wife's death. All of those years of tactical and gunnery experience would be focused in a stream of unleashed fury transferred through the medium of American firepower and technology. The enemy would not know what had hit them, and Abbot's crew would be in for one heck of a ride—if they could keep up with his fire and maneuver commands.

Or, the platoon sergeant could simply fall apart right there and refuse to go on.

Worse, maybe he would draw his sidearm, put it to his temple . . .

Hansen shuddered violently to suppress the thought as he neared the tank line. He paused, looking back for the chaplain, but he didn't see the man. Should he wait? *No.* Because if Abbot saw him approaching with the chaplain, he would know right away that something very bad had happened. It was better to ease him into it.

Damn, going into battle was hard, but maybe this was even harder. Where would he start? What should his voice sound like? He should have asked the captain for more pointers, but he had felt too embarrassed.

Abbot was sitting on top of the turret, speaking quietly with his loader, Paz, who was standing in his hatch. "Hey, Lieutenant," Abbot called, his tone almost jovial and sending a shiver down Hansen's spine.

"Hey, Matt. Can we have a word?"

"Yes, sir." Abbot slowly climbed down from the tank and hopped onto the snow. He glanced up at the dark clouds beginning to blot out the night sky, his cheeks stained by snowflakes. "Damn, we're in for another bad one. I hope we get moving soon. What's up?"

He's talking about the weather, Hansen thought. *And I'm about to ruin his life.*

"Hey, Lieutenant, are you all right? You don't look so good."

Hansen thought a curse. He was getting choked up already, gasping, feeling a little dizzy, wringing his gloved hands, and about a half second shy of running away. Once again, he looked for the chaplain and thought he saw him approaching.

"Sir? Really, are you okay?"

"No, I'm not so good."

"You want to see a medic or something? Come on, I'll get you over there right now."

Biting his lip, Hansen shook his head, then said, "Matt, I got a message from Karen. She must've met up with your wife at the field house."

"Oh, that's great. I was hoping they would. I told Kim to look out for her. So where are they now?"

Hansen's lips came together. He needed to carefully measure his words, carefully select his tone.

But he should not have paused, because during that few seconds of silence, Abbot's expression turned from wide-eyed anticipation to wide-eyed fear. Then his voice dropped in a hard request, "Lieutenant . . ."

"The busses were attacked on their way to Uijongbu. They must've gotten out of there, run into the mountains or something . . . but Matt, Karen said that your wife—"

Abbot held up a palm and averted his gaze. "It's okay, LT. It's okay."

But Hansen needed to say it, as much for himself as for the platoon sergeant. "Karen said your wife was killed. She didn't say how or anything else. Matt, I'm so sorry, man. I'm so sorry."

Ironically, Hansen was the one crying. It was all just so

fucking sad that he couldn't take it. What was he supposed to do or say next?

Abbot lowered his palm and just stood there, kicking snow with one boot for a few seconds before finding his voice. "She had to come here. She's as stubborn—*was* as stubborn—as anything. Couldn't talk her out of it. What're you going to do?" Abbot glanced up, the tears welling now.

Hansen was about to say something, but then he remembered:

Sometimes all you have to do is listen.

The platoon sergeant's gaze drifted far away. "Thing about her . . . she just got it, you know? Maybe you found the same thing in Karen. I hope so. Kim just . . . she let me be a man. I hope she knew how much I appreciated that."

Abbot's quiet acceptance left Hansen standing there, admiring the incredible strength it took to remain composed after hearing such grave news.

Amazingly, Abbot even smiled, drawing the deep lines in his face as he proffered a hand.

Feeling utterly awkward, Hansen shook hands, and the platoon sergeant read the confusion on his face. "Lieutenant, this must've been really hard for you—and you did good."

"Matt . . ."

Abbot took a step back and waved him off. "I've been here before, Lieutenant."

"No, you haven't. Not like this."

"Maybe not like this. But everything happens for a reason. And I'll deal with it."

Hansen lowered his head. "I, uh, I talked to the captain. He's going to send up word for us. Maybe they can get with the 2nd MP Company to find out more. Soon as I know, you'll know."

"Thanks, LT. That was a good idea. God willing they'll find her. I just . . . I don't want her left out there." Abbot's voice finally cracked.

Hansen took Abbot by the shoulders. "We'll raise heaven and earth if we have to—and we'll find her." He released the platoon sergeant.

"And they'll need to find Karen, too, right? So she's out there, alone?"

"Yeah, with the storm coming. I don't know if she's dressed for it. I don't know if she found shelter. Van Buren says that special forces guys have already penetrated that area. Jesus . . ."

"Now it's my turn to say sorry," Abbot began. "Fuck . . ." He whirled around, rubbed his chin in thought.

"And hey, the chaplain's on his way," Hansen said.

"Thanks, LT. I'm going to let my crew know what happened."

"If you want me to, I'll—"

"That's okay, Lieutenant. It's important for me to do that."

Hansen tightened his lips and nodded. "Do you want me to keep this quiet?"

"I wouldn't volunteer the information, but if somebody asks, go ahead. My crew deserves to know. Besides, I won't be able to hold it in around them." Abbot moved back toward his tank, reached the rear deck, lowered his head, and paused a long moment. He mumbled something to himself, then climbed up.

Heaving a great sigh of exhaustion, Hansen saw the chaplain coming over and gave an awkward wave. The white-haired man with deep blue eyes that reached out like a wave to settle over you hurried over. His voice complemented those eyes, coming in a soothing lilt that was practiced but didn't sound so. He just sounded like he really cared. And he did. "Hi, Lieutenant."

"Hello, Father."

"The captain told me about Sergeant Abbot."

"I've already told him, but I'm sure he could use you."

"Not me, Lieutenant."

"Right. Well, uh, thanks."

"Lieutenant, if you need to talk—"

"I know where to find you. Thanks." Hansen moved on down the row of tanks. As he passed Keyman's track, the TC rushed out from behind the forward deck and accosted him. "Sir? Can we talk?"

"Can it wait?"

"Negative, sir."

Hansen snorted, and his shoulders slumped. "What do you want?"

"Are you and Abbot trying to get rid of me?"

"Shit, Keyman. You think it's all about you. Why do you have to be such an asshole?"

"Sir, are you trying to get rid of me?"

"I want you in this platoon."

"What?"

"Yeah, I want you here. I also want some hundred-mile-an-hour tape wrapped around your mouth, but that's another story."

Keyman turned his head, spit a bullet of chew, then drew back, finally revealing his surprise. "You really want me here, sir?"

As usual when he was around the staff sergeant, Hansen found his hands balling into fists. "Yeah, I want you here. Because you're a better tanker than I am."

"Excuse me?"

"You heard me."

"Yeah, and I don't believe it."

"Your problem." Hansen started to walk off, but Keyman jumped in his path."

"No, don't go yet, sir. What do you mean I'm a better tanker?"

"Look, we all know you should've been Top Tank. But you made a mistake. Shit happens. That's all. And I like to think I'm a pretty good PL because I can admit that, even to an asshole like you. Of course I'd be an asshole if I didn't keep a guy like you on my wing—but enough with the second-guessing me. Enough with the bullshit. You just do the fucking job and shut up."

An odd little grin curled the TC's lips. "You really think I'm better than you?"

"In the turret, yeah. Your management style is way too rough to ever lead a platoon, as evidenced by your little slugfest, but as far as commanding the track, you got the edge."

"Are you kidding me, sir?"

"No. But don't let me hear that you've gone back to your men and told them that I'm kissing your ass now."

"I won't, sir. It's just . . . surprising. I saw you talking to Abbot over there. I figured you two were—"

"No, we weren't. Did you see me talking to the chaplain, too?"

"Yeah, so . . ."

"Well, if it makes you feel better, I was notifying the platoon sergeant that his wife was killed on her way to Ui-jongbu." Hansen immediately regretted using the news to make the TC feel bad, but the guy inspired the worst in him.

Keyman lowered his head, pursed his lips. "Oh, God. That's horrible. Shit. I feel like an idiot." He cursed again, then added, "You know, Abbot loved her like you wouldn't believe. When he wasn't trying to get me to like you, he was talking about her. Christ, he won't be worth jack now. He's going to be all emotionally bummed out, screwed up. What're we going to do?"

"He'll be all right," Hansen said, his tone hardening as he read the selfishness coming loud and clear through Keyman's words. "In fact, I think he'll be our secret weapon."

"Payback is still a motherfucker," Keyman said with a nod. "If you're right, then I hope he really goes animal, just like Neech."

Hansen smiled bitterly. "Just what I need now . . . another loose cannon."

Keyman gave an exaggerated wink. "At least you got me, sir."

"Right." Hansen rolled his eyes.

"Now that we're buddies, I'll play by the book." Keyman's voice wavered between sincerity and sarcasm. The son of a bitch would keep Hansen guessing.

"Okay, buddy. I'm going to my track to get warm," Hansen told him. "Van Buren should be back soon with the OPORD." Hansen started away, but Keyman called after him.

"You know what, Lieutenant? I'm glad we had this little talk. Makes me feel better about dying."

"Guys like you don't die."

"Yeah, we live in infamy, huh?"

Hansen waved off the sergeant and hurried away, wondering if he had really gotten through to him. Given the circumstances, he could use a small miracle to boost his morale, but he wouldn't hold his breath.

SERGEANT LEE WAS, according to Deac and Gatch, stinking up the turret with his kimchee again. While he did not want to offend his crewmates, Lee felt it was his right to eat what he wanted. Moreover, he disliked the MREs almost as much as the cold weather and almost as much as the criticism he received from the loader and driver. He, like any other solider, had become acutely aware of his sense of taste. No matter how chaotic or surreal his military life became, he could always rely upon the flavor of kimchee or *soju* or any of his other favorite foods and drinks to reestablish a connection to the outside world. Those tastes never changed. And in a strange way, they reminded him of what he fought to protect.

"I don't know how you eat that stuff," Deac said. "What

is that, like pickled cabbage? It reminds me of something spicy and something dead."

"Yeah, but that crap is why you don't see any fat Koreans," said Gatch from his driver's station. "The stuff smells so bad you can't eat a lot. And they have it at every meal. That's portion control for you. And they ain't worried about low carbs or fat content, right, Lee?"

Although he grew rigid over the remark, Lee kept eating and displayed no reaction.

"Lee, you know we're teasing you, right?" Deac asked.

Cocking one eyebrow, Lee gave the loader a quick, emotionless nod.

"Hey, man, we're serious, you know?" Deac went on.

"Serious?" asked Lee.

"You're just so wired now, dude. I don't know what it is, but for the past couple of days, you haven't been yourself. Way too quiet—even for you."

"I am still me, but I am tired."

"No, Lee, that ain't it. Gatch and I, we get the feeling that something's going on here. Maybe now with the lieutenant gone, you can talk about it. Are you okay? It seems like you're on edge or something."

At that instant, Hansen lowered himself into his hatch, then shut it against the cold. He took one whiff of the turret and grimaced. "Whew, Lee, man, whoa . . ."

"I am sorry, Lieutenant."

"Gatch, get out of your hole and come up here for a minute."

"You got it, LT."

Once the driver had squeezed himself down near Deac in the loader's station, Hansen said, "Now Gatch, I owe you an apology for snapping at you. I just got some bad news, and I needed to deal with it."

"Sir, if there's anything we can do . . ." Gatch began, but Hansen was already gesturing that there wasn't.

Lee studied the lieutenant's expression. He, like many

Americans, had a hard time controlling his emotions. Something was giving him great pain. Perhaps his girlfriend had left him. Or maybe he had received bad news from back home. Whatever the case, he was definitely preoccupied, and that unnerved Lee almost as much as revealing his own troubles. Deac and Gatch could already see that something had come over him.

But they would never know what it was like to be an outsider struggling to belong yet wondering whether it was worth the effort. That same struggle, along with all of the annoyances, continued to feed his anger.

And the food reeked.

"Guys, enjoy this little break. I'm sure once the captain gets back from his meeting, we'll be moving out."

"Probably down into TDC, huh, LT?" Deac asked.

"I think so."

"Maybe the North Koreans should level that big shithole. Then we can come in and rebuild it right. Put in a couple hundred titty bars."

"Yeah, that'd be cool," added Gatch.

"You guys are sick," Hansen said.

Lee wanted to tell Gatch and Deac to shut up as images of civilians and soldiers strewn across TDC's snow-covered alleys left an ugly feeling inside.

Then Lee saw himself climbing down from the turret and walking away. The lieutenant would come after him, and he would say that he was sorry but that he had decided he could only work with men of honor, not animals. He was a man. He had made a decision. And if they wanted to shoot him for desertion, then they had better get on with it—because he was leaving.

"Lee, I asked you a question," said Hansen.

"I am sorry, sir."

"Lee, man, what is wrong with you?" Gatch asked. "You're not even listening to us anymore."

"I said I am tired." Lee lowered his gaze and took in a long breath.

Deac folded his arms over his chest. "Bullshit. You keep saying that."

"Deac, leave him alone," Hansen said. "We're all tired. We're all really tired. But we can't let that stop us."

"Yes, Lieutenant," said Lee. "I will do my best." Lee hadn't been lying. He would still obey orders and be the very best gunner he could be—not for them now, but for himself. He was beginning to hate Deac and Gatch. And worse, his thoughts strayed to some very dark places as he plotted ways to get rid of one or both of them. Working aboard a tank was a dangerous job, even when you were not in combat. Anything could happen . . .

PLANES RACED OVERHEAD, their blaring engines wrenching Karen from sleep. She held her breath, looked around, suddenly panicked as the events of the night flashed through her mind and ceased on the single image of Kim Abbot, eyes open, body lifeless, blood all over . . .

Karen almost screamed but held back just in time.

How long had she been asleep under the tree? She checked her watch. *Thank God. Just fifteen minutes.*

Okay. She was still alone, still in the woods, still trying to escape.

Head south. Keep the road on your left. That's how you'll know. Keep the damned road on your left.

Oh, crap. Her legs felt so frozen that she could barely move them. She sat up, stifled a groan, thought she heard something.

The forest looked even darker, and the shadows seemed to drain the life from her.

Sounds? No, just the wind. Wait.

The message! She had sent Jack a text message.

She yanked the phone from her jacket pocket, thumbed a button, saw that he had replied. He would pass on the news to Abbot about Kim's death. He would do everything he could on his end to send help. *Thank God!* At least he knew she was still alive. *He knows!* And now she felt a rekindled energy surge through her aching muscles and bones.

He loved her. He had said so. *Nothing could stop that, right? Nothing!*

She opened her mouth and nearly cried. Her lips were so dry and frozen that they cracked and were probably bleeding. She licked them. Yes, they were. *Screw it.* She pulled down her cap, then balanced herself on the tree and slowly rose. The effort brought tears to her eyes.

Off in the distance, far below where she thought the main highway lay, came the steady humming of engines, big engines, and beyond it came an even more distant rumble. Bombs were being dropped somewhere out there, and with a shiver, Karen imagined that one of those pilots would be given orders to bomb the mountains in order to kill the special forces guys, and, in turn, kill her. Maybe Jack could call them? She hoped so.

After a wary glance across the forest ahead, she slowly started off toward the next group of trees that rose from a ridge and were huddled up like loitering teenagers.

If she could imagine her escape as simply connecting the dots between stands of trees, she could hold off some of the fear and make the course seem more manageable. The distances didn't matter. It was all about getting to the next tree. That's all. And that was the damned teacher in her, always analyzing, looking for solutions to problems, and trying to instruct even herself.

She stumbled but made it. After catching her breath, she tried to call Jack, but the network was a joke. They had to continue with the text messages, and they were lucky to have them. With near-frozen fingers she told him she was still moving south and would try to text him as much as possible. She ended, the message with a simple: *I love you* and a smiley face that seemed incredibly ironic.

Just as she pressed the button to send, a faint shuffling noise came from behind. She put on the night vision goggles and panned along the forest.

"Don't these assholes ever quit?" she whispered.

About a dozen men in heavy winter coats carrying machine guns high-stepped toward her, coming in from about a city block away and closing steadily, though the shin-high snow hindered their pursuit. She had a choice: try to move quickly ahead of them or dig in and hide.

If she remained, more soldiers might come behind the first group, and the odds of being discovered would increase. She had to keep moving. It was a race now, with Jack and Reese depending upon her to win.

That meant she had to stop crying. Right now! She rose again and charged away, descending closer toward the road, toward that hum of engines which she imagined were trucks driven by guys from places like Chicago, Denver, and Orlando. "Why, ma'am," they would say as they rescued her. "What the hell were you doing up there?"

"Well, I wasn't snowboarding," she would say, feisty and full of attitude, just like the Karen everyone back home knew and loved, the Karen crazy enough to travel all the way to South Korea to teach English.

"*Mom-cho-ee!*" shouted one of the soldiers.

Yeah, right, like she would stop so they could shoot her.

Gunfire erupted in lines that came within a few feet, puffs of snow continuing on, while more rounds chewed into the trees ahead.

As more bullets flew, she rushed up to another ridge, saw the bottom lying in shadows about six feet below.

"Oh, shit," she muttered, then held her breath and

jumped toward the mounds of snow, praying they were deep.

ABBOT SAT QUIETLY as the chaplain's words of solace came like soft music, the meaning lost but the tone comforting. That was all Abbot really needed: just a moment of peace to reflect. He already knew God had a purpose for his life and that God had taken Kim for a reason that might never become evident in this world. Abbot should continue to be resigned and not let her death cloud his judgment. He would go through the stages of grieving even while helping the LT run the platoon. They would fight. They would win.

However, Abbot could not accept God's mysterious purpose without first becoming angry.

After all, he could still smell Kim in his imagination, still feel her lips and smile over that sensuous look she gave him after they made love. The damned woman had become so Americanized that she had started collecting Precious Moments figurines, like one of the other wives she had befriended. She had several curio cabinets jammed with those little statues. What the hell was Abbot supposed to do with them? And what about her clothes and all of those crazy shoes? Those shoes?

It was odd how his thoughts shot back and forth between the important things he needed to do and the strangely trivial. He was worrying about clothes, shoes, and figurines when they had yet to recover her body.

Oh my God. Kim is dead. The chaplain was still talking when it really hit Abbot. His eyes narrowed, his cheeks grew tight, and he leaned over and began to sob. The chaplain draped an arm around his back and spoke more soft music. Abbot allowed himself another moment before he sat up, wiped his cheeks.

After saying twice that he was all right, he muttered a

prayer, thanked the chaplain, then quickly returned to the turret.

So many people needed to know about Kim: her parents, Abbot's, more relatives, friends, the whole fucking world. Abbot wished he could tell them all. He wished they could share the burden of her loss, but at the moment, that burden fell solely on his shoulders.

Then again, he had told the crew. Paz had actually become teary-eyed himself. Sparrow had assured Abbot that they would rip out the dark hearts of the motherfuckers responsible, even if that meant killing every North Korean combatant on the peninsula. Park had quietly offered his condolences.

So maybe they did share the burden, and he should rely upon them to get through. Yes, he would push them harder than they had ever been pushed before, but he would also protect them more fiercely. They were his only family in Korea. And he wasn't about to let them die, too.

All of a sudden, he knew exactly how Neech felt, and the pain clutched his stomach, turned it in knots. He cried once more before he reached the tank, then stole a minute to compose himself before getting into the turret. They couldn't see him weak. They just couldn't. Even when he had told them about Kim, he had not shed a tear. His voice had come evenly, his eyes steady.

Paz immediately offered him a cup of hot coffee, which he gratefully accepted.

"Sergeant, we've been thinking that if it's all right with you, we'd like to say a prayer." Sparrow stood near the ammo doors, sipping his own coffee. He raised his brows and waited for an answer.

"Well, I just said one with the chaplain, but go ahead."

The driver squeezed his eyes shut, then bowed his head. "Lord, God, we seek your peace and your guidance at this most difficult of times for your servant, Sergeant Matthew Abbot. We ask that you show him—and us—the way, the truth, and the light when it seems so dark right now. And we ask it all in Jesus's name. Amen."

Paz echoed the amen, and Park offered his polite nod of agreement.

"Sparrow, if you don't get that job as president of the United States, you can always become a preacher," Abbot said, wearing a weak grin.

The sharp-jawed black man gave a curt nod. "Either way, my mamma would be happy."

"I bet she would."

"Yeah, man, and if you get on TV like one of those televangelists guys, then you could make some serious cash—way more than you'd make as president," said Paz. "But then again, God likes to strike down those guys, doesn't he."

"He sure does," Sparrow said.

Abbot leaned back in his seat, closed his eyes.

There she was. His Kim. Where she would always be.

WEBBER GLANCED OVER his shoulder and frowned at Keyman, who had been sitting in his seat for the past five minutes, wearing a seriously large shit-eating grin, a grin so uncharacteristic of the man and so surprising to Webber and Smiley (king of all grins) that they could do little more than simply look at him before getting up the nerve to comment.

"Sergeant, what so funny?" asked Smiley.

"It's the fuckin' lieutenant. I got him on the run now. He's scared I'm going to bail on him. Now he's kissing my ass big time. I knew it would come to this."

"He's scared you're going to bail on him?" Webber asked. "What, go AWOL or something? Give me a break."

"Watch that, Webber. I still owe you for this face."

Now Webber was the one smiling.

"Wipe off that look," yelled Keyman.

"What?" Webber cried. "You can't see me from up there."

"I got eyes everywhere, asshole. Just remember that."

An icy gust cut down through the open hatches and stung Webber's cheek.

"This air is colder than death," Keyman said. "Colder than death."

CHAPTER
NINE

HANSEN'S CELL PHONE felt glued to his hand. It was his lifeline to Karen, and he guessed that the next time it beeped, signaling the arrival of a text message, he would jolt so violently that he would bang into something and hurt himself.

Word finally came down from Captain Van Buren, who was actually still at the OPORD. Their next defensive mission would be at Casey Creek, which ran from west to east across the Korean National Railroad, MSR 3, and right through Camp Casey. Van Buren had ordered the company to finish up critical actions in the AA and then haul ass back to the camp, where they would hit their very own motor pool so they could finish up maintenance and refit. Ironically enough, they were about to defend both TDC and their own home from the North Koreans, and the task force commander was doing everything he could to exploit that home court advantage, including using the motor pool they had worked out of day in and day out to prepare for the fight.

Within fifteen minutes Red, White, and Renegade Platoons were on their way, rolling back toward Casey, carefully navigating the treacherous mountain passes. Hansen remained in his hatch, dividing his gaze between the road ahead and the small screen glowing in his palm.

NEECH WAS NOT a quitter, but exacting payback on the enemy now seemed out of his reach. He could not kill enough of them to feel good. He would never reconcile with Batman's death. He was scarred forever. What was the point of going on?

But could he just walk away from his men, from the mission, from his career?

What was he thinking? Had he gone insane?

Or had he just had enough?

He stood in his hatch, wearing his night vision goggles and wishing they would allow him to see more than just the road ahead. He needed to vent. But one second he wanted to talk to someone, the next he didn't.

Strange, though, the dialogue in his own head would not cease. He wished he could stop thinking so much, but he had prided himself on his intellect. He had always wanted to be more like his father, the professor; he wanted to be a soldier and scholar.

Now his brain conspired against him, forced him to play out scenario after scenario.

If he refused to go on, he would be hurting his men, and while that pained him, he wasn't sure he could go into battle and muster the same anger and vengeance as he had before. Everything seemed wrong. Even Mother Nature was reminding him of that, making it so unbearable outside that no one would want to fight. Maybe he had nothing to worry about. Maybe they would just call off the war. The North Koreans would surrender, and Red Platoon would be called back for the celebration party. Everyone would eat too much, drink too much, and get laid. The ROKs would thank them and worship them like Gods.

Neech smiled bitterly. There was a snowball's chance in hell of that happening. He was fucked, plain and simple. He could accept his fate or try to change it. Those forces were threatening to tear him in two. And the more they pulled, the more they revealed a single notion that dominated them all:

He should already be dead. From the moment that Batman had taken the bullet meant for him, the clock had started ticking, and Neech had begun living on borrowed time.

AS GATCH STEERED them into the motor pool, Hansen felt an odd tingle work across his shoulders.

"I don't know about you guys, but this is feeling pretty weird," said Gatch.

"You got that right," Deac added. "Never thought we'd be defending from our own turf."

"Guys, if this is fate at work, then we're in good hands," said Hansen. "We've come home for war."

"Red One, this is Red Four," Abbot called over the platoon net.

"Go ahead, Four."

"I'm sending out Paz and Park to see if they can scrounge up some twelve gauges. I'm betting those KSG guys left some behind, over."

"Sounds good. You get 'em, send one over here, will you?"

"Roger that."

Members of the Korean Security Guard (KSG) who normally guarded the gates and walls of Camp Casey were preparing to fight alongside their American counterparts, using their Vintage shotguns and M14 rifles provided by the US units.

Meanwhile, the men of the Forward Support Battalion were rapidly repairing all combat vehicles they received for direct support maintenance in order to get them back into the fight. Some tanks and Bradleys that couldn't be fully repaired would be pulled into defensive positions in west Camp Casey and TDC, where they could still use their turret weapons. Even without engine power, those combat vehicles could and would still fight. Also, those Paladin howitzers and mortars whose engines had been pulled were being towed into position and employed manually.

The ammo storage areas on Camp Casey and Hovey were being emptied completely, and surplus ammo, including rounds used for training on rifle ranges, was being distributed in abundance to everyone.

While Hansen and his men were going to defend from the Casey Creek area, just north of TDC, they were but one element of a much larger defense. Ever since the North Koreans had first breached the Demilitarized Zone, military personnel and civilians in, near, and around the town had been preparing for an attack.

Those residents who had chosen to remain to protect their homes and businesses from looting were taking every bottle they could find and making Molotov cocktails with gasoline, diesel fuel, and even *soju,* the bitter-tasting Korean liquor. They would add soap flakes or soap powder to form a sticky gel. Molotovs were frequently used by rioting students and labor protestors who had become adept at making the classical weapon and would demonstrate their prowess on the NKPA. People would throw their flaming bombs from the upper floors of apartments and business buildings. They would also take bicycle inner tubes, convert them into slingshots, and fire Molotovs over those buildings or at targets they wanted to hit quickly. Their attacks were like mini napalm strikes and could prove amazingly deadly.

Meanwhile, propane bottles used for cooking and heating in most TDC homes and businesses were being rigged into improvised explosive devices and would be command detonated using car batteries and wires. Cooking oil from all of the restaurants would be poured onto the icy streets and set on fire with Molotovs when mounted and dismounted enemy personnel tried to move through the town.

At the TDC train station, where coal was stockpiled, the railroad staff had already pulled up some of the track and had sabotaged the local car switching station to prevent the enemy from using the station to transport personnel and vehicles. The 25th Transportation Battalion, which owned all of the American military railroad cars, had positioned cars on every crossing to block enemy mounted forces. They were also welding the car wheels to the tracks, which would definitely piss off those North Koreans who thought they could simply push the cars out of their way.

On the west side of MSR 3 lay a drainage canal, where cars and other barricade materials had been thrown in, blocking that high-speed avenue of approach. Used tires from all of the repair shops and junkyards had been piled into those barricades and others and would be set on fire to help slow enemy breaching efforts.

Any other weapons civilians could fashion would be employed, all in an effort to keep opportunists and combatants away from their valuable property. Those who truly hated the North Koreans would fight as boldly as any ROK soldier.

However, the presence of those civilians, numbering in the thousands, would make target acquisition all the more difficult. The enemy would, of course, seek refuge in those built-up areas and exploit structures they knew were on the Americans' restricted target list, and that worried Hansen a whole lot. Additionally, civilians would be used as human shields, and that was, arguably, a soldier's worst nightmare.

Still, while the enemy would launch an asymmetric offense, they would face a similar defense, with unpredictable civilians standing in their way. Then again, those ROK locals could just as easily turn on the US defenders, believing the Americans were more of a threat to ROK security than the North Koreans, according to one recent opinion poll.

Military preparations besides those initiated earlier by the Division Cavalry, task force scouts, and by First Tank and the Manchus, included the use of brigade "Knight Teams," which were Forward Observer teams with their own up-armored HMMWVs packed with digital, high-tech gear just like a BFIST. They were positioned even farther north than the task force scouts and would designate targets for laser-guided munitions.

Moreover, GPS units were being used to locate every road intersection where American and ROK forces could engage the enemy with mortar and FA fires. Air assault "light" infantry units from the 1-503 IN were situated in the built-up areas to help prepare and conduct the defense. They would use locally "procured" trucks and SUVs to move around town and rapidly reposition during the attack.

Maintenance units with M88 recovery vehicles were helping to push cars and barrier material into place. Once that job was done, they would join the battle with their .50-caliber machine guns.

REMBASS was probably being used along the highway and dismounted trails to provide early warning and targeting for the FA and mortars. GSR teams were no doubt setting up their dishes on the tallest buildings in town and would look up the MSR to track advancing forces. During the OPORD, Van Buren would definitely add to the list, describing ROK operations as well.

While all of the physical preparations were being made, it was up to each man to gather his thoughts and prepare himself for battle. No one could do that for you. Hansen, a kid from the suburbs of Long Island, New York, needed to rise to the occasion no matter what happened.

But as fate would have it, the occasion was a MOUT fight. Military operations on urban terrain posed one of the greatest challenges to American forces on the peninsula. Despite the many lessons learned during the wars in Iraq, tankers like Hansen did not engage in such fights without feeling apprehensive. Back then, insurgent forces had used schools, mosques, and hospitals as headquarters, ammo caches, and sniper positions. They had played the dirtiest of pool, beheading their captives and testing American soldiers' moral and ethical principles by forcing them to make less-bad choices in an imperfect world, which was a fancy way of saying that sometimes you had to sacrifice the good guy to kill the bad one.

And later, you had to live with yourself for making that decision. God, Hansen would rather be up in the mountains, defending a defile—or even back at that low-water crossing. But then he remembered that kid on the turret, the look in his eyes, the shot . . .

As Red Platoon was quickly rotated through the motor pool, with last-minute maintenance checks being initiated and fuel tanks topped off, Hansen received word that Van Buren had finally returned and had called for the OPORD briefing.

After meeting up with Thomas and Ryback, all three headed off for the Charlie Company garrison headquarters, where they would assemble with the rest of the command staff in the company classroom. Again, it would be absolutely bizarre to receive an actual wartime OPORD in the very same classroom used for so many practice orders before the war had started. Hansen would have to remind himself that this was real, even though his surroundings would suggest otherwise.

They entered the room and exchanged a few curt hellos with the company XO and first sergeant, received the acetate map overlays laying out the team's mission, then took their seats. Various poster-sized diagrams and charts of the Republic of Korea were hanging all over the room, and nearby stood a large sand table so they could study a relief model of the terrain before heading out. The battalion S2 had just printed out some blowups of more maps and satellite photos of the area the task force was defending from, and he had sent a runner to distribute them to the companies.

"Is everyone here now?" Van Buren asked the XO, who scanned the faces.

"Yes, sir."

"Good. Prepare to copy. A mechanized brigade of the follow-on North Korean echelons has seized Chong Gok to the north and is preparing to attack south directly down MSR 3 through TDC in an attempt to make a run for Seoul. Their lead scouts are likely observing Camp Castle just a few miles north of here right now. We can expect the main body to attack sometime within the next six to eight hours, depending upon what Mother Nature throws at us."

Van Buren crossed to the wall and utilized the maps and satellite photos as he spoke, indicating positions with his laser pointer.

"To our north is the 5th ROK Armor Brigade defending MSR 3 from South Chong Gok to Dong An station. They are reinforced with a ROK Army Reserve infantry battalion, and they are using the permanent, preexisting defensive positions and obstacle systems."

Hansen was aware that those bunkers and other strongholds had been in use for years and were annually cleaned up and reinforced by those same ROK reservists.

"To our east, Team Alpha is defending in sector with the mission to prevent penetration of Casey/Hovey Cut and protect our brigade's right flank.

"To our west is Team Delta, who will defend in place to prevent penetration of Highway 56 and to protect our left flank.

"To our south the 56th ROK Homeland Reserve Division is continuing to defend in place in the event we have leakers and if we have to withdraw.

"Also, to our immediate rear, colocated with our company team trains, is Bravo Battery from 1-15 FA. They're our dedicated Paladin battery, as usual, and will provide fires to the brigade Knight Teams, TF scouts, and us as required. Expect to hear them firing anytime, day or night.

"So then . . . the brigade's mission is to defend in sector and prevent enemy penetration of TDC and use of MSR 3." The captain glanced up from his notes, his expression never more serious. "Gentlemen, I cannot stress enough how important this mission is to the defense of the ROK. The primary North Korean objective is Seoul, and the ROKs will protect the city at all costs. Don't expect the ROK brigade up north to withdraw. They have orders to die in place if necessary."

Ryback lifted his brows at Hansen, who returned a nod. Neither of them doubted the ROKs' tenacity.

"Our mission is as follows: On order, Team Cobra defends Battle Position Casey to destroy enemy reconnaissance and lead elements of the mechanized brigade to prevent penetration of Phase Line Blue. I say again, on order, Team Cobra defends Battle Position Casey to destroy enemy reconnaissance and lead elements of the mechanized brigade to prevent penetration of Phase Line Blue. If you look at the graphics you'll see that Phase Line Blue runs east to west, right through Camp Casey and parallel to Casey Creek.

"Intent: Our mission is to prevent enemy mounted and

dismounted forces from penetrating across Phase Line Blue, and we will accomplish this with effective use of obstacles covered with direct and indirect fires. Ensure that you can both see and cover those obstacles from your positions and engage the enemy when he is slowed and stopped by them.

"Concept of the Operation: Red, White, and MECH Platoons will defend from positions just south of Dong An station vicinity grid 290995. Red will defend in BP Red from the Shin Chon River to the railroad tracks. MECH will defend in BP Infantry straddling MSR 3 with their left on the railroad and their right near the Camp Casey Golf Course Clubhouse. White will defend from BP White from the clubhouse to the Camp Casey Helipad. Secondary and tertiary positions will be prepared and occupied on order."

Mostly one-story repair shops, warehouses, and stores rose in and around the battle site area. There were also a lot of shacks and simple houses where civilians lived. Many of those buildings would provide excellent cover and concealment. HMMWVs could hide in car garages and even go to higher ground in multilevel parking garages. Hansen and his men could position their tracks inside stores or warehouses and fire through small openings such as windows or doors. Ryback's infantry could booby-trap doors and fire Javelins from within buildings, using them in a "bunker buster" mode to demolish buildings. Those TF scouts trained as snipers would exploit the urban area too, manning rooftop positions and providing precision head shots that would have a great psychological effect on the enemy.

Van Buren continued: "Red, your task is to destroy enemy forces if they attempt to use the frozen Shin Chon River or the railroad bed as high-speed avenues of approach. Engage them with direct and indirect fires, and tie those fires in with the obstacles that are being emplaced by the engineer battalion.

"MECH, your task is to first destroy enemy recon as they try to probe our positions and then to destroy main body enemy forces as they attempt to use the railroad and MSR 3 as avenues of approach or to bypass through Camp Casey. Provide one fire team to secure the FIST in his OP.

"White, your task is to destroy enemy forces as they attempt to bypass the obstacle belts and North TDC through Camp Casey proper.

"FOs will occupy Observation Posts on the roof of the Dong An Hotel and the North TDC truck stop. They will call for and adjust mortar and FA fires."

Van Buren stepped over to the sand table and took up a pointing stick as the rest of the group rose and gathered around. "The scheme of maneuver is as follows: We will occupy primary defensive positions and be prepared to fall back to secondary and tertiary positions on my order. TF scouts will conduct rearward passage of lines after they confirm the main body is approaching. Do not engage our scouts as they move through our lines. They are driving up-armored HMMWVs with CIPS panels on them, so you'll see those through your thermals for positive identification. After they're through the front obstacle belt passage lane, I'll seal it with MOPMS.

"We'll have a heads-up on the enemy frontline trace from REMBASS and GSR, and that'll be the initial trigger for our indirect fire plan. As usual, mortars will focus on enemy scouts, dismounts, and AT teams. FA fires and CAS will focus on mounted formations. As the main body lead elements come into range, engage targets on the river, the railroad bed, and MSR 3 at max range with TOW, main-gun, and Javelin fires. All of these fires will have maximum effect when the enemy is slowed or stopped at these obstacles. High payoff targets are enemy scouts, AT teams, and engineers. Once CAS is on station, enemy ADA teams will become priority targets as well. Linear targets for mortar and FA fires are planned in front of each obstacle belt.

"If the enemy begins to penetrate through the main defensive belt, I'll order the team to move back to the secondary positions. FIST and all other observation and target acquisition teams will move first, followed by MECH, Red, and White. When I give the command to move, light off the smoke pots we're giving you so there will be some obscuration smoke to help conceal your movement. Also, Red and White will each be receiving a dozen claymores, three per tank. You'll position these against likely infiltration routes and dismounted avenues of approach, and when you break contact to move to secondary positions, you'll detonate them as well. This should help us save some coax and .50-caliber ammo. When the last team is through I will close the passage lanes through the secondary obstacle belts with MOPMS.

"After defending from the secondary positions, be prepared to move on my order to the tertiary positions. If we go there, observers, Red, and MECH will cross on the MSR 3 bridge, and after we're set, the engineers will blow the bridges for both MSR 3 and the railroad. White, you will move to your tertiary position through the Camp Casey ford site, and I will close it with a MOPMS.

"When everyone reaches their secondary and tertiary positions, you can resupply there. The TF support platoon is dropping pallets of ammo and other supplies at each of the positions for each platoon. Other than that, all else is done IAW the SOP. At this time, what are your questions?"

The captain had barely finished speaking when Hansen's cell phone beeped from inside his jacket pocket. As Van Buren rolled his eyes, Hansen silenced the phone and didn't dare read the screen. "Sorry, sir."

"Sir, I have a question," said Thomas, who was kind enough to bail out Hansen by shifting the captain's attention. "We've got some serious weather coming in, and even without it, those streets are still hell for driving tracks."

"I've already directed the removal of alternating track

pads so the shoes can gain some firm traction. Maintenance teams should already be on this. If not, use your organic impact wrenches to take the rest off."

"Thank you, sir."

"Also, we'll be establishing some warm-up tents for dismounts, though MECH platoon should utilize those stores or shops with heat to rotate your men through."

"We will, sir," answered Ryback.

"As usual, Lieutenant, your platoon will have checkpoint duty along the road, and you'll have a few MPs up there to help out. Don't be surprised if those bastards try to sneak some recon guys through dressed like civilians or ROK soldiers. Use your challenges and passwords, and rely heavily on your KATUSAs. Some of the better guys can spot a North Korean almost on sight, then confirm based on his accent."

"Yes, sir. What about the sewer mains?"

Van Buren grinned. "You're pretty sharp, Lieutenant. We've had some men from the maintenance platoon already welding manhole covers shut, but they haven't sealed them all, and some are buried under ice. However, a few grenades dropped in usually solves that problem."

"Fire in the hole," muttered Ryback.

Hansen wished he had something to contribute to the briefing, but his thoughts were fixed on the possible message from Karen.

"All right, then. Let's go over this one more time on the sand table, then we're out through the main gate to occupy our BPs and begin preparations and mounted rehearsals."

Unable to stand the suspense anymore, Hansen stepped back behind Thomas and stole a glance at the message.

I'm okay, she had written. *Still moving south near MSR 3. Love you.*

"Love you too," he whispered, then turned back toward the sand table, where the captain was once again in the throes of simulated battle.

* * *

BEFORE HEADING BACK to the motor pool, Hansen learned from Van Buren that word regarding Karen's escape had been passed on and that there was nothing else they could do. He thanked the captain, then left the classroom. In the hall outside, he sent off another message to Karen, urging her to keep going. What else could he do?

Feeling a new wave of depression sweep over him, he dragged himself back to the tank line, where he gathered his TCs around the front of his track. "This won't take long," he began, glancing up at the heavily failing snow for a second before continuing. "We're heading up to Casey Creek, establishing our BP between the Shin Chon River and the railroad tracks west of MSR 3. We'll be getting set somewhere behind the second barricade. I want the platoon to find BPs inside some buildings and really exploit that cover and concealment."

"Sounds fucking beautiful, LT," said Keyman. "I want to come crashing out of one of those shacks and pounce on those motherfuckers."

"That's just how they describe it in the manual," Hansen quipped, but then, as he glanced around, his amusement vanished. Keyman, bashed up face and all, was the only one paying attention. Neech and Abbot wore the infamous thousand-yard stares. Hansen wished that was only sleep deprivation at work, but he knew better. "Hey, guys, are we good to go?"

"Yes, sir," Abbot said, snapping out of his trance. "And LT, my guys secured four shotguns, which they've already distributed."

"Excellent. How 'bout you, Neech?"

The sergeant took another moment before the gears in his neck finally got to work, producing a slow nod.

"All right, when we get up there, we'll dismount to recon, I'll go back over the OPORD, then we'll get set. Shit, while we're waiting for those knuckleheads to attack, we might even catch a few Zs."

"Sounds all right," said Abbot, who glanced back at his tank. "We've already loaded up the claymores. Maintenance guys are getting ready to remove some pads. We should be rolling pretty soon."

"Guys, I wish . . ." Hansen's thought drifted off. "Hell, I don't know what I wish . . . just . . . maybe that things were different."

"I wish for a pepperoni pizza," said Keyman. "A steaming hot pizza, dripping with cheese and oil. If I had one right now, I'd eat it, then I wouldn't give a shit if I died."

"Keyman, you suck," said Abbot. "I can smell that son of a bitch right now. Big, doughy crust, spicy sauce . . . Mmm . . ."

They had Hansen smiling. Maybe that was their intent. His tone had been far too grave, as though the words *Karen is out there!* had slipped out between every sentence.

But that tone didn't bother Neech, who remained a statue wired like a claymore.

Keyman shoved the TC. "Come on, Neechy. Wake up. I bet you can eat a whole pizza yourself."

Neech looked fire at the TC, then bit his lip.

"All right, we're done," Hansen said, giving Abbot and Keyman the high sign with his eyes. They understood and took off.

Neech was about to do likewise, but Hansen called out, "Hey, you did great back at the river. Really hardcore, man."

"Thank you, sir."

"Neech, I . . ."

"I know what you're getting at, sir. Do not worry about me. It'll pass."

"You know, I haven't heard one of your quotes in a while. They don't call you Neech for nothing, right?"

"Right. But there's nothing Nietzsche said that'll fix this."

"Yeah. Only you can."

"Me? Shit . . ."

"You already know what you have to do."

Neech made a face. "Really?"

"Yeah."

Neech wrapped wool-covered fingers over his frozen nose, then lowered his head and muttered, "Have to get back to my track, sir."

As he wandered off, leaving a trail of white boot prints in his wake, Hansen shivered as he considered not only Neech's mental stability but that of each man in his platoon. As he went through the roster, he realized he was more worried about the TCs than the loaders, gunners, and drivers. When he had first become a tank commander, he had wanted to believe that the men would be as simple to manage as the machines. They never were, never would be.

Hansen checked his watch. Almost five AM. He and the rest of the platoon had been up for nearly twenty-four hours, with a long day ahead. He reached for his cell phone, thought better of it as the maintenance team arrived. "Gatch? Deac? Get out here. Let's help these guys with the pads."

CHAPTER
TEN

BY FIVE THIRTY AM, Team Cobra rolled out of Camp Casey in the middle of the worst blizzard the peninsula had seen in nearly fifty years. A foot of snow had already collected on the turret and front slope of Hansen's tank, completely covering the driver's hatch, while the heat of the engine kept the rear deck wet, warm, and clear.

Hansen assured himself that the storm was a blessing in disguise. The North Koreans could not see well through all of the precipitation because most of their mounted and dismounted forces were not equipped with thermal sights. Every soldier in Ryback's platoon had the AN/PAS-13 thermal weapon sight mounted to their rifles or machine guns and would use them to spot dismounted infiltrators trying to sneak by the team's defense. That capability, coupled with the thermals on his Bradleys and those on the tanks, gave Team Cobra the technological advantage.

For years military strategists had been arguing that if North Korea invaded the south, the defenders, despite being outnumbered, would have the advantage because of

well-planned positions, familiarity with the terrain, and su-
perior technology. However, most conceded that weather
conditions could quickly level the playing field, giving those
invaders in the open more time to find and prepare positions
because Close Air Support elements would be grounded. In-
deed, the North Koreans had gambled on the weather, and
their strategy was paying off. At the moment, nothing was
flying, and they would have that time to better prepare their
positions and attack.

Still, Hansen guessed that even if the battle began, it
would come to a halt during the worst parts of the storm.
The Chinese had tried to fight in similar conditions during
the first Korean War and had wound up walking on frozen
feet and dying of hypothermia in their foxholes. Hansen
wouldn't be surprised if whole platoons of NK grunts
froze to death, forcing their unit commanders to halt and
warm up the others.

Either way, it was not a good day to die. Hansen would
have wanted better weather. He would have wanted his
girlfriend tucked into her bed, safe and sound and not out
there, somewhere, possibly freezing to death herself . . .

The platoon, spearheaded by Keyman's tank, headed
west toward Casey Creek, which ran through the middle of
the western end of Camp Casey. To cross the creek, those
driving HMMWVs and trucks used a bridge, while tank
and Bradley crews steered for the all-weather, cement-lined
ford site, which could support the weight of their vehicles.

Once on the north side of the creek, they turned left,
heading west again to the release point: Camp Casey Gate
#2. From there they embarked on the last leg of their short
drive, veering left to move parallel with the railroad tracks
and advance about one hundred and fifty meters to Dong
An station. The terrain between the gate and their battle
position was relatively flat, allowing the engineers to move
in quickly and construct an impressive array of defenses.
They had pulled up more railroad ties, had cut them into

smaller pieces, and had welded them into "hedgehogs" patterned after those obstacles used on the beaches of Normandy. The hedgehogs had been placed all along the frozen surfaces of Casey Creek and the Shin Chon River and tied together with crisscrossing tangle foot barbed wire and AT/AP mines. They stood like snow-covered scarecrows and hinted at the battle to come.

Continuing to move north between the tracks and the river to their left, they headed toward a long barricade of old cars, trucks, tires, and wire marking the north side of their secondary battle position. With binoculars in hand, Hansen observed that the barricade extended from about halfway between the tracks and river all the way out across MSR 3. It was an imposing wall of defense, one the enemy would have to disassemble to bypass, even as he took direct and indirect fire.

Just off to their left were several narrow side streets lined by ramshackle buildings and terminating at the river. Many power poles had been cut down and laid across each other to make abatis obstacles, with the tops pointing toward the enemy's avenue of approach. The poles were also rigged with barbed wire and mines to deny mounted access into those areas. Yet more railroad ties had been buried end up to make pole obstacles, they, too, spanned by wire and booby-trapped with mines to cordon off the streets.

Keyman led them carefully around the main barricade ahead, and the platoon trundled forward, passing another trio of hedgehogs nearly covered by drifting snow. Beyond them, cars, trucks, busses, trailers, and even a few dumpsters formed the next barricade, this one running from northeast to southwest across the river. Hansen imagined the PCs and tanks slowing before the wall of metal as his men targeted them or called in mortar or FA fires—that is, if those enemy tracks survived the mines.

"Red, this is Red One," Hansen began over the platoon net. "We should be getting close now."

The overlays he had received showed the team's three main Target Reference Points, which were barely discernable through his binoculars. TRP 01 was the tall smokestack of a textile mill slightly off to their northwest and to the left of the Dong An train station. The commander had chosen a tall radio tower to the east of MSR 3 as the second TRP, while a water tower with a red checkerboard pattern rising to the northeast was marked as TRP 03.

During MOUT operations, tall objects were routinely chosen as reference points, the same way mountain peaks and other high or plainly visible terrain features were chosen during defenses of defiles and other operations in more remote regions. That smokestack, radio tower, and water tower made excellent references for calling in mortar and FA fires as well as guiding CAS personnel to their targets. Trouble was, the storm made seeing them all the more difficult. The smokestack would show up because of the heat, but the radio and water towers would be more difficult to spot. Weather notwithstanding, the mortars and howitzer battery were already fighting the counterecon fight, being directed to long-range mounted and dismounted targets via the brigade Knight Teams and TF scouts, the booming like distant thunder seemingly muffled even more by the storm.

Two more barricades had been arrayed just behind the train station, which told Hansen that they had reached the general vicinity of their primary BP. He ordered Keyman and the others to slow down.

Just west of the railroad tracks was another network of narrow streets, home to random clusters of one-story buildings, including an auto shop and two warehouses at the end of a long alley whose east entrance had been left open by the engineers. The rear walls on those warehouses faced north, inviting Hansen to further scrutinize the position. More hedgehogs had been set up about fifty meters ahead of the buildings, standing behind another barricade that ran the length of the river and could be mistaken for a wall of snow, were the occasional patch of metal from a car or rail-road tie not peaking through.

Hansen panned east with his binoculars, where through the faint light and snowflakes he saw a Bradley near the checkpoint barricade along MSR 3. A few men quickly dismounted, then the vehicle moved off. There were too many other walls and rooftops obscuring Thomas's tank platoon in the east, though they, like Hansen's men, were probably looking for suitable cover between the Golf Course Clubhouse to their west and the helipad to their east.

"Red One, this is Red Two," called Keyman. "Do you see those long, blue buildings to our left? They look like warehouses, over."

"Yeah, I saw them. They look real good, over."

"I see big garage doors out back. We might fit through there, over."

"Roger. We'll push through whatever they have inside. Let's do it, out."

They plowed through much deeper snow drifts, working along a row of old trees, then Keyman's driver turned left down the long alley, and Gatch followed, uttering, "Whoa, this is getting pretty tight." They had but a meter clearance on each side of the tank.

"Just keep going," Hansen insisted.

After about twenty meters, the passage grew much wider as they neared the warehouses.

Suddenly, the door on a small shack to the right of Keyman's tank flew open. A figure bundled in a heavy parka rushed out and raised her arm.

A shot boomed!

Hansen jolted, looked to Keyman, whose arm was extended, his 9 mm in hand, faint smoke wafting up from the weapon.

The figure staggered back to the wall, then dropped hard to the snow.

"Red Two, hold your fire!" Hansen screamed over the platoon net. "Red, stop!"

All four tanks slowed to a halt. Hansen was so intent on getting out of the turret and to that fallen person that somehow he made it past all the snow without slipping. Keyman's track had already rolled by the victim's shack, but Gatch had placed Hansen right in front. He raced to the figure, dropped to his knees, and pulled back the parka's hood.

An old Korean woman, her face deeply grooved and framed by graying hair, her eyes creased in pain, stared back at him. Her mouth moved slowly, one lip quivering.

Lee, who had risen to stand in Hansen's hatch, cried, "She had no weapon!"

"Lee, get below!" Hansen ordered. "And get Deac out here with that lifesaver bag!"

"What the fuck does she want?" Keyman yelled. "She comes blasting out of the fuckin' door, waving something. I thought she had a weapon. I thought she was going to shoot me!"

Hansen unzipped the woman's jacket. Her shoulder was bloody. He placed two fingers on her neck and found a weak but steady carotid pulse. "Well you're lucky. She's not dead yet."

From the corner of his eye came the rushed approach of someone wearing rubber boots. He looked up, this time into the eyes of yet another old Korean, a man with a leathery face bearing jagged gray teeth. Two more old men followed him, all barely filling out their ratty parkas. "We not enemy!" screamed the first guy with the teeth. "She not enemy!"

"Well she fooled me," Keyman spat. "Why did she come out, waving her fist, then, hey, motherfucker?"

"You wake her up! You G.I. always wake her up!" the old man hollered back.

"You're kidding me! You hear that booming? That's

artillery fire out there," said Keyman. "She was going to sleep through that?"

"Keyman, shut the fuck up." Hansen stood and lifted his palms to the old men. "All right, just calm down. I'm going to get help for her right now."

Deac charged up, carrying the combat lifesaver bag, which was loaded with about half the gear that real medics carried. He was the tank's "combat lifesaver" and had been cross trained in basic combat medic skills but apparently not trained in the art and science of navigating icy roads on foot. He took another step forward, slipped, and a second later, was on his ass. Were the situation not so dire, Hansen would have burst out laughing.

"Sorry, LT," groaned the loader as he picked himself up, moaned again, then knelt before the woman. "All right, let me see what we got."

Keyman snickered. "Should we call a medic for you?"

Deac flashed an ugly smile, then began rifling through his bag.

Meanwhile, Hansen hustled back to the tank, climbed into the turret, then grabbed the mike. "Black Six, this is Red One, over."

"Red One, this is Black Six," answered Captain Van Buren. "Go ahead, over."

"Black Six, we have a ROK civilian fratricide incident and request MEDEVAC, over."

"Red One, this is Black Six, roger. State the nature of the incident, over."

"The Red Element accidentally shot and wounded an old ROK woman who appeared to be a guerrilla attacking one of our victors. She's hit in the shoulder with a nine-millimeter round and needs medical attention. Break.

"I have a combat lifesaver aiding her now and request the company medic take over while I continue moving the Red Element to BP Red, over."

"Roger, Red One. Keep moving to the BP and give me

the grid to the injured civilian. The company medics are on the way, over."

Hansen issued the grid, then he dropped a hand on Sergeant Lee's shoulder. "Don't worry, man. She'll be okay. Those medics will bust ass to get here."

Lee nodded, but residual lightning still lit his eyes.

Swearing under his breath, Hansen climbed down from the tank. Deac and Keyman had carried the woman into her shack, laying her down just inside the doorway. Deac had placed a big trauma bandage on the woman's shoulder and was applying pressure.

"Was it okay to move her?" Hansen asked.

"No, but I thought she might freeze to death before she bleeds to death," said Deac.

"She ain't gonna die," Keyman spat.

"Back to your track," Hansen told the TC. "MEDEVAC's coming. We're moving out."

"Yes, sir. And hey, bro," Keyman called to the old Korean still scowling at them. "You might want to go bye-bye, because by tonight this whole place will blown to shit."

"You G.I. trouble! Nothing but trouble!"

Hansen pointed at Keyman. "I said back to your track!"

"All right, all right," sang Keyman, throwing up his hands.

"Deac, show this guy what you're doing," Hansen told the loader. "We have to leave."

"Okay, LT." Deac waved to the old man, who reluctantly came closer. Deac took his wrist, placed his hand on the bandage, and said, "Pressure. Keep pressure. Okay?"

"You shoot her and just go!" yelled one of the other old men. "Just go!"

Hansen wanted to grab the man by the shoulders and get into his face. Instead, he widened his eyes and pointed north. "Enemy coming. Enemy coming soon. We have to go and fight."

The old man shook his head and walked back toward

the shack, passing Deac, who had already shouldered the lifesaver bag. "Okay, LT, I think she'll be good till the medics get here."

"Seriously, how bad is she?"

"Not too bad. But when they're old like that, even the fall could've killed her."

"That'd be our luck."

"I just wish we weren't giving God more reasons to hate us, is all."

Hansen gave a long exhale in frustration. They crossed to the tank and mounted up. Once in his hatch, he gave the order. "Red, this is Red One. Move out."

GOD HAD TO be on her side, Karen thought, because after she had jumped onto the mounds of snow, the men pursuing her had broken off. She had no idea why. She had hid near the base of the ridge, tucking herself up tightly against the cold, hard earth, and had stayed there for maybe a half hour, maybe more.

She had received the message from Jack in which he had urged her to keep going, and she had made a promise to herself to do so.

But now dawn was coming. She might be spotted. Shot on sight.

And her whole life, all the years of hard work and dedication, all the years of trying to make her parents proud, all the years of struggling to find a man who would make her happy . . . and then finally finding him . . . would be . . .

For nothing.

No. It couldn't come to that. She wouldn't let it. Dawn would come, yes, but the snow was falling much harder and might get even worse. She couldn't see more than fifty feet ahead, and she realized with a start that she had drifted down to within a dozen yards of a wide clearing that must be the main road. She stumbled along the embankment, the snow rising to her ankles, then suddenly to her knees.

She fell. At least the snow had cushioned her fall. She rolled onto her back and just lay there, breathing, the wind blowing so hard. The air so cold. Snow all over her now. An icy tomb. Time to give up. It was just too much. Her face felt dry and brittle, her lips like stone. Her bones ached.

Then she thought of her and Jack at the Flower House, how wonderful that had been, how absolutely amazing he was. She thought of Reese lying up there on the mountain. And she got angry at herself for even thinking about just lying in the snow and letting it all be for nothing.

She sat up, forced herself to her feet, and trudged on, worrying only about her next step. A gust nearly knocked her over. She steadied herself. Moved her legs, hunkered down a bit more as yet another gust struck.

Ten steps later, the silhouette of something large grew like a rogue wave across the sea of white. After drawing a bit closer, she dismissed the silhouette as a massive drift, but then, as she came within a dozen feet, she realized it was a car, an old Daewoo sedan that had swerved off the road to become encrusted in ice and buried in snow.

Seized by a reckless abandon, Karen rushed toward the vehicle, feeling almost drunk. She didn't give a shit about being in the open, about the possibility of snipers targeting her, or about the chance that someone could be inside the vehicle. She just needed to get there, out of the cold.

But when the car was almost within arm's reach, a massive chill rocked her body as logic kicked in, reminding her of the danger, though it was too late to turn back. She put everything she had into the next few steps.

Completely out of breath, she seized the driver's side door, and wrenched it open. Snow dropped from the roof and door, falling onto the empty driver's seat. Only then she thought of drawing her pistol, but a quick glance inside confirmed she wouldn't need it. With an audible shiver she climbed in and shut the door after her. First thing: Keys? No, she wasn't that lucky. Besides, the engine probably wouldn't start anyway, which was why its owner had abandoned it. She crinkled her nose over the stench of cigarettes and that distinct, almost spicy smell of Korean people, yet anything was better than being outside.

I'll wait out the storm here, she thought. But maybe she couldn't. Wasn't she a sitting duck? Any special forces guy who saw the car would want to look inside. But she would have her pistol ready.

All right. She would stay. For how long, she didn't know. Time to send Jack another message. She pulled off her gloves, blew warm air into her frozen hands, and then fumbled for her phone. *Damn it.* She was going to cry.

WEBBER TIGHTENED HIS grip on the shotgun they had procured from the KSG. He drew up closer to Keyman's shoulder as the TC used a heavy pair of wire cutters to snap off the lock on the second warehouse's big rolling door.

That done, they shifted to one corner of the door, while the lieutenant stood at the other. After the LT's go ahead, they, along with him, lifted the door in unison, bringing it up about four feet while keeping tightly to the wall. Hansen nodded, and they let go. The door hung in place.

While Keyman, Webber, and Smiley, who had come up behind Webber with his rifle, dropped to their bellies and inched closer to the corner of the open door, Deac, Lee, and the lieutenant did likewise.

Long rows of metal racks buckling under the weight of boxes of auto and machine parts stood between the tanks and northern walls, which were about forty feet off. Webber couldn't see any movement inside, but that meant jack. They lay there a moment more, breath steaming.

Webber imagined some pissed off warehouse owner sitting inside, rifle drawn. The thought shortened his breath, but thankfully, he had no time to worry about another panic attack. The LT gave the signal, and he and Smiley got up, kept hunched over, and darted inside to the left. Deac and Lee, also armed with rifles, entered to the right. They would clear the warehouse using standard infantry techniques, each man taking his assigned corner and calling out "Clear!" when he had completed his sweep.

The clearing went off without incident, then, once the tanks' antennae were folded down, Hansen and Keyman guided the drivers inside. The doorway was tall enough to permit the tracks but about a foot too narrow.

Morbid revved the M1's engine and blasted through one side of the wall, taking a long strip of sheet metal with him. Gatch came in behind, whooping from his open hatch.

Then the real fun/destruction began as each tank plowed into the warehouse's inventory, knocking over metal shelving, both drivers now hollering like preschoolers on a toy store rampage. There was something wonderfully powerful about watching those two sadistic maniacs crunch everything in their paths as they made their way toward the wall. The roaring engines echoed even more loudly inside the building, so loudly, in fact, that Webber's CVC helmet only partially dampened the sound. The crashing and smashing continued until the last two shelves tumbled and were eaten by tank treads. As Webber might later put it when he wrote his bestselling memoir, "I would never witness a more heartwarming display of mechanized mayhem."

The lieutenant used an old broom to bust out a rectangular shaped window in the northeast corner of the building, while Keyman did likewise in the northwest so that the tanks' gun tubes would fit through. The drivers maneuvered the tracks into position, while Webber and the others made sure the surrounding area was clear of any debris that might slow their exit from the building.

After that, Hansen issued the order for the claymores to be positioned outside, just south of the hedgehogs. Keyman and Smiley took care of that for their tank while Webber took care of a few more routine checks of his equipment.

About fifteen minutes later, Hansen walked up and said, "I've got good news. You and Deac are going outside to set up an LP/OP."

"How's that good news? I bet it's colder out there than it was on Christmas Eve."

"Probably. But the good news is you'll be the first ones rotated back inside."

"You got a funny way of seeing things, LT. I'll try to feel the love here."

"So will I." The lieutenant lowered his voice. "Can I trust you with this?"

Webber was about to lower his head self-consciously, but then he realized that he needed to show the lieutenant that he was the right man for the job, that he wouldn't pass out again. He lifted his chin, glanced unflinchingly at Hansen, and hardened his voice. "Sir, you can trust me with anything."

"Before this day is over I may have to." Hansen gestured toward a rear door near another set of windows. He was about to speak when an odd look came over his face. He reached into his pocket, yanked out his cell phone, and read the screen with widening eyes.

Webber thought of asking if everything was all right, but he decided against it. He had heard about Abbot's wife. No one in the platoon could keep a secret. He had also heard the rumor that the LT's girlfriend was in trouble.

"She's still okay," Hansen mumbled. "She found a car. Fuckin' A! She found a car!"

"Are you talking about Karen, sir?"

Hansen suddenly looked embarrassed. "Let's go out for a second. We'll pick a good place for that OP."

"Sir, it's okay. We know you're worried about her."

"I'm more worried about us."

"We'll be okay. But yeah, I know that's hard to believe, coming from me."

Hansen draped an arm over Webber's shoulder. "Sergeant, I have the utmost faith in you."

"Thanks, LT."

ABBOT WANTED TO remind Neech to boresight again since they had made a move. The boresight ranges would correspond to their sectors of fire. They also needed to perform some last-minute maintenance, like checking fluid levels and such. Hansen was sending out Webber and Deac to establish the LP/OP, so Abbot wouldn't have to worry about that, and radio communications between the tanks wasn't too bad, with only minimal interference caused by the buildings. The fewer things Abbot needed to think about, the better. His thoughts were scattered everywhere like the auto and machine parts, and he was still trying to collect them, organize them, even as he tried to forget that he would never kiss his wife again.

He leaned back on the tank, rubbed his aching eyes, then shivered himself back to reality, and a cold one at that. He and Neech had already situated their tanks along the north wall and had set up their claymores outside. They were ready to restart their engines and move up about six meters so that their gun tubes would jut from the windows. If they needed to move farther forward, they would bust through the metal walls and advance across the next alley, into the open field and toward the hedgehogs.

Abbot pushed off the tank and gazed across the warehouse. To his mild surprise, Neech's guys were already boresighting their tank, so he whirled and faced his own men, who were still clearing debris that had fallen onto the M1's hull and bustle rack. "Paz? Park? Let's boresight again."

The KATUSA gave a quick nod, but Paz shook his head, bit his lip, as though biting back a curse, then rolled his eyes and turned to head after the gunner.

Abbot grabbed Paz's shoulder and yanked him around. "HEY, WE NEED TO BORESIGHT AGAIN!"

The words, shouted very slowly for effect, echoed away.

Park stopped dead in his tracks.

Even Neech's crew turned their heads.

Platoon Sergeant Matthew Abbot wasn't prone to outbursts like that. His sense of calm—even in the most horrific of situations—had become famous.

But the enemy had crossed the line. Taken his wife. There was nothing left now but the job. He no longer had any tolerance for complaints or whining.

Paz's mouth fell open, and his eyes grew teary. "Sergeant, I . . ."

"GET ON IT! NOW!"

"Yes, Sergeant!"

Abbot shoved him away, then glanced down at a small box near his feet. He cursed and booted the box across the warehouse, then he marched a few steps toward Neech's tank. "Fuckin' show's over! Those cocksuckers from the north are coming, and they won't wait on us!"

INSIDE THE TURRET of Neech's tank, Romeo, who sat in the gunner's seat, craned his head to face Neech, who was at his TC's station. "I think Abbot's losing it."

"And you thought I was," answered Neech. "Or maybe you still do."

"We're all crazy. The whole fucking world."

Neech waited until Romeo and Choi were finished with

the boresighting before he spoke again. "You know, it's funny that we've never talked about this before."

"Talked about what? Going crazy?"

"About you becoming a TC."

"I bet some people would call it crazy to put a little spic like me in charge."

"Not crazy. And it could happen sooner than you think."

"Maybe I don't want it."

"Bullshit."

"Hey, who cares about that now? This whole place . . . it's going to be total chaos. And when the shit goes down, we have to stick together, right?"

Neech closed his eyes. It took a long moment before he could muster a nod.

"Hey, man? What're you thinking about?"

He opened his eyes and shrugged. "Nothing."

"Well, let me plant this thought: pretty soon we'll get some serious payback, even better than we got at the river. Batman'll live forever because you, me, and little Choi up there will make sure of that, right?"

How could he tell the poor guy that he didn't believe that anymore? How could he tell him that he felt like climbing out of the turret and shedding his Army career like a bad skin? How could he do anything but nod?

GATCH HAD SELECTED menu no. 2, "pork rib" from the packets of MREs standing tall in their brown plastic pouches. Nutrition, according to the labels on the narrow boxes inside, was a force multiplier, and those were two of the Army's favorite words.

Along with the boneless imitation pork rib (with smoke flavor added), the pouch contained some New England-style clam chowder, wheat snack bread, cheese spread, some lemon-lime beverage base powder, and the usual condiments like salt, sugar, Tabasco sauce in a tiny bottle, and packets of instant coffee and nondairy creamer. You also got a book of matches, a napkin, a moist towelette, two pieces of Chiclets-like gum, and a light green packet known as the MRE heater, which as the package warned, was (like the meal itself!) not intended for human consumption. You added water to the heater packets, slipped your imitation pork rib or clam chowder packet inside, and the chemical reaction did the rest. The reaction in your gut was another story altogether, not to mention the dreams such meals produced . . .

Gatch stared down the beach at the long lines of tank tracks being slowly erased by the incoming tide. He glanced ahead, looking once more for the tank that had produced those tracks.

Instead he found Jesus sitting on a Harley, his long beard bound in front by a single rubber band and wandering down like a weird tail between his pierced nipples. The Almighty had taken a small American flag and had folded it into a bandana that he had tied around his head. An angel's wings and halo had been tattooed on his right bicep, above the word *Mother*.

And seated behind Jesus was none other than Dale Earnhardt Jr. in full race car driver regalia, helmet tucked into the crook of his arm, moustache neatly combed.

Gatch asked them what they were doing there, but when he spoke, his words came out in Korean.

Jesus and Dale Earnhardt Jr. shook their heads and frowned. "We don't understand you. Don't you speak English?"

"But Jesus, you're . . . Jesus. Don't you speak all languages?"

"I'm sorry, but we don't understand you," said Dale Earnhardt Jr. He slid on his helmet.

Jesus throttled up, wheeled the bike around, and rumbled away, as Dale Earnhardt Jr. gave a mechanical wave.

A familiar rattling and clanking sent Gatch whipping

around—just as the wide treads of an M1A1 filled his view. The tread slammed him down. He felt his back break, his ribs pop, his skull shatter beneath the pads and shoes.

He shook awake in his driver's seat, burping up some clam chowder and pork rib. "That's what you get for falling asleep, you motherfucker," he whispered.

"Gatch, you all right in there?" the lieutenant asked.

"Yes, sir. Just talking to myself to stay organized."

He winced over that explanation. How complicated was his job, just sitting there, unable to even observe the area through his vision blocks since the wall stood in the way?

At least the lieutenant ignored the remark and got on the company net. "Very well. Black Six, this is Red One. Red is sct in BP Red and is REDCON-3, over."

"Red One, this is Black Six, roger. Scouts from the 5th ROK Armor Brigade to our north report mounted recon elements on the move toward their position. Our Knight teams and scouts confirm. Stand by, REDCON-3, out."

CHAPTER
ELEVEN

WITH THE COMMO wire unrolling behind them, Webber jogged across the alley and into the open ground behind the warehouses. Deac kept close behind, sweeping the area with his rifle. They moved about twenty meters, buffeted by winds and snow, then dropped into a ditch between the buildings and the barricade of hedgehogs. They would have had a clean line of sight between the eastern and western barriers were it not for the morning gloom and snow. As it was, Webber could only see about thirty meters ahead with the naked eye.

Donning his night vision goggles, he squinted to pick out TRP 01 and the factory smokestack in the distance. Off to the right stood the train station and the other two barriers behind it. Satisfied with their position, one of three he and Hansen had discussed, he pulled out the field phone from his ruck and plugged in the commo wire, which ran all the way back to Keyman's VIC 3, effectively hot looping them into the rest of the tanks.

"Red One, this is Red Two Golf, radio check, over."

"Red Two Golf, this is Red One. You're loud and clear. Do you have good observation of our sector, over?"

"I can barely see the smokestack, out near the station. Can observe both the east and west side of our sector, and about fifty or so meters up the tracks to the station, over."

"Roger, will rotate you in about thirty minutes. Hang tight, out."

"This is the coldest it's ever got here," Deac said as the biting wind ripped across their cheeks and a sudden flurry of mortar fire resounded somewhere far off.

"And we're out in it—again. The question is, who's got the bad luck? You or me?"

"Uh, that'd be you, Sergeant," Deac said. "And can I ask you something?"

"What?"

"Did you really pass out in the tank? That's what we heard."

"I just banged my head, got stunned. Fuckin' asshole Keyman blew it way out of proportion."

"He does that, doesn't he. You think he feels bad about shooting that old Korean lady?"

"Are you kidding?"

"Damn, he's just one of those guys you'll never forget. Not exactly human, you know?"

"Yeah, well he got his."

"I saw that. Nice fuckin' shiner. Beautiful work, man. Just beautiful."

"Whoa, whoa, whoa, what do we got up there?" Webber shifted his goggles to a row of shrubs running between the half-hidden railroad tracks. He focused on a sign bearing the station's name in English and Korean. For a second, he thought he had detected movement.

Deac had a pair of conventional binoculars in hand. He pushed up on his elbows and took a look for himself. "All I see is snow. Like everywhere . . ."

Webber probed once more, lowering the goggles just a little.

There!

A group of dismounts, maybe four in all, shifted stealthily from shrub to shrub, rifles slung across their backs. They were nearly lost behind fluttering drapes of snow. If you blinked at the wrong second, you would miss them. Webber no longer blinked. Were they ROKs, Americans, or North Koreans? He was damned sure that no matter who they were, they weren't supposed to be there.

"Red One, this is Red Two Golf," Webber said nervously. "We've spotted four, maybe five dismounts about fifty meters north our location. They're moving south along the shrubs between the railroad tracks. They just passed the sign, over."

"Roger. Continue to observe," Hansen ordered. "Let me call higher and see what's going on."

"They're still coming," said Deac. "And I don't think they're ours, man."

Mortar and artillery explosions, along with the booming of tank guns, now came distinctly from the north, the sounds remote—but coupled with the presence of unknown dismounts, they were enough to scare the living shit out of Webber.

"The ROK armor brigade is engaging," he said, beginning to lose his breath. "And these must be more recon motherfuckers who've slipped on through. We have to stop them before they get eyes on our position."

"Okay, let's go," Deac said, starting out of the ditch.

Webber yanked him down. "You asshole! I'm not talking about us!"

"I know. I know."

"Stop fucking with me."

"Sorry, man. Guess I'm ready to shit ice cubes myself. But we have to calm down."

"I'm calm!"

"Dude, you're as puckered up as it gets."

Cursing through his teeth, Webber grabbed the field phone and called Hansen to see if he had anything on the dismounts.

Meanwhile, Deac *tsk*ed as he stared through his binoculars. "I don't know why we make plans, when nothing ever goes according to . . . These guys shouldn't be here. But here they are. And what're we going to do about them?"

"RED ONE, THIS is Black Six. A squad from MECH platoon is en route to intercept your dismounts. Have your guys continue to observe and report. Hold your position and do not engage, out."

Hansen got back on the horn to convey the order to Webber, whose voice had begun to crack. "Well, I hope those guys move their asses," said the loader, " 'cause these guys are."

"Just sit tight and observe, Sergeant, out."

A gust of wind rattled the warehouse's metal walls and forced a chute of snow through the window in front of Hansen's tank. He straightened in his hatch, continuing to peer intently through his NVGs while Lee searched for the dismounts with his thermal sight, though his field of view was severely limited by the window.

"Red One, this is Red Two," called Keyman.

"Go ahead."

"I don't like this. A shitload of dismounts could've slipped right by the ROKs, working along the mountainside, then pushing right on through all these backstreets and alleys."

"Or they could just have a couple of recon squads working through to call in FA and mortars."

"That's too obvious, man. They won't play it by the book. Let's get Deac and Webber out of there now."

"Thanks for the unsolicited opinion. Now shut your hole and observe."

"I'm telling you, we should pull them out."

He was never going to stop with his second-guessing, was he? What would it take? Did Hansen need to climb down from his turret, go over there, and scream in the sergeant's face?

"What're we waiting for?" Keyman raised his voice. "If I'm right, then you're leaving them to die."

Sergeant Lee cleared his throat. "Sir, I think that—"

"Not now, Lee!" Hansen screamed. He tore himself from the hatch, climbed down from the tank, and jogged across the warehouse toward Keyman's track. "Dismount right now!"

Keyman lowered his goggles and stared at Hansen in utter disbelief. "What are you doing?"

"I said dismount!"

"Are you serious!"

"Sergeant Key, if you do not get down here—"

"All right! All right!"

Hansen's heart slammed against his ribs, and his hands trembled in anger as Keyman lowered himself to the ground and faced him, his eyes narrowing in a challenge.

AT FIRST, WEBBER wasn't sure from which direction the shouting originated. *"Ee-dee-wa! Ee-dee-wa! Jon-cha! Jon-cha!*

He craned his head, scanned the walls of the warehouses with his goggles, then found the source:

A parka-clad man stood off to the east, near a rickety wooden fence behind a row of shacks. Webber zoomed in. It was one of the old Korean guys who had confronted

Keyman and the lieutenant after the old lady had been shot. The guy was holding his own pair of binoculars and waving to the recon guys ahead. *"Ee-dee-wa! Ee-dee-wa! Jon-cha! Jon-cha!*

"That motherfucker," grunted Deac. "He's calling to them. What do you think he's saying?"

"He's saying, 'Come here! Tanks, tanks!'" Webber said, growing even more breathless. "Red One, this is Red Golf Two, over."

No response.

"Red One, this is Red Two Golf, over!"

"We need to shut him up," Deac said. "I'm going."

"Wait!"

But the big loader sprang to his feet, rifle at the ready. He charged toward the old Korean and was consumed in seconds by a fluctuating wall of white.

"Red One, this is Red Two Golf!"

NEECH HAD NOT had a cigarette in probably two years, but he had decided to bum one from Romeo and pump a little nicotine into his veins, which would go well with all the lukewarm coffee he had been guzzling. He was in his hatch, taking long drags and releasing columns of smoke that reached toward the warehouse's ceiling when he heard faint cries in Korean coming from outside. He ditched the cigarette and called Abbot, who wanted to immediately dismount for a look.

His pistol leading the way, Neech went to the warehouse's rear door, cracked it open, and peered out, just as Abbot came up behind him. "I just called Hansen. He didn't answer. I sent Paz over. What do we got here?"

"Oh, man," Neech said, taking it all in and just reacting. "I gotta go!"

"Wait!" cried Abbot.

Neech burst from the door and sprinted along the warehouse wall, racing up toward the jagged teeth of an old fence as Deac tackled someone to the snow.

"Neech!" Abbot hollered, thumping up behind him.

"What are you doing, old man?" yelled Deac as he threw down his rifle and grabbed the guy by the throat. "You're giving up our position, huh?"

"Deac, let him go," cried Neech as he hunkered down. He flicked his gaze forward, toward the railroad tracks and the station beyond. Holy shit, they were out in the open. *Not good. Not good at all.*

"Deac," Abbot said in a warning tone. "What are you doing?"

"He's waving to the fucking recon guys out there!"

"They can't even see him," said Neech.

Deac tightened his grip and shook the old man. "He was screaming that we got tanks."

After a quick nod from Abbot, Neech slid his arm around Deac's throat and ripped him off the old man. "What the fuck are you doing?" cried the loader, struggling against Neech's grip.

"We're big boys, Deac. Just calm down."

They caught their breaths, then Neech relaxed his grip and finally released Deac, who sat there, rubbing his neck.

In the meantime, Abbot spoke rapidly in Korean. While he had never claimed to be fluent, living with a Korean woman for all those years had certainly helped to hone his skills.

"What're you telling him?" asked Neech.

Abbot put a finger to his lips.

The old man uttered a few words, his voice burred, lips cracking. Then he lay there, a toppled monument of old-school Korea, eyes tightening to slits.

Abbot yelled at him in Korean.

He folded his arms over his chest.

"What did he say?" Neech asked.

Abbot snickered. "He wants us to let him go or shoot him."

Deac crawled toward his rifle. "I'll shoot the rat fuck."

"No, he doesn't get what he wants," said Abbot. "We're taking him back."

HANSEN FACED KEYMAN, suppressing the urge to find a metal pipe so he could bash in the guy's head. "Staff Sergeant Key, I want to know what it'll take? I thought we worked this out. I thought we were buddies?"

"Lieutenant, please!" shouted Lee, standing in the TC's hatch.

"I said not now, Lee!"

"Trouble outside!"

Lee had not finished speaking when small-arms fire popped and cracked, first in the distance, then rounds beat hard on the wall, some ricocheting, some cutting through, all of them rattling the metal and echoing hollowly through the room.

"What the fuck?" Keyman asked angrily as he spun and mounted his tank, ducking as two rounds sparked off the turret. "Shit!"

Hansen raced back to his own track as the fire continued, three rounds drumming the wall to his immediate left. "Lee, what the hell's going on?"

"Dismounts moving up along the riverbank! Enemy recon engaged by our infantry. Abbot, Neech, and Deac are outside with a civilian. Webber is still at his post."

Slamming into the hatch, Hansen quickly plugged his CVC helmet's cord back into the intercom, then called up Webber. "Red Two Golf, this is Red One. Get out of there!"

LITTLE LATE FOR that, Webber thought as he propped up on his elbows and took aim at the guys who had dropped along the frozen riverbank, their rifle muzzles flashing. "Get inside!" he shouted back to Deac, Abbot, and Neech. "I'll cover you!"

Webber couldn't believe what he had just said. He had obviously lost his mind. He was a one-man show, taking on how many dismounts over there? Ten? Twenty? Or was it just three or four recon guys? He just couldn't tell.

At the same time, Ryback's men had approached from the east and had taken up positions in the high ground about twenty meters away from and overlooking the tracks. They traded fire with the recon guys, then, during a sudden lull, a grenade exploded, shattering the railroad sign and whipping up a thick cloud of gray smoke.

"Webber, come on!" yelled Deac.

Rounds booted up chips of ice and clumps of snow in front of the ditch, and it seemed like Webber was damned if he moved, damned if he didn't.

He guessed the real question was, would he rather be shot while fighting back or shot while trying to run away?

The answer kept him leaning hard on his trigger, cutting loose round after round, keeping those audacious North Korean assholes at bay.

One guy rose, trudged forward, slipped, dropped to a knee—his last mistake. *Bang!* Webber dropped him. He couldn't believe it. "Yeah!"

He was smiling. Actually smiling. Loving the shit. Amped up. Unafraid. And breaking orders to boot. He wasn't supposed to engage. *Fuck the order. Fuck the enemy!*

What the hell had happened?

Well, the moment was his—and his alone. His life wasn't in Keyman's hands.

Up until that moment on Christmas Eve, when Keyman had broken down and had shared his problem with his father, Webber had always felt safe around the TC, a man so cocky that even God wouldn't want to piss him off. But when Keyman had revealed his weakness, Webber had realized that he wasn't safe. In fact, he would only be safe if *he* determined his fate, which was why being pinned down and alone made him feel like a million bucks. He called all of the shots, both literally and figuratively. He took aim at two grunts jogging toward the hedgehogs.

He fired. *Down one.*

Yet even as he squeezed the trigger for the second time, missing that son of a bitch, Deac seized his arm and began pulling him out of the ditch. "Back to the warehouse, man! Let's go!"

"Wait!"

"Fuck you, man. We're out of here!"

"**RED, THIS IS** Red One. Renegade will handle those dismounts. I don't want to crash the party just yet. I do want everyone mounted and ready to go, REDCON-2, out."

Abbot was standing in his hatch, watching Neech finish wrapping hundred-mile-an-hour tape around the old man's mouth. They had already bound his hands and feet and had positioned him atop a small shipping container.

"All right, that's good," said Abbot. "Back to your track. If our grunts don't stop those dismounts, they'll be moving in."

"So we're leaving this old fucker here?" asked Neech.

Abbot nodded. "He won't freeze. And he can't run or talk."

"I hear that." Neech tore off the roll of tape, then shoved the hood up on the guy's parka. Suddenly, he grabbed the old man by the collar. "You think those guys are your friends? Don't you remember the first war? Don't you remember anything?"

The old man remained stoic; he'd had a lifetime of practice.

Neech shoved him, then took off running for his track.

"Red One, this is Red Four. We have secured our prisoner and will hold him until the first sergeant arrives, over."

"Roger, Red Four. Good work, out."

The old man glanced up at Abbot, the defiance still smoldering in his eyes. Abbot looked away. Then looked again. The old man's expression grew even more dark.

Abbot was about to dismiss the look, but then he glared back, his thoughts running wild. He imagined an old man just like him tipping off the special operations guys, telling them about Kim's bus. Kim had been killed because some asshole South Korean had betrayed his country and the Americans who were helping to defend the nation against communist aggression. An old man just like him had been the reason why Kim had died.

No, not an old man just like him.

It was this guy. Him! He killed Kim! Put a bullet in her head!

Abbot went reflexively for his pistol, came up with it. He took aim at the traitor seated below, the man who would pay for killing Kim!

The old man grew more erect, thrust out his chest, ready to take the bullet. He almost begged for it.

And Abbot could already smell the gunpowder, already see the man slump, already feel his heart surge with revenge.

One shot, and it would all be over. *One shot.*

Boom!

What the hell was that? he thought. *Not gunfire.*

Someone had booted open the rear door, and even as he swung his head around, automatic weapons-fire rattled below.

A grunt had penetrated the warehouse! Abbot saw him dash along the wall. He took aim, fired. Hit the wall behind the soldier. The guy kept moving, raised his weapon, fired a salvo that beat across the turret, one round caroming off Abbot's hatch.

"Neech!" he screamed. "They're inside!"

A second grunt rushed into the warehouse through the open door, dropped to his gut, fired, rounds punching the old man, who wailed against the tape covering his mouth. He rolled off the shipping container and onto the floor as Neech's words echoed:

You think those guys are your friends? Don't you re-member the first war?

Neech was standing tall in his hatch, pistol drawn. He took two shots and leveled that second guy.

Meanwhile, Abbot had lost the first guy behind a fallen shelf. Paz had already climbed up into his loader's hatch and was bringing around his 240. Abbot signaled that he thought the guy was behind the shelf, then put a finger to his lips. He pulled himself from his hatch, then climbed silently down from the turret.

"Grenade!" Paz screamed.

Had Abbot not been crouched down and shifting in front of the tank, he would have been killed. The enemy grunt had lobbed a grenade over the tank, from right to left, where it dropped just on the other side.

With a white-hot surge of adrenaline coursing through his veins, Abbot threw himself beneath the tank, sliding be-hind the big road wheels for cover—just as the explosion shook the walls, sent deadly metal fragments hurtling every-where, and would have wreaked havoc with his ears, had he not been wearing his helmet.

Just then, Paz, who must've ducked down then re-merged into his hatch, opened up with his 240, hosing down that entire side of the warehouse. Abbot rose. "Hold your fire!"

Then, coughing, his eyes tearing from all the smoke of the grenade's explosion, Abbot shifted slowly forward.

Ahead, a pair of legs peaked out from near the fallen shelf.

He drew closer, came up on the man, who lay supine and mortally wounded, blood bubbling at his lips, though he was still alive.

"Did I get the motherfucker?" Paz asked.

Abbot gritted his teeth and without a second thought put a bullet between the guy's eyes. He holstered his pistol, then turned back for his track. "Yeah, Paz. You got him."

HANSEN HAD BEEN trying to call Abbot over the platoon net, when Neech had called to report that a dismount had infiltrated their warehouse. Now Abbot was back on the net, saying that they had killed two enemy grunts and that their prisoner had been caught in the cross fire. Hansen called Van Buren to convey the news, and the captain acknowledged, adding, "Mech platoon reports ten enemy killed at the railroad tracks, with another eight near the riverbank."

The captain was still talking when artillery fire began dropping heavily behind the warehouses, perhaps only one or two hundred meters away. Hansen broke in to convey the grid coordinates.

"Roger, Red One. We are observing that indirect fire," answered the captain. "Enemy scouts must've called it in before Mech got to them. Hopefully, there's no one left to adjust. The ROKs already report heavy losses to their armor brigade, so you can bet we'll be facing some mounted forces. Hold your position. Black Six, out."

So maybe Keyman had been wrong for once. They had just faced a couple of recon squads, not "a shitload of dismounts" who had slipped by the ROK brigade.

But something deep down told him that he shouldn't be so cocky, that if he were a good platoon leader, he would get creative, utilize his environment and prepare for the worst.

So he imagined that Keyman was right. He imagined what else they could do to slow the advance of, say, multiple companies of dismounts. They had the claymores and smoke pots. What else?

He glanced around the warehouse at the hundreds and hundreds of cardboard boxes and all the shelving.

They were so obvious yet forgotten. Why hadn't he thought about them earlier?

He had been too much in a rush to set up their BP. He had been worried about the LP/OP and about making sure they had good concealment.

He had been thinking about Karen.

"Red, this is Red One. I have an idea. I want everyone to dismount. Pile up the shelving in front of all the doorways. Then I want you to move the boxes of inventory to the north wall. Everything you can. We'll build ourselves a little barrier inside, and we'll light it up on the way out, over."

Neech and Abbot acknowledged. They, of course, bought into the idea big time, since they, like many tankers, were pyromaniacs given licenses to burn.

Keyman got on the net and said, "Oh, I think that's a waste of time, LT. You were right. They only had a couple of recon squads out there. And by the time their dismounts get close enough, we'll be falling back to our secondary BPs anyway, over."

A breath-robbing explosion lifted earth and snow just thirty meters in front of the warehouse, then a trio of secondary booms sounded as Hansen peered through his binoculars and realized that the shell had detonated his three claymores. *Shit!*

"Looks like that last one took out my mines. Oh, well. Anyway, Red Two, I want you to help build the barricade. That's an order, out."

Hansen then reported to Van Buren that the enemy FA fire was getting way too close for comfort. Either someone was helping adjust fire, or the NKPA was getting awfully lucky out there.

Now it was up to the guys from Bravo Battery 1-15 FA to silence those enemy guns before they gave Hansen and the others unrecoverable headaches.

"**FUCKIN' GUY HAS** us dismounted during an artillery attack," muttered Keyman under his breath as he and Webber threw boxes of auto parts at the wall. They had been doing so for about fifteen minutes, and Webber's muscles were beginning to burn, despite the cold. He stretched, yawned, and reached around to rub the small of his back.

"This doesn't bother you?" asked Keyman.

"Come on. I think we'll be all right. And this is a good idea. We light the smoke, blow the claymores, then light up all this shit to create more smoke and cover our withdrawal. What part of this don't you get?"

"The part when we get killed 'cause a fucking shell hits a little closer and—"

The explosion sent them dropping to their guts. A half second later, the concussion passed through Webber, and in the next heartbeat, he thought the end had come.

Yes, Keyman had predicted their deaths, revealing that the man did, in fact, have a deal with the devil and would be moving into one of the less fiery suburbs of hell.

Webber, on the other hand, was headed straight for a ghetto of molten lava reserved for loan sharks and other losers.

He waited another moment. Chuckled. *I'm still alive.*

Slowly, he glanced up—just as one wall in the south corner buckled and began to collapse, allowing black smoke to pour in from outside.

"Jesus Christ," Keyman hollered. "LT, we have to mount up, man, come on!"

"All right, that's it," said Hansen. "Everybody back in the saddle!"

"See, he knows how to listen to reason," said Webber, as they scraped themselves up, then double-timed back to their tank.

"Why, Webber, are you saying I'm a reasonable guy?"

"Hell, no."

"Well, I'm still proud of you."

"Of me?"

"See this shiner on my face? I love it. Makes me look more scary."

"You don't need the shiner. That face is ugly enough."

The TC was about to say something when the next shell struck somewhere east of the warehouses. They flinched anyway.

Two seconds after the blast, debris struck the roof in a cacophony of little pings and thuds.

Webber guessed that the row of shacks where the old Korean woman had lived, along with her politically misguided friends, had been blown to kimchee and kindling, as had the rest of the block.

"Hey, you not sick anymore," said Smiley as Webber dropped into his gunner's seat. "You look like badass motherfucker ready to get on."

"That's get *it* on."

"Okay. Ready to that's get *it* on!"

"Whatever. But you're right. I'm feeling pretty good now." Webber beat a fist on his CVC helmet, remembering that his fear could rear up at any second.

If he could imagine that he was in command and not Keyman, then maybe he would the one who initiated attacks and did not succumb to them.

Yet he felt more compelled than actually ready to command. Of course he wouldn't need to imagine being a TC were Keyman out of the picture. The man had said he wouldn't live through the night, but he had.

Still, there was a weird aura about him that Webber had never noticed before. He seemed far less uptight and somehow resigned to whatever would happen.

CHAPTER TWELVE

DEAC WAS SUCKING Tabasco sauce straight from the miniature bottle that came with some of the MREs. He quickly devoured the red-hot liquid, then kept the bottle in the corner of his mouth like a stubby plastic cigar, chomping on it with crooked teeth.

The loader's oral fixation repulsed Sergeant Lee so much that he wanted to turn back from his station, smack the bottle from Deac's lips, then scream at him to behave like a professional soldier.

Soon they would be going into battle. They would be taking lives. They might sacrifice their own lives to defend the great nation of South Korea. They should be meditating about that, coming to terms with it, envisioning themselves and the mission in order to assure their victory.

But no. Deac was spending those precious moments burping, farting, scratching his crotch, and making sucking sounds with the bottle.

Even worse, Hansen had also lit Lee's fuse by dismissing him like a dog when there had been trouble outside.

At least Lee had not borne witness to the shooting of Abbot and Neech's prisoner. While he had not condoned the old man's behavior, the TCs could have found a safer place for him. Instead, they had left him to be shot by the infiltrators. Lee was not surprised. Both Neech and Abbot had most likely developed an especial hatred for all Koreans that dictated their decisions.

Americans, Lee had observed, often chose what made them feel good or justified rather than what was right, what was honorable. Their culture emphasized being self-centered and self-indulgent, yet they greatly admired altruistic individuals, probably because they were rare finds. Unsurprisingly, many in their military claimed to be brave, courageous, and often said they would die for their country—but South Korea was not their country. Were they fighting as aggressively as they should? Were they fighting for the right reasons?

Lee had once thought so. However, during the past two days he had concluded that going into combat was, for many of the Americans, a perfect way to boost their egos, and they fought hard for that reward. Saving his people was just an added benefit to make them feel good.

Even Lieutenant Hansen, arguably the most sincere man in the entire company, had succumbed to that temptation. His actions in the defile and at the low-water crossing were more about enhancing his career and gathering souvenirs to show to his friends. His motivation was not pure.

"Hey, Lee, don't your eyes hurt?" asked Deac. "You've been scanning forever."

Lee drew back from his primary sight and glanced at the loader, allowing his contempt to tighten his expression. "Yes, my eyes hurt. But that doesn't matter. The enemy is coming. Of course we need to watch for them. We are here to defend the citizens of South Korea from this invasion."

"Whoa, dude. Don't get all formal and serious on me.

It's been what, two hours since the shelling stopped over here? We're pounding the shit out of them now. By the time they make it down here, we'll be mopping up what's left. Why are you looking so paranoid?"

"Why are you looking so cocky?"

"Hey, bud, there's a fine line between being confident and cocky."

"And you know this line? Even when you load wrong ammo or jam one aft cap? You should know humility."

Lee regretted opening those old wounds, but he couldn't help himself. Back in the defile, Deac had, during two critical moments, made grave errors that had nearly cost them their lives. And that was another interesting thing about the Americans. Many of them dealt with failure as though it hardly mattered. For them, there was always a next time to improve. The consequences seemed unimportant. Most would never survive in the ROK military, where failure was the ultimate disgrace.

"Hey, man. Now you're insulting me?" Deac's eyes seemed to glow above his round, red cheeks. "What happened to Mr. Fucking Polite? Y'all have gone nasty on us."

"Deac?" Hansen called sternly. "You and Webber are rotating back outside to relieve Park and Romeo. Get your gear and dismount."

"Okay, LT." Deac glared at Lee. "That's good timing for you." He yanked the Tabasco bottle from his mouth, tossed it onto the floor.

Deac knew full well how particular Lee was about keeping the turret spotless—but he hadn't realized that the gunner would challenge him. "Pick it up."

Deac hesitated, locked gazes with Lee, then swore under his breath and fetched the bottle. "You know, we're here to bail out your fuckin' country—and ya'll should be kissing our asses."

"Whoa, whoa, whoa, Deac," cried Hansen. "I hear a remark like that again and—"

"Hey, I'm sorry, LT. That nap did nothing for me. Still grumpy as hell, I guess."

"Don't interrupt me. If I hear a remark like that again, I will have you removed from this crew, understood?"

"Yes, sir."

"Good. Now apologize."

"Uh, Lee? I'm sorry for that, man. I didn't mean it."

But Lee had already returned to his sight. He held his breath, clutched the control handle, and would not answer. Two thoughts collided: he wanted to end his life. Never breathe again. Just turn blue and die.

At the same time, he wanted to pummel Deac, make him beg for mercy, and tell him that his half-hearted apology meant nothing.

Then he would force the loader to admit that ROK solders were the most fearsome and disciplined on the planet. The ROKs would rather die than kiss the asses of the American scum who considered their tours in Korea as one-year pit stops to drink and whore and do whatever they wanted because they thought no one was watching.

Well, the ROKs were. And very closely at that.

Now, like some of his KATUSA brothers, Lee had received final confirmation that he could no longer trust his crewmates. And he sensed they felt the same. They abided him. They hated him. There was no other truth.

"Hey, man, I'm *sorry*."

Finally, Lee took a breath. "I heard you."

"All right, Deac," Hansen called, trying once more to defuse the situation. "On your way."

Once the loader had left the turret, Hansen spoke quickly, his tone a mixture of frustration and embarrassment. "Lee, he didn't mean that. He's just strung out. That's all."

"Okay," Lee replied. "I understand."

Yes, he did. *Perfectly*.

* * *

WITH HER EYES closed, Karen had been drifting in and out of sleep. At the moment, she lay back on the car seat, listening to the sound of her breathing, a sound that soothed her. She pictured a lush valley on a warm summer night, with thunderclouds gathering near the mountaintops. She and Jack lay on a warm, comfortable blanket, searching for shooting stars.

She rolled onto her side, knocking over the empty wine bottle. "Oops."

Jack laughed. "You're drunk."

"So are you."

He frowned, glanced over his shoulder. "Who's that?"

Karen pushed up on her elbows. She couldn't see anything, but a sound, one much too rhythmic, gained her attention. Suddenly, Jack vanished, the stars winked out, the mountains shrank, and night turned into day.

She jolted. Opened her eyes. Listened.

Footfalls!

They were faint but there. *Getting closer.* She turned her head slowly to the left, glimpsed out the driver's-side window, which was draped in a thick layer of snow, allowing only vague impressions to filter through.

A uniform. American? She wasn't sure.

The car door flung open.

All she needed was a second's worth of recognition, but she feared any delay.

She blinked, fired!

The man looked at her in shock, his narrow eyes growing wide as he fell back onto the snow, clutching his chest, his rifle falling from his hands.

And for a terrible heartbeat she wondered if she had shot an American or a North Korean.

But her answer came quickly. *"Hang-bok-ha-ra!"*

Even as he lay there, bleeding profusely, he was ordering her to surrender.

And he was definitely not alone. She glanced up the mountain, saw another soldier dodge between trees. Two more followed him.

A gurgling sound came from her victim. His head fell to one side, his tongue slipping from his lips. Even as his breath vanished, so did Karen's. *Oh my God.* She had killed him.

Her hands shook violently, but her mind screamed to get out of there. She grabbed his rifle, slung it over her shoulder, then practically vaulted from the car and began a haphazard trot down the road, snow rising to her ankles, then her knees, then shrinking again as she headed for the right side of the embankment.

Jesus, she had forgotten how cold it was, how the storm was raging, how the car had been such a great sanctuary.

She stole a glance back, saw one guy, then another slogging down the mountain, their weapons held across their chests for balance.

She charged harder for the trees ahead and a small hump that might have a ditch behind it.

Her cell phone beeped with a message from Jack. He usually had better timing.

Then again that single beep provided all the motivation she needed. Actually, his timing couldn't have been better.

She raced for the trees, her determination to see him blazing again. She rose up and over the hump, dropped behind it, pushed herself into the snow and lay there, listening, breathing, her runny nose ignored, as was the wind's stinging cold.

What was that? *An engine.* From where? *The south.* She rose tentatively from the ditch, hazarding a quick glance below.

Two HMMWVs rumbled up the road, soldiers manning their big guns. They would roll by her position. She needed to scream at the top of her lungs. She opened her mouth.

Gunfire cracked, striking the trees above her.

The HMMMV drivers hit the gas, and the gunners up top opened fire, sweeping the mountains, their rounds striking just a few meters in front of the ditch.

They were firing at her!

She threw herself back behind the mound, as the trees cracked and the rounds continued to thump. But she couldn't take being so close yet so far.

She leaned back, cupped trembling hands around her mouth: "STOP IT! I'M AN AMERICAN! I'M AN AMERICAN!"

A brilliant white dot appeared amid the trees, followed by a horrible whoosh as a rocket tore across the valley. Three, two, one, and it struck the lead vehicle with a powerful explosion that echoed like sick applause across the mountains.

A second rocket was already in the air and *bang!* it hit the hood of the second HMMMV. Red and orange flames swelled in a ball as the gunner hurtled through the air, more fire whipping across his shoulders as yet another explosion resounded.

It was all happening again, a nightmare repeating itself before her weary eyes, only this time there weren't any busses full of military dependants, just those poor, unsuspecting soldiers. She couldn't bear to look as more gunfire raked over the now burning vehicles. They were finishing off her rescuers, killing her hope. Then panic took over. She started running, her vision going blurry, her footing reckless, her pulse the only sound.

HANSEN AND THE rest of the platoon had sat in their BPs for nearly five hours, listening to the far-off drumming of mortar and FA fire, taking turns catching a few Zs, and trying to keep warm.

During that time, the snow had begun to taper off, if just

a little, but the winds continued to rattle the warehouse's walls. Finally, just twenty minutes prior, the long-awaited call from Captain Van Buren had come in.

The task force scouts and brigade Knight Teams had confirmed that the enemy mechanized brigade's main body was approaching and had completed their missions of early warning and initiation of delaying artillery fire plans. The scouts and Knight Teams were conducting their rearward passage of lines, and at the moment Hansen was watching their up-armored HMMWVs with CIPS panels roll down MSR 3, toward Ryback's checkpoint. The CIPS panels showed up as "cold" spots against "hot" HMMWV body/engines in the tank thermal sights, thus confirming they were friendly. Three trigger-happy platoons held their fire as the scouts reached the barrier where, one by one, they were allowed to pass by Ryback's men.

The indirect fire plan was underway, with REMBASS and GSR having already provided the heads-up on the enemy's front line trace. The mortars were, as ordered, targeting the enemy scouts, dismounts, and antitank teams. FA fires were focusing on the mounted forces, as would CAS, once they got back in the air, which might be sooner than later.

Huge pillars of smoke, perhaps ten in all, rose from points north of the train station and were collecting into a single wall of gloom. Between the smoke and the lingering snow, nothing was visible to the unaided eye, save for the dim outline of mountains on either side of the road and railroad tracks.

Abbot, who was as usual monitoring the company net, conveyed the most recent target grid coordinates from FSO Yelas, who was refining his targets and relying upon all three of the company team's platoons as field observers. TCs or gunners often jotted down the numbers on the stiff cardboard back of MRE entrée packets, which, when cut apart, made great 5×8 note cards in the field. Some TCs would then tape the cards to their map boards or to the back of their .50-cal mounts. Others like Hansen would use a clipboard that had been taped to the .50-cal mount, which also held a map, so they could operate hands free.

Hansen sent out word, reminding Neech and Keyman to update their overlays and continue scanning aggressively for targets. He then reached into his inner coat pocket for one of his alcohol pens and made his own updates. Abbot had once reminded him to keep the pens close to his body during cold weather operations, otherwise they would freeze up, and "as you know," the platoon sergeant had added with a wink, "every man needs a well-functioning pen."

After one more glance at the overlay, Hansen leaned into his sight, impatiently surveying the railroad tracks, the river, and the glowing image of the smokestack rising from the built-up valley.

"Red One, this is Black Six, over."

"Black Six, this is Red One, go ahead."

"GSR team reports movement of mounted forces pushing south along the railroad bed and along the bank of the Shin Chon River. Break.

"We'll first see what's left of their recon company. Next you should expect companies of PCs led in by tanks. You will engage these forces with indirect fire first, per our OPORD. Those that make it through will slow as they approach our obstacles, and that's where you'll report their position, have the FSO assist you with the indirect fire fight, and engage them with direct fire. Break."

The captain wasn't conveying anything new, but it was absolutely imperative that Hansen and the other platoon leaders understood—and remembered—the enemy's intent and their plan to stop him. With stress and sleep deprivation taking their toll on soldiers, it was far too easy to become confused, distracted, and forgetful on the battlefield. Van Buren's update was meant to help them stay focused and serve as a brief version of his last pep talk.

"Red, also be advised that GSR indicates at least one battalion-size force of light infantry and possibly a second force of motorized infantry crossing the frozen river in an attempt to move dismounts along the west bank to skirt around our barriers. Break.

"Red, you will engage these forces with mortar and direct fire. Use your AP rounds wisely. Do not allow yourself to be overrun. Notify me immediately if infiltration is too heavy, and we'll fall back to secondary positions. Set REDCON-1 and report when set. Let's give 'em hell. This is Black Six, out."

Hansen ordered the platoon to start their engines in unison, though he would wait until the last moment to have them move up into firing positions, with gun tubes jutting from the windows.

"Crew check. Driver?"

"Driver ready."

"Weapon safe. HEAT loaded. Loader ready."

"Gunner ready."

Keyman, Neech, and Abbot checked in and reported that they were set.

And then, as though God had cued the North Koreans, they appeared in the thermals.

"Moving PCs," cried Lee.

Hansen checked his extension and saw the three glowing silhouettes, their outlines betraying them as BRDM-2 recon vehicles equipped with antitank guided missiles along with the usual 14.5-mm and 7.62-mm machine guns. The PCs were way up the railroad bed, range approximately 2,500 meters. Though he would rather take out the vehicles himself, Hansen got on the horn to FSO Yelas, making the request for FA fires and conveying the grid coordinates and speed of the vehicles. While there wasn't much glory in simply calling for the big guns, doing so helped them conserve ammo, and Hansen had a strong premonition that they would need every main-gun and small-arms round they already had or could acquire.

At the start of the war, a fire brigade of ammo vehicles had begun passing a continuous flow of ammunition from the rearmost ammo storage depots on the peninsula, all the way forward to the breeches of the field artillery cannons. That was what FA was all about—delivering those projectiles from the warehouse to the enemy's position at a time and place of the commander's choosing.

A few moments later, the heavens woke, and the three BRDMs succumbed to the blistering FA fire, with secondary explosions swelling into the first. Hansen relayed the news to Yelas, even as Keyman spoke rapidly over the platoon net: "Red One, this is Red Two. We have dismounts moving along the west side of the riverbank, couple thousand meters . . . wait! We got more right here. Thirteen hundred meters. How the hell . . ."

"Red Two, this is Red One. What do you see, over?" Before Keyman even replied, Hansen shouted, "Lee, scan left!"

No, it wouldn't be a nice, clean, long-distance battle of tank vs. PC or tank vs. tank. The NKPA infantry forces promised to make the late afternoon as aggravating—and hair-raising—as possible.

"Red One, I see at least two companies of infantry pushing along the west mountainside, overlooking the river."

"Red Two, stand by," Hansen snapped. "Lee, what the hell is he seeing out there?"

"He's right. There are dismounts about two thousand meters out on the west side of the riverbank. Also, there are more, perhaps two companies, up in the mountain. Then there is a smaller force on the riverbank very close, about thirteen hundred meters and moving fast."

"Red One, this is Red Two," Keyman called, his tone more urgent. "They're maybe a thousand meters north of the first barrier now, over."

"Red One, this is Red Four. I've confirmed the position of those dismounts. Mortar fires are on the way, over."

"Roger that, Four."

The mortars were able to fire within two minutes or less and were close enough so that Hansen and the others could hear the booming begin—which it did in earnest. Time of flight was about thirty to forty seconds, but once they started firing, Hansen figured it would be one volley after another as soon as they could drop the rounds down the tubes.

Damn, Hansen had not expected so many dismounts so soon. He and his men needed to do everything possible to delay firing their main guns until absolutely necessary. He did not want to give up their location—not just yet.

But those damned grunts could infiltrate much sooner than anticipated, forcing the platoon to engage.

And all the enemy needed was one bright guy with a good radio. The bastard would call for 152-mm howitzer fire to be placed on the warehouses, thereby ruining Red Platoon's day.

"I've lost the nearest dismounts," said Lee.

As he finished, the mortars dropped hard and fast along the west side of the riverbank, some falling a little wide or a little short, but if you were one of those North Korean grunts trying to haul ass along that frozen bank, you had just been given pause.

"Moving PCs," said Lee. "Three coming down the east bank."

"Red One, this is Red Two. Three more PCs just east of the river, over."

"Roger that, Two. We have them."

"Red One, this is Red Four. I have those PCs. Calling in fires right now," said Abbot. Two seconds later his voice sounded over the company net as he began rattling off the coordinates to FSO Yelas.

Meanwhile, many more volleys of mortar fire hammered

the western banks. The first barrier of cars and debris spanning the river lay below a thick shroud of blowing smoke.

"Black Six, this is Renegade One," called Lieutenant Ryback over the company net. Despite it being Abbot's job to monitor that net, Hansen routinely listened in as well, though not as intently as the platoon sergeant. "At least a full company of enemy infantry have infiltrated the train station and are preparing to push on toward the next barrier."

"Roger, Renegade. I was hoping we wouldn't have to level the station. Fires will be on the way. After that you will engage with direct fire once those remaining men hit the first obstacle. Engage and report, out."

"Black Six, this is White One," called Thomas from his BP on the east side of MSR 3. "We have enemy tanks, PCs, and dismounts moving southeast of TRP 02. Looks like they'll try to bypass the obstacles on the southeast side of the train station, over."

"Roger, White One. Continue to put fires on them. When they slow at the barriers, hit them with direct fire and keep me updated regarding infiltration. Engage and report, out."

The chatter went on, even as the field artillery Abbot had called for arrived as violently as it was timely.

But then he grimaced as the blasts lifted behind the incoming vehicles.

"Red Four, this is Red One," Hansen called. "Our fires are long, over."

"I see that," answered Abbot. "Calling to adjust."

"Red One, we have dismounts at the first obstacle," said Keyman. "We got a couple squads moving through. And you know there are more on the way. They'll be here in five minutes. And I still can't find that first group, over."

"Red One, this is Red Two. Looks like one of those PCs just got stuck, over."

Hansen took a look for himself. Yes, one PC had halted

for some reason. It could be stuck, but then again . . .
Hansen began to pick out an irregular line of blips coming
in from behind the stopped vehicle. He recognized a pair
of silhouettes immediately. Tanks. T-62s to be sure.

"Hey, Lee?"

"Yes, yes, I see them. One company there. They are part
of the lead battalion."

That battalion, Hansen knew, was probably comprised
of three mechanized infantry companies each with about
ten BTR60s or VTT 323 personnel carriers. Between eleven
and thirteen dismounts rode in on each PC, and those
VTTs were armed with Saggers in addition to the usual
machine guns.

Because the area was so built up, it was impossible from
his vantage point to tell exactly how many vehicles were
approaching and how they were arrayed, although the first
company had formed a column just east of the smokestack.
The T-62s became the column's deadly tip.

The stalled PC began moving again, though the two
tanks were already slipping past it. Hansen tried to envi-
sion which avenue of approach they would choose.

If the company veered west of the obstacles behind the
train station, they would steer directly into Red Platoon's
sights—if artillery fires didn't finish them first. If they decided to utilize the railroad bed for a much swifter approach, they would run smack into the barriers. The frozen
riverbed posed the same problem.

Hansen confirmed the battalion's position with Abbot,
who then relayed the coordinates to FSO Yelas. At the
same time, Hansen called over to Keyman to see if he had
an update on the first group of dismounts near the river
barrier.

"Negative, Red One. Lost those two squads behind a
bunch of shacks down there. Don't see any more movement. They're waiting on their buddies. I don't like this."

"Well, you're not alone. Continue scanning."

* * *

WEBBER FELT ONE with the machine, his gaze never leaving his sight.

"Smiley, get up top and man your gun," said Keyman. "Cover the opening out back. Webber, bring the turret around so you can do the same with the coax."

Webber complied. Still, he had to bitch about it, if even a little. "Hey, Key, I don't like taking eyes off our sector."

"Indulge me for a minute, asshole, okay?"

"It's Sergeant Asshole. And this is a bad idea."

"You know, if I wanted your opinion, I would've asked you to bend over and issue it."

"And I would have. Trust me."

A SHADOW FLUCTUATED near the rear of the warehouse, where part of the wall had collapsed from that enemy artillery shell.

Hansen turned his head fractionally—just as a shuffling of metal sounded in the distance. His pulse bounded as he probed the gloom, repeatedly whispering, "Where are you?"

Something creaked. He cocked his head. Another creak. *Shit!*

Wait . . : there he was!

A North Korean grunt stood beside the tattered sheet metal, bringing his RPG to bear on Hansen's turret. He had a perfect shot at the engine and ammo compartment.

Hansen felt utterly helpless. He had no time to get his pistol out of its holster, no time to duck into the turret and shut the hatch, no time to order his men to swing the turret around and shred the Korean with coax fire.

He had just enough time to stand in his hatch.

And die.

But suddenly, the loader's machine gun atop Keyman's

tank woke in a menacing blaze of fire, ripping through the debris and punching the Korean back outside, into oblivion. Several muzzle flashes shone from along the collapsed wall before they, too, went silent under the 240's onslaught.

"Hold your fire!" Keyman cried.

During the engagement, Hansen had ducked partly into his hatch, but now, choked up and stunned, he rose, just a little, realizing what had happened.

Keyman had swung his turret forty-five degrees in anticipation of dismounts trying to infiltrate through the damaged rear corner. He had put the tank's coax and loader's weapon within reach. His clever thinking had saved them.

Hansen slumped against his hatch, then shrank into his seat, rocked by the chills of near death. He pursed his lips, swallowed, as Keyman called over the net:

"Red One, this is Red Two, over."

"Red Two, go ahead."

"Well, big surprise, we got dismounts outside. My loader killed one, but there could be two squads or more, with buddies coming to join the party, over."

"Roger. That guy was about to fire an RPG at me."

"Yeah, I saw that."

"Thanks for the help."

"Hey, it's all about the beer. You buy."

Hansen was too blown away to smile. "I guess I will, stand by. Red, this is Red One. I want all loaders to man their two-forties. Traverse your guns over the rear deck, just like we do during convoy ops to watch for aircraft. You know the drill. Excellent work so far, guys. This is Red One, out."

All right. He had to think, think, think. He had hoped to remain within the warehouse and engage those tanks and PCs. It would have been audacious, cunning, just beautiful.

Time for a new plan. His more idealistic self wanted to believe all would be well. His cynical side reminded him that everything would go to shit and that being flexible and

thinking quickly—as Keyman had—was the way to stay
alive. All bets were off. If he ignored the infantry guys,
they could run cover for antitank teams, who would unload
their Sagger missiles and prepare to shoot them into the
warehouse. He needed some feedback. It was time to call
higher and share the news.

"Black Six, this is Red One, over."

"Red One, this is Black Six, go ahead."

"We have at least two squads of dismounts in our sector.
They have already infiltrated our BP. Request Mech displace one squad to assist, over."

"Red One, stand by."

Van Buren spoke rapidly with Lieutenant Ryback,
whose tone said he was having one hell of a time holding
off the dismounts who had advanced from the train station
to begin pushing toward the barriers. He wasn't happy
about losing a squad to Hansen, but he would send them.

Breathing a weak sigh of relief, Hansen informed the
rest of the platoon: "Red, this is Red One. Black Six is giving us a Bradley to swat those dismounts. The bastards
have probably called for fires on our location. Red Three?
Red Four? Do not fire on that Bradley as it enters our sector. It'll be coming in from the east, across the railroad bed.
Break.

"Red, we will remain in position, ready to move up and
engage tanks and PCs. If that arty does come in and it gets
too heavy, then we'll light smoke pots, blow claymores,
and fall back to secondary positions. Guys? Good luck and
God Bless. This Red One, out."

CHAPTER
THIRTEEN

NEECH WAS WORKING a kink out of his neck when Romeo called down from the loader's hatch. "So we're staying here with those motherfuckers still outside? That Bradley won't be here for what? Five, ten minutes? Maybe more? What if the Koreans get up on the roof?"

"Man, why are you so afraid to die?" Neech returned his gaze to his extension, smirking over the kid's rant.

"If I die because I obeyed a stupid order, that would really suck, you know?"

"Maybe all orders are stupid now. Maybe this whole fucking thing is a joke, and we're out here pretending it means something, when it doesn't mean jack. Batman didn't die to save me. He died for nothing. It's all a waste of time."

"Oh, dude, don't even go there."

Neech lightened his tone. "Just kidding."

"No, you weren't. Come on. We have to keep our heads straight, right? Okay, so this sucks, but we'll get payback, right?"

"Don't you get it, Romeo? That'll never happen. There is no payback. There's just this, just us, sitting here, realizing what a terrible mistake we've made with our lives."

"Oh my god. You can't be serious."

"I need another smoke."

Neech was about to open his hatch. He didn't give a fuck about scanning the sector anymore. A cigarette sounded really good.

"Grenade!" screamed Romeo as he dropped into the tank, slamming the hatch after himself.

An explosion rocked the track—then came another, less powerful burst that still earned their attention.

"I saw 'em throw the first one!" screamed Romeo.

"Jesus, calm down," Neech hollered. He slowly rose in his hatch, smelled the smoke, and realized what had happened.

The bastards outside had tossed in a couple of grenades through the open window, just to harass them.

Maybe Neech hated the Army, hated war, hated everything now. But those North Korean scumbags who were denying him his smoke would pay dearly.

He grabbed the KSG shotgun, opened his hatch, and burst up, firing two rounds out past the open window. "Fuck you, assholes! You're going to eat our shit and die. Do you hear me?"

Swearing again, he tucked the shotgun under his arm, pulled out a cigarette from his breast pocket, then lit it with the Zippo he had borrowed from Romeo. He took a long drag, then glanced across the warehouse at Abbot, who had brandished his own rifle and was shifting his gaze between the window ahead and the back doors.

"Red Three, this is Red Four. Was that a couple of grenades?" asked the platoon sergeant.

"Yeah, it was. Assholes."

"Three, are you . . . all right?"

Neech liked Abbot. He didn't want to challenge the man's authority. They were in the same boat so to speak, trying to fight and grieve and somehow remain sane. He knew Abbot was really referring to him having a smoke—especially in the turret. Still, he needed the nicotine. "Four, I'm okay. And I'll take care of this."

Romeo rose into the loader's hatch and resumed the controls of his 240. "Let's just roll outside and whack these guys. We can't wait for Renegade. Enough is enough."

A rush of air much louder than the wind came from beyond the window, then an explosion boomed, sending a quake through the tank and rattling the entire warehouse.

"Red, this is Red One. Those enemy fires are coming in. Get in your open protected positions and stand by!"

Neech rolled his eyes, took another drag on his cigarette, then leaned back, wondering how long he could push his luck. Long enough to finish his cigarette? He hoped so.

THE MUFFLED RUMBLING of enemy artillery fire continued from points somewhere south of Casey Creek and Phase Line Blue, reminding Abbot that they weren't the only ones in the line of fire. The enemy had every intention of softening up Camp Casey, along with the rest of TDC.

But Team Cobra was responding in kind, and Abbot kept a steady gaze through his extension so he could report the effects of their own fires on that first battalion.

The lead tanks were already junkyard worthy, lying in heaps about thirty meters west of the train station, with small fires still rising from their hulls. Neither had taken a direct hit, but both had been close enough to exploding shells—and when it came to artillery fire, being close was being dead.

About half of the PCs had been taken out, but the other five or six drove on, weaving through lanes of devastation, their crews neither frightened nor demoralized, Abbot knew. They might even be jealous of their comrades who had already died as heroes for the Dear Leader in Pyong-yang. And those fanatic-filled PCs were followed by yet another company.

TOW and Javelin fire flashed across the sector just east of the train station, as the MECH platoon got into the fight, picking off yet another company barreling down MSR 3. Even an old grease monkey tanker like himself felt awed in the presence of all that firepower.

However, he wasn't there to watch the show. He got on the net and spoke tersely with FSO Yelas, not exactly requesting but demanding more FA fires on the mounted forces pushing into their sector. However, the Paladins were putting fires on both the enemy forces in White's sector as well as beginning to demolish the train station in front of Ryback's BP. They would get on Abbot's tanks and PCs as soon as they could. In the meantime, mortars would keep coming to disrupt dismounted movement around those vehicles.

The effects of all that fire were clearly evident in the sky, which had grown eerily dark. Of course, the storm had picked up again, along with the wind, making it feel as though you could exhale, catch your frozen breath, then throw it like a chunk of ice at the enemy. If it could, even his watch would rub its hands together.

Through the thermals, Abbot watched one wall of the train station collapse under two huge blasts that also consumed a car that had been abandoned nearby. Two of Ryback's Bradleys rumbled east about a dozen meters to better attack the fleeing dismounts, while the one he had displaced to Red had just headed into the alley behind the warehouses, getting ready to bushwhack those godless grunts out back.

Abbot's neck tingled for a second, then a shell struck so close that he swore the warehouse outside must have exploded around them. A glimpse through the opening between his hatch and cupola proved otherwise, though the wide metal door to the rear had collapsed inward, and the buildings and shacks across the street were fully engulfed in flames. A dark form appeared against those bright orange curtains, rolling by as though unfazed by the destruction. It was Ryback's Bradley, safe and sound, the vehicle's driver having either God-inspired navigation skills or the luck of the Irish.

Ahead, the second pair of tanks, along with the remaining BTRs and VTTs of the first company and the full complement of personnel carriers for the second company, suddenly opted for the railroad bed approach, rolling in at full throttle toward the pair of barriers behind the train station.

"Red One, this is Red Four. Second company moving in along the railroad bed, over."

"Roger. Keep directing fires on them. We'll wait to engage until they hit the first obstacle," Hansen answered.

Another artillery shell struck, and as the thunder shook through the tank, a metallic scraping and thudding came from above, as though someone were trying to get inside the tank.

"Is that us?" Paz asked, heading up for a peek through his vision blocks.

"I don't know."

Abbot craned his neck, glimpsed through the gap in his hatch. A huge piece of the metal ceiling had been torn away and had fallen across the tank's deck. "It's just debris."

"Sarge, you think we could get trapped in here?"

"Trapped? Nah. Hit by artillery? Probably. Red One, this is Red Four, we are taking heavy fire here, over."

"Roger, all right, Red. We're not waiting anymore. Move into firing positions and report when set."

"Driver, move us up!" Abbot ordered, then opened his hatch and stood tall to guide Sparrow into position. The tank jerked as they rolled closer to the wall and the gun tube began to push through the warehouse's broken window. Another meter. One more. "Okay, stop!"

Abbot lowered into the turret, returned his hatch to the open protected position. He could see himself giving the order to fire. He could hear it. Taste the words. Feel his fingers digging into his palms.

He wanted to lash out at them for taking his Kim. Just like Neech, he wanted to know revenge in the most intimate way possible. The feeling scared him. He sensed how easy it was to forget who he was, forget the mission, forget everything. His sole purpose in life would be to draw blood, and he would use the platoon as means to that end.

No. He wouldn't go there. He was better than that. He would tap into all that cold outside, let it freeze his heart and turn him into just another component of the tank, a mechanism of death running on a cool, steady stream of adrenaline, his anger, like everything else, in check. And better yet, he would provide a positive role model for Neech, allowing the younger man to see that you could still fight without letting a personal loss cloud your judgment.

Abbot took a long, frigid breath, savored the ice, then turned practiced eyes on his extension.

DESTRUCTION ON A rural battlefield was one thing, but to watch the outskirts of a city succumb to all that artillery and mortar fire—especially when Hansen knew civilians were still inside many of those buildings—was just hard to watch. If you didn't know better, you'd believe that a thousand pyromaniacs armed with gasoline canisters and matches had been bussed into TDC and let loose on the city.

Fires raged from the crumbling train station, from the smaller buildings near the radio tower, and from those below the water tower far off to the east. Even if a structure didn't take a direct hit, red-hot artillery and mortar fragments, along with other battlefield incendiaries, could easily penetrate thin walls to ignite both the walls and whatever was inside.

Some of the barriers had been set ablaze as well, as had most of the repair shops adjacent to Ryback's position on MSR 3. What wasn't burning would be soon, and the falling snow did little to extinguish the flames. All those hot spots glowed brilliantly in the thermal sight, making it harder to distinguish crouching dismounts from burning rubble. However, those infantrymen would, in fact, stand out better to the naked eye, making it harder for them to sneak up on Red's position.

Fires and fear notwithstanding, the platoon had a job to do, and while Hansen worried about Neech, Abbot, and the rest, he had to believe they would be there for him and for each other, as they had been in the past. He had to believe that all they had been through during the past few days— all they had lost—would not interfere.

That was a scary thought.

Once all the tanks had reported in and were set in their firing positions, he gave the order: "Red, this is Red One. Tanks, PCs. Frontal. Alpha section, fire sabot. Bravo section, HEAT. Tophat, tophat! Fire!"

Lee had already targeted and identified the T-62 rolling straight toward them at a range of 1,450 meters. The second the main gun boomed and rocked the tank, Hansen widened his eyes, waiting in breathless anticipation for the enemy track's turret to blow sky-high above a rush of flames.

He got his wish. Direct hit, center of mass. The tank blew apart, as did the one Keyman had fired upon. "Target!"

"Yee-haw!" bellowed Deac.

"Loader, battlecarry HEAT." Hansen felt the old magic again. He took a deep breath, smelled the cordite, and grinned. He was that kid again, inside the turret for the very first time, enveloped by raw, jet-fueled power and feeling like Superman.

"Red One, this is Red Two. Renegade is engaging troops with chain-gun fire. He's driving most of them back toward the river, over."

"Roger. Continue to engage, out."

"Three moving PCs," said Lee.

Hansen checked his extension. "Near one first."

Deac armed the main gun and slid clear of the path of recoil. "Up!"

"Fire!"

"On the way!"

As the PCs ate HEAT and burped fire, Gatch, who had been notably silent for a while, yelled in a lame Korean accent, "Oh, he no like die. He no like at all!"

"GATCH, YOU SHUT UP! YOU SHUT UP!"

Hansen and Deac were stunned into silence. They had never heard Sergeant Lee raise his voice. Ever. "Gatch, you do as he says. Lee, next target. Let's go!"

The gunner turned his burning eyes back to his sight.

Keyman had taken out another of the PCs, while the third turned left—right into artillery fire.

Lee hunted one more for another target.

Meanwhile, two more BTRs neared the first obstacle, their gunners putting 12.7-mm machine-gun fire on suspected dismounted positions dead ahead, though their suspicions, like their fire, were misplaced since Ryback's men were well to their east.

One BTR suddenly lurched into the air as it hit a mine, but Lee had the second one. "Moving PC—identified!"

"Up!"

"Fire!"

"On the way!"

The BTR was about to plow between two cars and a

wall of burning tires when the HEAT round blew it—and that entire section of the barrier—into a huge, flickering bonfire that cascaded over the ground.

"Target!" Hansen cried, then he shot a quick look to Deac, squelching the loader's smile and probable desire to make a comment that might incite Lee.

Unfortunately, Gatch was still the live wire up front. "They spread their cheeks for that one, didn't they . . ."

"Gatch, save it."

"It ain't fair, LT," said Deac. "We can't be glad these fuckers are dying cause Lee's got a conscience now? That's bullshit."

"No, it's bullshit if you don't shut up and do your job. Got it!"

Deac's lips tightened. "Yes, sir."

Lee had not looked up from his sight. Hansen was about to ask how we was doing, but then thought better of it.

"Red One, this is Red Two," Keyman called, his voice even at first, but then his tone suddenly shifted. "Whoa, this is fucked up now! Hang on. Shit! Renegade is getting overrun. He's got troops on his Bradley. They must've been hiding behind the rubble back there. And the rest of the company is moving through, probably with AT teams. Request permission to move up outside and assist them, over."

Well, there it was. Time to rock 'n' roll without cover and with guns blazing. According to the OPORD, they would blow claymores and light off smoke pots just before they fell back to secondary BPs. But the rest of the company team was not ready to fall back yet. It was time to get a little more creative. "Red, this is Red One. Stand by to blow our claymores so we can take out the rest of that company. After that, we'll move outside. Alpha will engage the troops and assist the Mech squad. Bravo will continue to engage the PCs at the barriers. Prepare to detonate claymores and report when set, out."

Hansen then called Captain Van Buren and issued a quick SITREP of his intent to reposition the platoon. As expected, Van Buren concurred and approved the move. Now the CO was informed, the other platoons knew what kind of movement they would see in Red's sector, and everyone was kept up to date on their situational awareness. Moreover, that squad from Renegade knew help was on the way.

After a few seconds, Keyman, Neech, and Abbot reported that they were good to go. Hansen wished he could detonate his own mines, but the damned North Korean artillerymen had dropped that lucky shell on his party favors.

"All right, Red, blow claymores on my command." Hansen took a deep breath, waited until the troops, shifting like a fluctuating snakes along the riverbank and down the railroad bed, got a little bit closer. "NOW!"

The pound and a half layer of composition C-4 explosive within each of the nine claymores detonated, sending harsh and chaotic bangs echoing off the buildings.

A nanosecond later, the seven hundred steel spheres within each mine were blown outward in fan-shaped patterns that swept over the North Koreans charging south. Though Hansen couldn't hear them scream from inside the warehouse, he saw those troops closest to the mines get blasted apart, their arms, legs, and heads tumbling. Though the thermals spared him some of the gore, his imagination filled in the blanks. For a few seconds, he sat there, transfixed. The human body could tear apart in so many different ways that no matter how many deaths he viewed, he might never see them all.

He blinked, realizing with a start that he was supposed to give the next order. "Red, this is Red One. Move out!"

"Hang on to your panties!" Gatch hollered, throttling up and blasting through the warehouse wall, metal peeling back in great folds as a sixty-eight-ton fire-breathing dragon was suddenly set free.

Hansen opened his hatch and stood, never feeling more pumped.

Then his cell phone beeped. A message from Karen. *All right! Thank God, she is still alive!* Should he steal a second to read the message? Not now. . . . After allowing himself a brief sigh, he barked, "Driver, turn left!"

Thick clouds of smoke whipped over the turret as Hansen coughed and lifted the NVGs hanging around his neck. He peered through the goggles, looking past the warehouses as Keyman's tank turned, the turret traversing, the coax flashing and rattling as a gale whipped in more smoke and falling snow. He switched between his NVGs and his naked eye, gaining better peripheral vision with the latter, though the smoke did burn his eyes.

Meanwhile, Abbot and Neech divvied up their targets via the platoon net. Knowing they were about to fire their main guns, Hansen dropped back into the turret, sealed his hatch to open protected, and began scanning for troops as they roared toward the riverbank.

As predicted, main guns boomed from near the second warehouse behind them, and a few seconds later, Abbot reported that two more PCs had been destroyed and that he was continuing to coordinate more fires with FSO Yelas.

Hansen was about to tell the platoon sergeant "good work" when a flurry of enemy artillery fire dropped into the river, blasting through the first obstacle, devouring several hedgehogs, then striking the next barrier.

"Holy shit! That's some heavy fire!" cried Gatch.

"Yeah, don't make a wrong turn, okay?" Deac asked.

"Hey, man, that's the hand of Jesus out there. My driving can't do nothing about it."

Hansen voiced a question of his own: "Uh, can you guys fight the battle instead of bullshitting about it?"

Deac and Gatch kept quiet.

They neared the corner of the warehouse and turned to find Keyman's tank engaging dismounts holed up behind some lean-tos and inside two shacks along the riverbank. Webber was tearing the shit out of the place with his coax, while Keyman delivered sporadic fire toward points farther north up the river.

"Red Two, this is Red One. Coming up right behind you, over."

"Roger. The Bradley's clear now and bugging out. Suggest we do the same and get back in the real fight, over."

Before Hansen could respond, small-arms fire jackhammered all over the left side of the turret. He peered beyond his hatch. The fire originated from along the hills adjacent to the railroad tracks.

"Troops to the left," said Lee.

"Coax troops!" Hansen ordered.

"Do it, Lee! Cut 'em down!" added Deac.

As Lee opened fire, Hansen shouted, "I don't need you repeating my orders!"

Deac flinched and nodded. "Sorry, sir!"

Lee's fire raked along the hills, though it was hard to tell if he was hitting any of those grunts. They had, of course, ceased fire, and those not dead were assumedly on the move again.

Two massive explosions more powerful than anything Hansen had experienced thus far shook through the tank. And while his CVC helmet and the M1's armor dulled most of the sound, the concussions themselves were absolutely amazing.

"They dropping nukes or what?" he muttered, then craned his head in the direction of the warehouses. The small gap between his hatch and cupola severely limited his field of view, but even so, he saw enough.

Both warehouses were gone, replaced by flames and choking black smoke. The NKPA artillery had no doubt conducted a time on target mission. All rounds from a single unit had fired to impact on the warehouses at the same time, thus achieving a massive effect.

"LT, you seeing that?" asked Deac, looking through his own blocks. "We got out of there just in time!"

Abbot hollered over the platoon net as he called to Neech: "Red Three, this is Red Four. I got the tanks! You take the PCs, over."

"Roger. Man, they're rolling in fast. Got two already pushing through the first obstacle. I thought the engineers mined the shit out of those barriers . . ."

The net fell silent as main guns thundered, and, in the distance, a sabot and a HEAT round found their marks.

"Lieutenant, we have trucks moving south down the river," said Lee. "Motorized infantry. They're stopping near the east bank. Troops dismounting."

Hansen counted over a dozen vehicles with North Korean soldiers streaming out of them and heading out, across the broken ice, fighting their way through the heavy winds and swirling snow. "Red Two, this is Red One. Battlecarry AP rounds and stand by to fire on my command, over."

"Roger, One. Battlecarry AP and stand by."

After stealing a few seconds to eavesdrop on the company net, Hansen learned that the enemy brigade was hitting them hard and fast, exploiting their infantry in a classic attempt to overwhelm the defenders. Both White and MECH platoons were reporting heavy infiltration.

So it was no surprise when, a few seconds later, Captain Van Buren sent out word: "This is Black Six to all Cobra elements. Fall back to secondary BPs. I say again. Fall back to secondary BPs. FIST and all the other teams will move first, followed by MECH, Red, and White. Blow your claymores, light your smoke pots, and move out!"

"Red Two, this is Red One. We've been ordered to fall back to secondary BPs. But let's get off these AP rounds first, over."

"Roger that. Target identified."

"All right. Fire!"

The AP rounds ripped from the tanks' turrets, arced in the air, and, once they reached their set ranges, detonated over the troops, releasing their flechette projectiles into the snowstorm.

"Aw, look at that," said Deac, just after he had reloaded the main gun with a HEAT round. "Fuckin' massive slaughter. Unbelievable!"

Lee turned away from his controls and looked daggers at Deac, who just shrugged and asked, "Y'all mad again?"

"Deac, not now, man! Not now!" Hansen snapped. "Red, this is Red One. It's time to light smoke and get ready to fall back to secondary BPs, over."

"Red One, this is Red Four. Just give us a minute to take out a couple more and we'll join you, over."

"Roger, Four. Don't take too much time, out." Hansen regarded Deac. "Get the pots and meet me up top."

The smoke pots resembled gallon-size paint cans, and once lit by the attached match or electrical squibs, they produced large, billowing clouds of hexachlorexane zinc smoke that obscured vision to the naked eye and, in very heavy concentrations, could even blind thermals. In years prior tank and Bradley crews had been able to inject diesel fuel into their exhaust systems by employing the Vehicle Exhaust Smoke System, thus producing their own screens. But when the switch had been made to JP-8 jet fuel, the practice had ceased since that fuel would set the vehicle on fire. Sure, you still got smoke, but you got it the hard way.

Deac passed one smoke pot to Hansen, while he took the other. They removed the matches, lit the canisters, then tossed them upwind, accounting for how the smoke might blow to best cover the sector. If Hansen had the time, he would have considered how to conceal the hot spot produced by each pot. They could have even stacked several pots on top of each other so as one ran out, it would light the next.

But when enemy dismounts were still firing, you lit 'em, chucked 'em, and got going. Getting killed while trying to establish the perfect smoke screen would earn you immediate, posthumous indoctrination into the Knucklehead Hall of Fame.

Keyman and Webber had just lit off their own pots, and the wind churned the smoke into a broad wall that closed the curtain on act one of the battle. The screen could even restrict nap-of-the-earth and contour approaches for aircraft, but the storm was already taking care of that. In fact its winds, snow, and temperature inversion were allowing the smoke to produce better obscuration results than normal.

Van Buren's voice abruptly crackled over the company net. "Red One, this is Black Six, over."

"Go ahead, Black Six."

"MECH is falling back to secondary BP. You're up next, over."

"Roger. We've blown our claymores, lit smoke, and will fall back to secondary BPs now, over."

"Good work. After you and White have moved through the passage lanes of the secondary belts and I've received confirmation from White's last track, I'll be sealing the lanes with MOPMS. Get in position, then engage and report, out."

With his engine revving, Keyman's tank did an about-face and rolled off, trailing rooster tails of snow as it dug a path around the west side of the destroyed warehouses. Hansen ordered Gatch to drop in behind the tank. They would keep their turrets reversed so they could continue to engage the enemy as they moved toward their next BP. The loaders would man their machine guns and face "forward," while Hansen and the other TCs would turn sideways or all the way around to help guide the tanks. If things quieted down enough, Deac and the other loaders could begin transferring ammo to the ready racks.

However, the small-arms, mortar, and FA fires suddenly increased into a near steady thrumming as the enemy sensed what was happening and attempted to unload their guns before losing their targets.

Abbot's track appeared like a ghost tank behind them, outlined in white and slicing through the snowstorm, with Neech bringing up the rear.

All four tracks turned left down the alley behind where the warehouses, repair shops, and small shacks had stood. The enemy mortar and FA fires had turned the block into a great maw of jagged, black teeth, burning out of control as a few civilians darted here and there within the rubble, searching for precious mementos, for loved ones, for whatever . . .

"This is it. We found it," said Gatch. "The highway to hell."

No one commented, not even Deac.

They reached the end of the alley and turned right, heading down a narrow road toward a row of shacks on their right that had, quite remarkably, remained intact, while the buildings across the street and around them had crumbled and were still burning. Hansen was reminded of how tornadoes often did the same thing, leveling one house while the neighbor's was left unscathed. Acts like that inspired some to believe in God or the devil, depending upon which house you owned. It was definitely strange, though, how just one block had survived, as though its residents were in cahoots with the North Korean artillerymen.

As Keyman's tank neared the first shack, people emerged into the street from doorways and hiding places between the buildings, dozens of them armed with rocks, pipes, baseball bats, whatever they could hurl at the passing tanks. Many were teenagers or young adults, probably college students looking to vent some frustration. They didn't care if the invaders were Americans or North Koreans; they believed—and perhaps rightly so—that either side would destroy their property and take their lives if they got in the way of the battle.

Keyman raised his hands as the incoming pelted him and his ride. "Yeah, we love you, too!"

Hansen, who had been standing in his hatch, ducked down as something hard connected with the side of his CVC helmet, wrenching back his neck.

"Red One, this is Red Two," Keyman called tersely. "We're under attack. Permission to return fire, over."

"Red Two, don't even joke like that, over."

"Wish I were. You just know they're covering for some asshole with an RPG."

"What's he worried about?" cried Deac. "There aren't any dangerous old ladies out there!"

"Red Two, just speed up and get out of here," Hansen ordered.

"Roger. Let's hope one of 'em doesn't pull a Tiananmen Square on us."

Staving off the image of a civilian positioning himself in front of Keyman's tank to block their passage, Hansen stood a little taller in his hatch. He threw a last look back, then gazed ahead . . . and gasped.

Crouched on the roof of the last surviving shack in the row were two men in their early twenties, both wearing only sweatshirts and jeans, their heads covered in snow. Each held a flaming Molotov cocktail in his fist.

As Keyman's tank neared them, they wound up . . . and let their bombs fly.

CHAPTER
FOURTEEN

THE VOICES RESOUNDED all at once and sent lightning down Webber's spine.

Smiley, who had been standing in his hatch and manning his 240 until the civilians had attacked, was rattling off Korean at the top of his lungs. Keyman was hollering "Motherfuckers!" but extending the word into a battle cry that grew louder as he reached to slam shut his hatch.

Something thumped the turret, and a second later, Webber smelled gasoline or kerosene fumes, along with something burning.

"Fucking Molotovs!" boomed Keyman. "Driver, stop! Smiley, grab the extinguisher and get up top! Webber, traverse right and coax that last shack!"

"What?"

"Coax that last shack!"

The shack? Keyman wanted him to fire at civilians? *But this was self-defense, right?* As he brought the turret around,

Smiley fetched the fire extinguisher and rushed into his hatch. "Fire not too bad! Not too bad!"

"No, it's not," said Keyman, already up top with his shotgun in hand. "They must've overfilled one of the bottles and it didn't ignite. And they missed the engine with the other one. Missed the ammo, too. Fuckin' amateurs."

Webber scanned the last shack and couldn't find anyone nearby or on the roof.

"Fire, Webber! Coax that fuckin' shack!"

"No way. I think we should wait. Call the lieutenant. See what he wants to do."

"No way? You don't have a choice! Jesus Christ, what do I got here? I got a gunner who won't shoot. I got civilians attacking me. Shit! Nobody fucks with my tank! NOBODY!"

It was easy to imagine the rage flushing Keyman's cheeks. With a grunt, he ripped out his intercom cord and yanked himself out of the hatch, even as Smiley's extinguisher hissed and whooshed.

"Where are you going?" Webber shouted, leaving his seat and heading up into the TC's station. He ascended into the hatch, craned his neck.

Keyman was running straight for the shack, shotgun at the ready, as the lieutenant's tank pulled to a halt about ten meters back, the LT shouting Keyman's name.

Webber added his voice. "Key, it's not worth it, man! It's not worth it!"

Dodging left like a wide receiver, Keyman disappeared behind a buckling wooden wall.

Meanwhile, Neech and Abbot were coming up behind, taking the full brunt of the civilian assault. Some of the residents were throwing burning pieces of timber, perhaps taken from their own homes in an effort to say, "Look what you've done!"

"Sergeant crazy," Smiley said, putting out the last of the flames. "He crazy."

* * *

HANSEN HAD SEEN Keyman dismount, and though he had called out twice, he went for a third time, straining against the tanks' engines and the screaming crowd behind them.

Presumably, the staff sergeant was still in the alley between shacks, either ignoring Hansen or unable to hear him. That Keyman had succumbed to his temper was no surprise; that he was putting the entire platoon at risk so he could play Rambo enraged Hansen. *Fucking idiot!*

"Red Two Golf, this is Red One," Hansen called to Webber. "Get that track rolling right now!"

Webber, who was still standing in the TC's hatch, raised a thumbs-up, though he never looked more torn.

Hansen needed to get the platoon away from the shacks and the crowd. Ironically, their passage lane through the second obstacle belt ran on the west side of the next barrier, just five minutes away. They had been so close . . . yet so far. "Red Four, this is Red One, over."

"Go ahead, One."

"Red Two has dismounted and gone after the bad guys. We're pulling ahead without him, over."

"Roger. Let me dismount. Pull up fifty meters. I'll bring him back, over."

Hansen beat a fist on the turret. "Negative. We're rolling now, out."

NEECH SNORTED. "YOU hear that shit, Romeo? We're leaving without our best guy."

"Well, he's an ass. You don't leave the tank. Death before dismount, right?"

"So he leaves the tank—so we should leave him? What happened to the Warrior Ethos? Guess the LT forgot all about that . . ."

"The LT'll go back for him. We just have to get out of here now."

"Choi, keep us idling. Do *not* move!"

Romeo grabbed Neech's arm. "Excuse me?"

Neech yanked away and popped his hatch to face the crowd. "I'm bringing him back."

"No, you're not." Romeo's voice grew shaky. "I know what you're doing, man. This is just making it easier for you."

"Nothing's easy."

"Where are you gonna go? Where?"

The little Puerto Rican had seen right through him, but Neech didn't care. Maybe he really would bring back Keyman. Maybe the crowd would get to him first. Or maybe he would just keep on walking until the North Koreans found him.

Neech had often heard that tanks were "cages of courage." You were trapped inside the vehicle, unable to keep your head down like an infantryman. And whether you were scared or not, there was always someone inside, usually the TC, with the will to fight. He forced you to go on.

But Neech's will was gone. And the cage door was open. He drew his pistol and climbed onto the turret while Romeo popped his own hatch, ducking as a piece of wood nearly struck his head.

"If you don't come back, then you were right. Batman died for nothing."

Neech didn't want to hear it. He crossed to the back deck, then hopped onto the ground. He raised his pistol and broke into a jog toward the nearest alley. Two old men moved from a doorway and shouted angrily at him, one waving a bat. Neech looked away as something struck him in the back. He winced but didn't miss a step.

"WEBBER, WHY YOU wait?" asked Smiley, back behind his 240. "LT say go!"

"Red Two, what's the delay?" Hansen called again.

"Morbid, just another minute," Webber told the driver. "Just another minute, and he'll come back."

"C'mon, Webber. Fuck Keyman. Fuck him good. Let's leave him like the LT says!"

Abandoning Keyman, leaving him perhaps to die, felt at once good . . . and bad. The guilt had already set in—yet at the same time Webber's fear was lifting. He was in charge of the tank, standing in the TC's hatch, being addressed as "Red Two."

And loving it.

"Red Two, I said move out!" cried Hansen.

Webber faced the lieutenant's tank, saw Hansen in his hatch, waving emphatically.

They weren't really abandoning Keyman. Just moving up. Webber needed to believe that. *Sorry, Key. I gotta go.*

"All right, Morbid let's—"

The shouts seized Webber's attention before he could finish the order.

A turn of the head left him in shock.

Four men had sprang from behind the rubble on the opposite side of the street. Two Molotovs were already in the air, launched from bicycle inner tubes and plummeting down, straight for him and Smiley.

Webber started to duck. "Smiley, get down!"

The first cocktail exploded over the turret. Flaming gel rushed up and over him, sticking to his uniform, his hands, his face, while Smiley shrieked in agony as the second bomb burst over him, flames hissing and spitting.

I'm not supposed to die, Webber thought as he frantically swatted his burning face, his nostrils clogged with a sickly sweet odor. *I'm not supposed to die! Keyman is. He said it, goddamn it! He said it!*

Oh, man, it hurts! It hurts so bad!

"We're on fire!" Morbid wailed from his driver's station. "It's coming through my hatch seals!"

The tank's halon fire suppression system kicked in with a roar, but it was too late to help.

Webber couldn't see, couldn't feel, couldn't breathe anymore. At least he was dying in the turret, where he belonged.

THE MOLOTOVS WERE already exploding over Keyman's tank by the time Hansen swung around, drew his pistol, and took aim at the last Korean, who was just winding up to pitch his burning bottle.

Hansen fired three shots. The first struck the guy in the chest; the second hit the bottle, causing it to explode and turn the bastard into a human torch; the third struck the guy in the hip, knocking him to the snow, where he lay writhing spasmodically, still engulfed in flames.

Deac got up on his machine gun and with a howl cut loose an unrelenting bead that punched down the other three Koreans as they tried to escape toward the burning shacks. He kept raking the area, expecting to find more bad guys lurking behind piles of broken cinder blocks.

Hansen snapped his gaze right, left, then to the rear as Abbot's tank neared them. The platoon sergeant had a fire extinguisher in hand and was climbing down from his turret while Paz covered him with his 240.

"Hold your fire!" Hansen ordered Deac.

"Come on, Lieutenant! Let me kill the rest of these fuckers! Look at the thanks we get! Webber? Smiley? Talk to us, guys! Talk to us!"

"LOADER, HOLD YOUR FIRE!"

"Yes, sir!" Deac was literally foaming at the mouth.

"Get the fire extinguisher and the fucking lifesaver bag and get over there," Hansen ordered him. "That ammo could start cooking off. Gatch, get us up closer to cover. Lee, man Deac's gun when he's out. Move! Move! Move!" Hansen waved back to Abbot and Neech, gesturing that they skirt around Keyman's track and pull forward. Paz shouted to Sparrow to move up, while Neech's tank hesitated, with only Romeo standing in his hatch.

Beginning to hyperventilate, Hansen got on the company net as the tank rolled closer then turned slightly to better shield Keyman's track. "Black Six, this is Red One, over."

"Go ahead, Red One."

"Black Six, we've been engaged by civilians throwing Molotovs. Red Two has been hit! We have two, maybe three wounded! I need a MEDEVAC here now!"

"Calm down, Red One. Now what happened out there, son?"

Hansen backhanded tears from his eyes. "I say again. We were falling back to our secondary BP when we were engaged by civilians throwing Molotovs. Red Two was hit. Engine's out. Looks like a mobility kill. I have at least two wounded that I can see. I'm sending out a combat lifesaver, but I need that MEDEVAC, over."

"Red One, at this time I need you to confirm whether you have wounded or killed, over."

"Roger, Black Six. Will confirm and report back, out."

Hansen should have better assessed the situation before calling the CO, but he could barely think straight. Still, at least he'd received some feedback. He trembled violently as he climbed down from the turret to join Abbot, who raced up to Keyman's tank and began putting out the flames on the rear deck, while Deac was working on the front slope.

As Hansen neared the track, he got his first whiff of charred flesh—flesh that had once belonged to his men. Smiley and Webber were slumped in their hatches, their faces burned beyond recognition, their Nomex melted into their bodies. Webber's arms were outstretched, as though he were crucified against the armor. Smoke from the fires and halon poured from the open hatches.

"Let me get up there," Abbot cried, then he crawled onto the front slope and slid open the driver's hatch, releasing another cloud of dark smoke. The platoon sergeant covered his mouth and nose. He glanced up at Hansen, shook his head.

First Batman . . . and now this. Webber, Smiley, Morbid, all young men with their whole lives ahead of them, just like Hansen.

He choked up, whirled to face the shacks. "Sergeant? I want to level this fuckin' block! Level this whole fuckin' block right now!"

Abbot jumped down from the tank and seized Hansen by the shoulders. "Call the CO. Tell him we need the M88."

"Dude, they killed your wife."

"Two wrongs don't make a right. Call the CO. Right now . . ."

Were it not for the platoon sergeant's even tone and unflinching gaze, Hansen might have pulled away and done what he wanted. But if Abbot could keep it together at a time like this—even after losing his wife—then the least Hansen could do was the same. "All right, Matt. All right. I'll call."

NEECH HAD HEARD the gunfire ahead, but it had only quickened his pace. He knew that if he hesitated, he wouldn't be able to go through with it.

Through with what?

He still wasn't sure. Was he going AWOL? Was he just walking away from it all?

Or was he really going after Keyman? His mind changed by the second.

Running felt good, though. Really good. He didn't care about the fires, the snow, the guilt. He just had to keep moving—toward what?

* * *

KEYMAN BURST INTO the shack, aiming his shotgun at two old women cowering in one corner. "Where are they? Where the fuck are they?"

The women shook their heads, then one muttered something.

He leveled his shotgun on her. "Where the fuck are they?"

The old woman pointed at the door. "Go away! Go away!"

Cursing, he stomped out of the shack, then kicked in the door of the next one, finding the small room with a tattered cot empty.

He whirled, shuddered.

It dawned on him: he'd been hearing gunfire from the alley, but his desire for payback had dulled his senses.

What was he doing?

He took off running for the alley, for his tank, for his men. He swore he would never abandon them again.

NEECH TRIPPED, CRASHED into the snow, and just lay there for a few seconds, breathing. He was about halfway to the river now. What would he do when he got there? He still didn't know. He had not gone after Keyman. He had obeyed the devil. He had . . . surrendered.

With his breath finally under control, he pushed up on his hands and knees, then glanced sidelong toward a row of demolished buildings.

Whoa. Two squads of enemy infantry were keeping tight to cover but shifting quickly down the street, heading for the platoon's position. Even if Hansen had already moved the tracks, they might still come under heavy fire since there wasn't much cover from the shacks out to the next barrier.

Neech dropped onto his gut, then crawled forward, turned around, and continued to observe the troops.

"If you don't come back, then you were right. Batman died for nothing."

Neech could return, warn the others, and maybe only he, Romeo, and Choi would know that he had left. He could even lie and say that he had searched in vain for Keyman. Of course he hadn't gone AWOL. Of course.

There was still time to save himself, but he just lay there, groping for an answer.

GATCH HAD OPENED his driver's hatch because he couldn't believe what he was seeing through the vision blocks. The stench immediately made him gag, and, a few seconds later, he pushed up on his elbows and vomited over the hull.

He closed his eyes and was back at the beach. He saw Jesus on his Harley, saw Dale Earnhardt Jr. lying in his shattered car as the waves swept in, threatening to carry him out to sea.

Why'd you have to let them die?

The Almighty rumbled over, pulled to a stop, and began speaking furiously in Korean.

"Gatch!"

Deac stood beside the tank, lifesaver bag on his shoulder. Gatch blinked again, as a wave of dizziness turned the world crooked, then back again. He wiped drool from his mouth and coughed.

"Your puke looks good compared to what I just saw," said Deac, his voice cracking, his eyes swollen with tears. "Dude, it's fuckin' horrible, man. Just horrible . . ."

"You know Morbid was real short," Gatch began, shaking his head over the irony. "He would've been out of here. Fuckin' Smiley. That guy was a character. And Webber . . .

God, he, uh, how can someone die like that?" Gatch slammed a fist on the tank, then stared up into the falling snow. "How could you let somebody die like that? Burned alive!" He broke down, slumped over the hull, and started crying.

"Shit, Gatch, come on. I'm the one who cries—not you. Come on, you fucking pussy."

Gatch looked up, brushed off the tears, and sniffled. "God's been trying to tell me something. I don't know what it is. I just don't know . . ."

"Deac, back up top to relieve Lee," Hansen ordered from his hatch.

"Yes, sir."

"Gatch?"

"I'm okay, LT."

"Good. Seal up. The first sergeant and the M88 are on their way."

"Ain't this a bitch," Deac said. "Tanks and PCs coming at us and firing . . . artillery and mortars going off everywhere . . . and our guys get whacked by civilians. What kind of shit is that?"

As Gatch sealed his hatch, he glanced up at his lucky Dale Earnhardt Jr. bumper sticker. Shaking his head, he began tearing it from the metal. The sticker hadn't kept him safe. Nothing had. Nothing at all.

ROMEO HAD DECIDED to cover for Neech. He had ordered Choi to move the tank forward, as Hansen had wanted. The lieutenant probably assumed that Neech was still on board.

However, if Neech didn't come back within the next few minutes, Romeo would be forced to tell Hansen because there was no way that just he and Choi could operate the tank. Sure, he could pick targets and fire rounds from the TC's position, but he would have to climb down and re-load the main gun after every shot, and that would take too much time.

"Red Three, this is Red Four, over."

"Oh, shit, Choi, Abbot's calling," Romeo said over the intercom. "What do I do now?"

"You talk, Sergeant. Tell him everything fine. Neech come back soon. I'm sure."

Romeo took a long breath before answering. "Red Four, go ahead."

"Who is this?"

"This is Red Three Golf, over."

"Where's Red Three?"

"Uh, he's, uh—"

"Right here, motherfucker," Neech said, sticking his head into his hatch.

Romeo breathed one of the deepest sighs of his life. "You piss me off, you know that?"

"I saw Keyman's track," Neech said, his voice dropping. "I thought they'd missed."

"They got him the second time. The whole crew's dead. Now get in here and talk to Abbot."

KEYMAN REACHED THE shack used by those two Molotov-throwing meatheads. He rushed alongside it, then headed into the alley. With a start he realized that Abbot and Neech had pulled their tanks about thirty meters ahead and that Hansen's tank was, for some reason, shielding his track.

Only a few civilians remained in the street, mostly the teenaged boys who didn't mind risking life and limb for a glimpse of the action. *Assholes.* He shouted to a few of them, gesturing that they take cover, but two flicked him the bird. He rushed on, nearing Hansen's tank.

"Hold it right there, Sergeant," Hansen yelled from his hatch.

That smell? Keyman took a few more steps, his view widening past Hansen's track.

He looked to his turret, to the lingering smoke, to the blackened bodies.

"No, no, no," he muttered, breaking into a sprint. "No. No fucking way! NO!"

He staggered up to the hull, gaping at the body lying back across the TC's hatch and the other jutting sideways from the loader's. "Webber? God damn it, Webber? Smiley? Morbid?"

Just then an M88 recovery vehicle came around the corner, followed closely by an M113, probably the first sergeant's.

Keyman climbed up onto the forward slope, went to the driver's hatch. Morbid lay in his seat, his face ghastly, inhuman.

With a terrible gasp, Keyman rolled back onto the hull, arms falling to his sides. He closed his eyes, feeling the snowflakes strike and melt on his cheeks.

They were all dead.

Since the beginning of the war, he had been having premonitions about dying. He had been trying to tell Webber that he needed to be ready. He had been resigned to what might happen, even glad about it. He knew that the ultimate way to best Hansen was to make the ultimate sacrifice, to die in battle like a glorious warrior, to become a legend among the men of First Tank.

He would be number one. He would be the best again.

Yet as lay there, beginning to comprehend what had happened, he realized that his premonition *was* coming true. He was dying. Inside. Now . . .

And they would remember him as the tank commander who had forsaken his mission and his men.

* * *

THE RECOVERY VEHICLE and the first sergeant's M113 were fast approaching, and Hansen needed to make sure that everyone—including Keyman—was good to go. As heartless as it sounded, the mission was not over just because they had taken casualties. Captain Van Buren had reminded him of that, and he had also implied that given the situation, the tank itself was more important than the crew. Getting it repaired and back in service was priority one. The company team needed to maintain combat power. Hansen hated what he was hearing, but he understood the CO's position, having to consider the big picture and a much larger number of men. He also remembered what he learned at an officer professional development session given by Van Buren last month. During the Yom Kippur War, every Israeli tank near the Suez Canal was knocked out by Egyptian AT fire. The Israelis recovered every one of their tanks, repaired them, and sent them back into battle. American forces on the peninsula would do no less.

"Sergeant?"

Keyman draped an arm over his eyes.

Hansen threw a look back at the recovery vehicle, then quickly dismounted and hustled up to Keyman's tank.

Remarkably, within those few seconds, his thoughts cleared, the proverbial lightbulb went off, and he knew exactly what he had to do. "Sergeant, come on," he urged the man. "Dismounts are moving up. You're riding with me as loader. I'm sending Deac over to Neech's track. You're going to fight my tank and let me fight this platoon."

Hansen had figured that showing Keyman downward loyalty would, at this most dire moment, really prove that he still respected the man, despite his mistake. In fact, he had every intention of downplaying the error—because he needed his best tanker in the fight. There was no way to prove whether or not Keyman's leaving had directly resulted in the deaths of his crew. If he had remained, he might have been killed, too. However, Hansen still did not condone the act; he merely understood it and would work around it until such time that he and the staff sergeant could have a long talk—the one Hansen had been waiting for since the day they had first met.

"Sergeant. Let's move!"

Keyman opened his eyes. "Fuck that. I'm not leaving my men."

"Yeah, you are—because we need you now." Hansen leaned onto the front of the tank. "Come on."

"You still want me in the platoon—after this? I'm a fuckin' murderer, man. A murderer . . ."

"Bullshit. You fucked up. But you're not a murderer. Come on!"

Keyman's breath grew ragged as he sat up, glanced back at the bodies draped over the turret. His voice came thin and small. "What happened?"

"More guys came from across the street. There was nothing Webber could've done."

"Yeah, but I could have—"

Small-arms fire ricocheted all over the hull, and Hansen grabbed Keyman, threw him to the ground. "Deac!"

As they began crawling back toward Hansen's track, Deac let his machine gun sing. He, along with Paz and Romeo, began putting fire on the row of shacks, as did the gunners aboard the M88 and the first sergeant's M113.

Hansen glanced back at Keyman to make sure he was still following. Though his expression was tortured, his cheeks wet, the staff sergeant was right there.

They reached the tank, and Hansen ordered Lee to suppress the dismounts with coax fire, buying himself and Keyman a few seconds to climb into the hatches after an unhappy Deac dismounted and charged off for Neech's track. Getting Deac away from Lee would give both guys a chance to cool off, yet another bonus of Hansen's plan to bring Keyman aboard.

"Red, this is Red One. Bravo section will fall back to secondary BPs now. I'll stay here to cover the M88 and the first sergeant's track. Move out!"

At first, seeing Keyman in the loader's hatch, gripping the 240 was quite an odd sight. But then the TC wiped his eyes and gave Hansen a stern nod.

He was at home, back in the fight. They both were.

CHAPTER
FIFTEEN

SINCE THEY WERE under fire and pressed for time, Keyman's tank, bodies and all, was being towed back to the Unit Maintenance Collection Point located well behind the battle lines. The supply sergeant would meet the tank there to perform mortuary affairs tasks, and the first sergeant would supervise from his M113. The battalion maintenance section at the UMCP would immediately address the disabled tank and either repair it or rape it for parts. If the tank could be repaired sooner than others at the UMCP, then a crew with a busted tank would transfer their bags, refit it, and roll out to fight.

Hansen guided Gatch into their secondary position. He had picked an alley beside a two-story building about fifty meters behind the third obstacle south of the train station. That particular barrier ran across the railroad tracks, over MSR 3, and extended out toward White Platoon's position. The railroad lay off to their right, with the creek running just south of them. Again, a collection of small hotels and stores sandwiched between apartment houses lay off to their west, blocking their view of the river. Once again, they had a clean line of sight up the tracks to the barrier and beyond. With all the restricted terrain, both the railroad bed and MSR 3 still remained the likeliest avenues of approach for PCs and armor.

The secondary battle position was not as well-fortified as the first because of available time. Some junk had been pushed into piles at the ends of the longest alleys, and engineers were waiting with M9 Armored Combat Earthmovers and other equipment to seal up the barricades and other smaller obstacles as Hansen and the others maneuvered into position. The ACEs, which resembled really mean-looking bulldozers, could breach berms, set up antitank ditches, prepare combat roads, bust through roadblocks, and establish access routes at water obstacles.

Captain Van Buren notified everyone that the company team had lost one tank from Red platoon, one from White, and one Bradley from MECH. The commander of the engineer company in direct support of First Tank was now being ordered to convert his combat engineer squads into their doctrinal secondary role as infantry. Each squad had an M113 with mounted .50-caliber machine gun, and they already carried the same weapons as an infantry squad. They would be, Hansen knew, really pissed off at the North Koreans for having to convert to their secondary role. They would employ every piece of C-4 at their disposal, and Hansen would not put it past one of those sappers to drop a whole building on a North Korean tank or squad. They would also strap ten to fifteen pounds of C-4 or TNT to the underside of manhole covers and blow them when enemy tanks, PCs, or unsuspecting dismounts drew near. One of the "old salt" sappers might even set up a Fougasse weapon, which was a drum filled with jellied gasoline and detonated with a white phosphorous grenade. The improvised explosive device was like a stationary Molotov, only much bigger, and it could be aimed down or across a street. There was no doubt in anyone's mind that the North Koreans would pay dearly once those demolition-happy engineers were set free on the city.

As soon as Gatch stopped the tank, they all dismounted and got busy unloading the nearby pallets of ammo and other supplies dropped off by the TF support platoon. Neech and Abbot had already procured what they needed. Keyman worked hard and fast, back to his old machine self. He had refused to speak to the chaplain, saying they were too busy and he would get to that later. He probably wouldn't, but that was all right. Every man had his own way to grieve, and the loss was hitting Hansen himself. Again. Webber, Smiley, and Morbid were Keyman's crew, but they were members of Hansen's platoon, and he felt as hollow as Keyman did. But he had to deal with it—especially when those bastards from the north were still coming in droves to kill them all. At times he balled his hands into fists, shuddered in fury, and imagined gunning down every scumbag who thought a Molotov would solve his world's problems.

They finished resupplying, which included having the fuel tank topped off, then went back over the M1 with a fine-toothed comb, looking for damage as the enemy mortar and artillery fire picked up, falling well short of their BP. The enemy would make their adjustments soon. But much to Hansen's relief, he learned over the company net that Apaches were finally in the air and beginning to target armor and PCs from long range. He wasn't concerned about being robbed of glory anymore. Let those pilots go nuts. He was completely exhausted. Ready to go home.

Back in the turret, he checked his cell phone again, wondering when Karen would send her next message. He had finally stolen the time to read the last one, just after he and the rest of the platoon had crashed through the warehouses.

She was still pushing south but being chased. She had seen some "guys" get killed but hadn't elaborated further.

Gooseflesh ran across Hansen's shoulders as he pictured her out there, stumbling through the snow. Her strength to go on had amazed him, yet he had an awful feeling that she had sent her last message.

BOTH KEYMAN AND Neech had left their tanks and had abandoned their crews . . . the only difference was that Neech had been given a second chance, and those were as rare as mercy on the battlefield. To ignore one was to ignore God.

Thus, Neech needed to seize the moment. Seize the day. Seize his life. The more he thought about how Keyman must feel, the more he realized that even if the war was wrong, even if Batman's death seemed meaningless, Romeo, Choi, and now Deac still counted on him, still believed in him. When it came down to the nitty-gritty, you didn't fight for ideological or political reasons. You fought to keep yourself and your brothers in arms alive. You fought to preserve the good memory of those who were gone. You fought to honor all of them. You had to look forward, not back.

Unfortunately, it had taken Keyman's mistake and the deaths of three men for Neech to finally realize that.

He had joined the Army because he had felt like a fat bastard with no will power. And now, for the first time since Batman's death, the great weight, the one he had thought would bury him, was being lifted—not by anyone else, but by himself.

"Red One, this is Red Three. We're REDCON-1 over."

"Roger, Three. Stand by."

"Hey, Deac?"

The loader leaned forward and raised his brows. "Yeah, Sergeant?"

"I know you've dismounted a lot these days, and I'm sure the FIST will keep us updated from his OP, but—"

"Yeah, I know. Get the old boresight spaghetti cord and go have a peek around the corner."

"You read my mind."

Neech had parked his tank near two intersecting alleys. To engage PCs and armor, he would need to move up, turn left, and fire, yet they still needed to maintain good observation of their sector. Deac would take the twenty-five-foot-long spaghetti cord and use it to remain connected to the intercom system. He could venture out as far as the gun tube's muzzle and have enough slack to glance up the alley, toward the railroad bed, and send back reports.

Wearing a somewhat disgruntled expression, the loader started out of the tank

"Hey Deac?" Neech called. "Glad to have you."

Deac shrugged then spoke in a deadpan. "Y'all got a good crew here. Makes up for being so ugly. It must suck, though, never getting laid."

"Yo, speak for yourself, redneck." Romeo grabbed his crotch. "Every time you spank the monkey, I get a real woman. Do the math."

"Sergeant, how do you work with this guy?" Deac asked.

Neech considered the consequences of not working with Romeo. He smiled tightly.

ABBOT SHOULD NOT have removed the wedding photo from his wallet. He should not have sat there at his station, eyeing it for over five minutes. He should not have been feeling sorry for himself when the bell for round two was about to ring.

But it was too late to punish himself for that weakness. He had always been the rock of the platoon, the foundation.

He wanted to continue in that role, the one that best suited him, but knowing Kim was gone made him feel like crying one moment, screaming at the top of his lungs the next.

When Hansen had wanted to now down that entire row of shacks, possibly killing more civilians, Abbot had been a breath away from agreeing. Vengeance made you feel good. It set everything right with the universe. When they took from you and you didn't take back, something was wrong. There was no justice. Worse, that feeling of being violated, being taken advantage of, made you hungry, and in combat only blood would satisfy the craving.

He couldn't deny it anymore. Kim was out there, lying in the snow, dead. He would never shake off that image. And now he felt sorry for his crew. He was about to take them on a ride the likes of which they had never seen. He would no longer suppress his anger the way he had at the first BP. He would bring his most merciless game to the battle. Athletes might call that their "A" game. He called it his "D," as in death to the enemy. *Death to them all!* He just hoped his crew and his tank could keep up with him.

"Hey, Sergeant?" called Paz. "Didn't you hear the lieutenant? He's on the radio. Wants to know if we're set. You didn't check in."

Abbot slipped the photo into his inner breast pocket, tapped it twice, driving it against his heart. If he died, she would be with him. "Thanks, Paz. Red One, this is Red Four. We are REDCON-1, over."

KAREN DID NOT remember collapsing in the snow and consequently had no idea how long she had been lying there. She had realized that she was giving up and had been profusely apologizing to Jack and to Reese for doing so.

"I think she's dead," came a voice from the darkness. "Frozen right there."

She couldn't open her eyes. Whether they were frozen

shut or what she didn't know. She tried to speak, but lips felt glued together. There was nothing there.

A pressure came at her neck. "Hey, she's still got a pulse. Sergeant! Sergeant!"

They spoke English. They were Americans. She was being rescued. If only she could feel something, but she was just too tired, too stiff, too empty.

"What's that in her hand? She's got a death grip on it."

"It's a cell phone."

She remembered Reese. *He's still out there!* Her mind screamed to tell them. She tried to open her mouth again. *Oh my god.* If she couldn't speak, he would die out there.

"She's trying to talk."

"Ma'am, we're from the 2nd MP Company, and we're here for you. You got some frostbite. Don't say anything."

Someone was approaching. Heavy footfalls. "All right, guys, what do we . . . holy shit. Is this her? The one they told us about?"

"Could be, Sergeant."

"Damn, what are the odds of that?"

"She stayed close to the road. That's what saved her."

"All right. Let's get her out of there."

Karen was overwhelmed with emotion. Tears wouldn't come, but that was okay. They lifted her from the snow and carried her toward the thrumming of engines.

THE SKY ABOVE TDC had become a gray tarpaulin spanned by threads of light as both sides traded mortar and artillery fire; as Hellfire missiles, 2.75" rockets, and 30-mm chain-gun rounds streaked overhead toward the enemy brigade; and as TOWs and Javelins launched by Renegade platoon burned up and across MSR 3, reaching out toward the water tower. Explosions rumbled and flashed, lit up the mountain peaks, then died, leaving fires and smoke behind.

Having Keyman in the turret was one of the best decisions Hansen had ever made as a platoon leader. If you would have told him twenty-four hours ago that he and the pain in the ass would be operating out of the same tank, he would not have believed it. If you would have added that he had been the one who had made that decision, he would have called you insane.

Yet now Hansen could concentrate much more on the enemy's movements, on helping Abbot call in FA and mortar fire, and on fighting the platoon the way he knew best. Keyman and Lee would service the targets, and there was no more deadly pair in all of First Tank.

While the Apaches had taken out over a dozen PCs and perhaps at least as many tanks, Team Cobra's work was hardly finished. Scouts, the GSR team, and REMBASS indicated that more armor and dismounts were still pushing south, while FSO Yelas continually updated them regarding the enemy's movements toward their sector. Oh, yes, there would be plenty of targets to go around.

"Two moving tanks!" Keyman shouted. "Coming right down the tracks."

"With PCs behind them," added Hansen. "Red, this is Red One. Tanks, PCs. Frontal. Alpha, fire sabot. Bravo, HEAT. Tophat, tophat! Fire!"

Three M1A1 Abrams main guns rocked the neighborhood, and then, almost instantly, two VTTs burst into impressive fireballs, while the sabot fired from Hansen's tank slammed into the nearest T-62. While its turret hadn't blown off, black smoke and fire shot up from the hatches and hull. The tank veered radically to the left and stopped. One crew member leapt from the vehicle, flapping his arms as flames rolled up his shoulders.

Hansen nodded with satisfaction. "Target!"

"See the guy on fire?" Keyman asked as he loaded the next round. "He thought he could fly."

The second tank's gun tube winked orange, even as Hansen yelled, "They fired! Driver, move—"

Gatch shifted them back and left, tucking them more tightly against the building as Hansen finished the command and cement began dropping hard onto his hatch. He glanced through his vision blocks, saw a gaping hole in the wall above. "Fuckin' sabot just missed us!"

But Keyman and Lee were too busy to hear, grunting their fire commands. As Hansen turned around, Lee had identified the tank and was squeezing his triggers: "On the way!"

The main gun drove Hansen into his seat, but he didn't mind. He jammed his face into his extension and watched a beautiful sight: one T-62 lighting up the frozen ground. "Target!"

"You're damned right," cried Keyman. He kneed open the ammo door, grabbed the next round, and loaded the main gun. "HEAT loaded, loader ready!"

Dozens more explosions sounded from across the tracks and MSR 3. White Platoon's guns were beating the big drum, as were Renegade's chain guns. Hansen also assumed that Captain Van Buren was setting off the MOPMS as dismounts and more armor approached.

The engineers had already kicked their plans into high gear as well, dropping at least two buildings lying closest to the railroad bed, debris spilling near the tracks. Those graduates of the twenty-eight-day-long Sapper Leader Course had worked hard for their sapper tabs, and those patches with the word *SAPPER* spelled out in an arc were proudly displayed above the unit patches on their left shoulders. They were most definitely putting all that vigorous, fast-paced, and specialized training to good use.

In short, the enemy was getting pounded by all of Team Cobra's assets.

"Troops to the front!" cried Gatch.

Lee had them in his sights. "Identified."

"Gunner, coax troops!" Keyman ordered.

Two squads of dismounted infantry were moving through

the burning barricade, keeping tightly to the embankment along the left side of the tracks. Lee's glowing bead of fire sent them scattering like field mice over the embankment, while others got hammered and punched to the snow.

"Target," said Hansen. "Looks like you got four. The others went over the side. Put a little more fire up near the barricade. I see movement over there." While Lee complied, Hansen got on the net, calling FSO Yelas and requesting immediate suppression of the dismounts.

Lee continued firing as Keyman started into his hatch, drawing Hansen's attention. "Hey, man, where are you going? Stay down!"

"We got bad guys on the roof!" Keyman popped his hatch and seized his machine gun.

In the meantime, a small pickup truck careened through an opening in the barricade, with North Korean troops piled in the back and two more hanging over the sides, firing wildly ahead. Hansen strained for a better look at the truck. He took a deep breath and swore.

The sick bastards had tied two women and a little kid to the hood of the vehicle, using them as human shields. Now he knew why the driver's head jutted from the side window.

Just then, mortars dropped into the sector ahead, sending quakes through the ground and shrouding the barricade in smoke pierced by flying shrapnel.

Lee ceased fire and began screaming something in Korean.

Hansen gaped at the man. "Lee!"

The gunner put his hands on his hips and leaned back from his controls.

"Lee, take out that fucking truck!"

SERGEANT LEE CLOSED his eyes. He had seen and done enough. He would not kill innocent women and children. Not for anyone—especially the Americans. He

had had a feeling it might come to this. And he was prepared.

A WARY GLANCE through his vision blocks had
proved critical for Keyman. Three civilians with Molotovs
bolted stealthily along the rooftop, heading north from the
far corner in an effort to get above the tank.

Setting his teeth, Keyman blew apart the concrete
ledge, the good old 7.62-mm rounds achieving far better
penetration than the wimpy 5.56-mm ammo in the M4
carbines and M16s. Debris and dust mixed with the falling
snow as rounds drilled the first attacker, knocking him
backward across the rooftop, his Molotov slipping from
his grip.

The second guy wound up for the pitch like some pathetic big-league wannabe. Keyman told him to keep his
day job with a salvo that opened his chest while the burning tracer turned his fastball into a bomb that went off
point-blank, draping him in a chute of fire.

Bastard number three, who had been standing too close
to his buddy, got caught in the burst. A second later, his
Molotov exploded as he writhed, staggered forward, then
plummeted over the side. He thumped onto the frozen
ground, rolled onto his back, then grew inert, hungry
flames eating his flesh.

There it was. *Three for three. An eye for an eye.* Maybe
it solved nothing, but it felt damned good. Okay, so these
were the same damned people whose city he was trying to
save. *You can't have it all, can you?*

Keyman swung the gun forward, heard Hansen screaming at Lee, flicked his gaze up, squinted, saw a pickup
truck bouncing toward them, guys jammed in the bed,
muzzles flashing. Small arms bit into the nearby concrete,
struck, and caromed off the tank's hull. The Koreans had
tied something to the hood of the truck, maybe sandbags.

He thought of lifting his NVGs for a better look through all the blowing smoke and snow.

"Lee, coax that truck!" Hansen repeated.

"I WILL NOT! I WILL NOT!"

Holy shit, that damned KATUSA was having a major meltdown, and Hansen wasn't the type of TC who would boot the gunner in the back of his helmet until he cooperated. That was old-school and more Keyman's style. Thus, for a split second, Keyman was torn between dropping into the turret to confront Lee and shooting at the truck.

But that second passed, and Keyman had always been a trigger-happy motherfucker. While trying to engage troops with an M240 in a pintle mount wasn't the easiest or most accurate way to deliver death and destruction, the pickup truck was within five hundred meters and his tracers reached out to nine. He got busy, realizing only after his third burst that the Koreans had tied people to the hood. *Oh, shit.* He had already killed them and had sent the guys in the flatbed running. His next thirty rounds hit the truck's fuel tank, and the vehicle shit a ball of fire. He got off the machine gun and lowered himself into the turret.

Sergeant Lee stood at the loader's station. He had drawn his pistol and now aimed it directly at Keyman's head.

"**SPARROW! MOVE UP** to the end of the alley," Abbot ordered, his pulse racing. They had just destroyed an enemy T-62 and had narrowly avoided RPG fire by rolling forward then turning hard down a cross street.

"Loader, battlecarry HEAT."

"Yeah, all right," Paz moaned.

"Come on, Paz, keep up with me!" Abbot glared at the loader, who slammed the next round home.

"Okay, Sparrow, turn right and stop!"

They rounded the corner and faced north, hugging the side wall of a clothing store, mannequins dressed in the latest chic outfits frozen behind the windows. Abbot surveyed the sector; they had a clean shot up the tracks.

"Two PCs," said Park, his voice steady as he identified the enemy armor rolling down the railroad bed.

"Near one first," Abbot cried.

Park should have immediately replied, "Identified." He did not.

Abbot tensed. "Gunner!"

"Got him! Identified."

"Up!"

"Fire!"

"On the way!"

Abbot didn't wait for the shot to either hit or miss the PC. If the round missed, Park's head would roll, and the KATUSA knew that. Instead, Abbot focused on Paz, who was moving as though he had just emerged from a coma. "God damn it, Paz, load that fuckin' gun! Come on! Come on! Come on!"

"I'm loading it, Sergeant!"

Abbot glanced into his extension. "Target! Second PC!"

"Identified."

Nothing from Paz.

"Loader!"

"Up!"

"Fire!"

"On the way!"

"If you people cannot keep up with me, then . . ." Abbot sat there, panting. *Oh, God.* He hated himself. His guys were dragging because they were exhausted. Really exhausted. He checked the extension. "Target!"

Normally, Paz would've drawn upon his keen sense of black humor, and Sparrow would've echoed the sentiment, but Abbot had intimidated them into silence. What had he done?

"Troops! Troops to the front," boomed Park.

"Gunner, coax troops!"

* * *

KEYMAN REFLEXIVELY STEPPED back, his eyes never leaving the pistol tucked into Lee's palm. The KATUSA's hand was shaking as though he'd just had a caffeine overdose. Because there had never been any real love lost between Keyman and the KATUSAs serving with First Tank, he felt all the more outraged that one of them had the balls to point a weapon in his direction. "What the fuck is this?"

"Move aside! I'm leaving! I won't fight this war anymore!" Lee's eyes were bloodshot, his cheeks red, his breath broken. He extended his arm, pushing the pistol closer to Keyman's head.

"Aw shit, we got no time for this." Keyman had been ready to die, and he'd be damned if some KATUSA would get the pleasure of offing him. "Jesus H. Christ, Lee, what are you, a fucking spy? A coward?"

"MOVE ASIDE! KEYMAN, I WILL SHOOT YOU!" Lee's hand shook more violently, his face now growing so tight that Keyman thought the little guy would have a coronary right there.

"Sergeant Lee, secure that weapon," Hansen said calmly, having drawn his own pistol.

"No!"

Hansen wasn't used to hearing that word. "SECURE THAT WEAPON!"

Shit, if the lieutenant was actually stupid enough to fire inside the turret, then all was lost. Then again, Lee didn't give a shit if he fired; he was wanting out.

"Troops to the front!" Gatch announced from his driver's station.

Keyman held his breath. They were wasting time with the fucking KATUSA's crisis of conscience while the bad guys altered their positions and set up for the kill outside.

No, he couldn't take any more nonsense. "What're are you going to do?" he asked Lee. "Go crying to your North Korean brothers, you spineless motherfucker! You traitor! You coward! You fuckin' coward!"

In fact, Lee was beginning to cry. And through his tears, he began wailing in Korean, the words like machine-gun fire, the spit flying.

He's going to shoot me, Keyman thought, then he regarded Hansen, pleading with his gaze.

"I say again," interrupted Gatch. "Troops to the front! I see two guys with RPGs! I see an AT team!"

REALIZING THAT ABBOT was engaging troops, Neech knew it was up to him to destroy the next three VTTs that were rolling in through the smoke. They stood out brilliantly in the thermals, or as new loader Deac might put it, "like a 'coon family in the glare of headlights."

Neech and Deac were getting along famously. Somehow, in the middle of all the shit, they were having fun. Neech felt almost giddy now as Deac, who had returned to the turret just in time from his OP at the street corner, reloaded the main gun and Romeo identified the nearest PC.

Deac was right there with his, "Up!"

"Fire!"

"On the way!"

Boom!

The enemy VTT and its crew experienced American firepower at its most accurate and audacious. You had to love it! "Target!"

All of them, even Choi down in the driver's station, sang together, "We will . . . we will . . . rock you!"

Freddie Mercury and the rest of the rock band Queen might have been critical of their rendition of the classic rock song, but Neech didn't care.

They serviced the next two targets with the speed and efficiency of men who had been born and bred to fight.

Hooah!

"LEE, LISTEN TO me. You don't have to fight," Hansen assured the gunner, forcing a calm back into his voice. "But don't leave this turret. Just stay on board and secure that weapon. We'll settle this later."

"Red One, this is Black Six, over."

Hansen glanced at the radio. *Shit.*

"Red One, this is Black Six, over."

Captain Van Buren's voice drove him into a panic. "Lee, I'm ordering you for the last time to secure that weapon!"

The KATUSA shook his head, then faced Keyman. "MOVE ASIDE!"

Hansen decided that forcing the issue wasn't worth it. They had a battle to fight. "Key, let him go."

"Are you crazy?"

"I said, let him go!"

Rolling his eyes and snorting, Keyman began to move.

But then he seized Lee's wrist with one hand and tried prying the pistol free with the other.

"Don't fire!" yelled Hansen.

Lee, a Tae Kwon Do expert, easily wrenched free, pistol still in his grip. He whirled, cocked the pistol's hammer, and was about to shoot Keyman point-blank in the chest.

There was no doubt in Hansen's mind that Sergeant Lee Yong Sung would take Keyman's life.

CHAPTER
SIXTEEN

WHAT HAPPENED NEXT took a mere two seconds, but they were the longest two seconds of Hansen's life.

He knew that a HEAT round was sitting in the breech and that the gun tube had been lowered to an almost level position when engaging their last target.

And he saw that Lee had unknowingly placed himself directly in the path of recoil.

Hansen had no other choice. He reached out and *BOOM!* fired the main gun from his position.

The breach block recoiled some two feet like a piston, the heavy metal slamming mercilessly into Lee's lower chest. The KATUSA dropped to the floor like an aft cap, pinkish blood frothing at his mouth and nose. His ribs had been broken, his lungs punctured. Beginning to wheeze, he dropped the pistol, clutched his throat, coughed once, then grew still.

Hansen and Keyman looked at the dying man, in shock, in awe—until Gatch broke their trance. "RPG guy is on one knee. He fired!"

Keyman started for the gunner's station. Hansen turned, looked into his extension, just as the RPG exploded over the tank's front slope.

Gatch was panting like a mad dog. "God damn it!"

"And God will," said Keyman. "By using us!"

With that, Hansen's former wingman put the coax to work, Z pattern after Z pattern taking down troops. Then, for a few seconds, he held his fire.

Taking the cue, Hansen popped his hatch and used the extinguisher to put out the flames on the hull. The grenade had struck some of the tank's heaviest armor, shattered one of the headlights and bent one forward flap, but overall it had done minimal damage, thank God.

Gatch's voice cracked as he reported: "Sagger incoming!"

One of those North Korean antitank teams had managed to unload their suitcase, set up their missile, and get the wire-guided sucker into the air.

"Driver, move back!" Keyman shouted before Hansen could give the same command.

The tank rolled parallel with the building, but Gatch got too close, shaving off some sheet metal and cinder blocks before they reached the end. "Turn left!" Keyman ordered.

An echoing boom sounded just ahead as the Sagger struck the front side of the structure and detonated, leveling a good portion of the wall and heaving enough gray smoke to fill the entire alley. Whatever was inside began burning furiously.

Keyman shifted to the loader's station, opened the ammo door, grabbed another HEAT round, and slammed it into the breach block. "HEAT loaded, loader ready!"

"Gatch, move out!" Hansen ordered.

They tore ass down the intersecting alley, between several two-story apartment houses, then Gatch braked as they neared the next corner. A series of dull thuds rocked the turret.

"They're jumping down from the roof!" Keyman grabbed his pistol, went up into his hatch.

Lee was lying in a heap, his chin now covered in blood. Hansen knew he shouldn't have glanced back. "Oh, God." He choked up and was about to bury his face in his hands when Keyman's pistol cracked.

With a surge of fear and adrenaline, he burst up top, his own Beretta clenched in his fist, a full mag of fifteen rounds waiting to be emptied.

Keyman screamed "Die!" and fired at a North Korean grunt mounting the rear deck, striking him in the heart. Another grunt came up behind the first, and once more, Keyman yelled "Die!" and fired again. He continued with that chant, as though issuing orders to the attacking troops—and they all obeyed. Keyman made sure of that.

Hansen joined the fray, shooting two grunts clinging to the front of the tank, hitting one in the cheek, the other in the groin. They both fell away. "Gatch, hit the gas!"

The tank lurched as Gatch accelerated. Hansen tossed a look up to the rooftop. Two troops were propped on their elbows, one with a rifle, the other with an RPG, both about to open fire. He shot the RPG guy, then ducked behind his open hatch as a salvo of automatic fire ripped over the hull.

"Get on the two-forty! Get the guys on the roof," Hansen told Keyman. "I'll get them here!"

Keyman holstered his Beretta, grabbed the M240, and pivoted, bringing the machine gun to bear on the rooftop troops, even as Gatch throttled up once more.

Meanwhile, Hansen almost laughed at the last NK grunt, who was actually swinging from the gun tube like a monkey. One shot ended his acrobatics.

Keyman leaned over and raised his palm. Though Hansen hardly felt jovial about all the killing, he couldn't help but return the high five.

"Do we kick ass or what?" the staff sergeant asked as they descended into their hatches.

"Yeah." Hansen's voice began to break up as he regarded the fallen gunner. "I killed him. I killed Sergeant Lee."

"You killed a deserter. And you saved me. In my book, that's a win-win."

"We should've let him go. Why did you try to stop him?"

"Because it ain't right. Because I figured he'd shoot me anyway. And because I thought I could take him."

"Did you think about disobeying my order?"

"Hey, man. I know what you're trying to do. Don't blame this on me. You did the right thing. No one forced you."

It took a moment, but Hansen recognized the truth in Keyman's reply. "You're right. But if the situation were reversed—"

"I would've killed him in a heartbeat. Because I love you."

Hansen almost smiled. "How can you joke now? Fuckin' wiseass."

"Red One, this is Black Six, over."

"You'd better get that," Keyman warned. "The captain ain't as forgiving as you are."

"No," Hansen answered slowly. "He's not. Black Six, this is Red One, go ahead."

"Red One, a little FYI to lift your spirits. A squad from the 2nd MP Company found your girlfriend. I say again, they found your girlfriend. Apparently some corporal helped her escape during the ambush. He didn't make it, but she did."

"Roger, Black Six, and thank you." An incredible feeling of relief seized Hansen's body, loosening all of his muscles and making his eyes grow watery. "Thank you so much."

Men from the 2nd Military Police Company and the Yongsan-based 8th MP Brigade were probably livid that they had failed to protect the dependants during a simple escort mission and had been out in force looking for them and their fellow MPs. Hansen hoped he would get a chance to personally thank the men who had found Karen.

In the meantime, he gave the captain a quick situation report that included food, fuel, and ammo status as well as the loss of Sergeant Lee. Van Buren acknowledged and went on to say that they now had close air support and that the mechanized brigade's remaining PCs, artillery pieces, and reserve tank company were under heavy attack by the Apaches and Warthogs. He expected that the battle would be over in a matter of hours but was still ordering everyone to remain in secondary BPs to rearm and refit. The engineer company was going to combine with the Renegade Platoon and the Korean National Police to cordon off and search the area for more North Korean dismounts. The KNP would also arrest any more unruly civilians and launch investigations into who threw the Molotovs. The 56th ROK Homeland Reserve Division to the south was well-prepared to deal with any enemy troops that slipped past friendly forces. ROK reinforcements were going to conduct a passage of lines north to replace the decimated 5th ROK Armor Brigade and clear/secure the Camp Castle area. Rumor had it that Team Cobra's next mission would be a counterattack to regain territory and inflict more damage upon the enemy.

Hansen directed Gatch to the end of the next alley, then they turned to face the railroad tracks once more. The snow had all but stopped, replaced now by literally hundreds of fires coughing up white, gray, and black smoke from both sides of the sector. Walls of fire spanned several streets, where as expected some of the locals had poured and lit their cooking oil to thwart enemy soldiers and local looters. Buildings struck by mortar and artillery fire were still crumbling as the fires within raged out of control.

Keyman had dragged Lee's body away from the breech,

removed the gunner's helmet, and used it to cover the KAT-USA's face. "I never trusted him," the staff sergeant commented, lifting his chin at the body.

"I did. But things change."

Hansen kept a steady watch through his extension, while Keyman did likewise at the gunner's station, though he would jump to the loader's to reload the main gun as needed. Most of the engagements were now happening well north of the target reference points, up along the river, out toward Camp Castle.

THE TIDE WAS coming in, and Specialist Rick Gatch shielded his eyes from the sun, squinted, and watched as the tank tracks began to vanish in the surf.

Behind him, Jesus was sitting on his Harley, revving the engine, and Dale Earnhardt Jr. was walking barefoot up the beach, ignoring the frantic calls of his pit crew as they tried to pull his demolished car from the surf.

Gatch took a deep breath, wiped the sand from his eyelashes, then marched up to Jesus. "Are we going to talk?"

"See them?" Jesus asked in Korean, but now Gatch understood.

"The tracks?"

"Yes. Two paths, side by side. I walk with you—not for you. But you have to keep up with me. Can you?"

"I don't know. What do you want me to do? Turn into some kind of preacher? A screaming bastard on cable with a bad toupee? I'm not sure that'd work out."

"It's your life."

"Yeah. And sometimes I feel bad about the way I've lived it. I was hoping you could help."

"You're learning to speak my language. That's good."

"You speak Korean? That's weird."

"No, I speak the truth, but sometimes it's hard to understand."

"Yeah, it is. Can I tell you something? I don't like myself anymore."

"That's okay. I don't like you either." Jesus smiled, revealing a gold tooth.

Gatch shook his head. "God's a wiseass. Of course. How else would I imagine him?"

"So we got a deal? You clean up your act, walk with me, and—"

"And what? You'll keep me alive?"

"Are you alive?"

Gatch snorted. "You're God. You ought to know."

"It's all very complicated."

"Are you saying I'm going to die?"

The Almighty pursed his lips. "I'm sorry, Gatch, but you're already dead."

"No way. Bullshit. I don't remember anything. I didn't feel anything . . ."

Jesus consulted his Rolex. "It happened very fast."

"But I didn't want to die. I wasn't ready. I wasn't right with you. Now I'm fucked."

Jesus sighed deeply. "Maybe I can cut you some slack— but if I spare you, then you have to get right with me."

Gatch opened his mouth to reply, but Jesus spun around, popped a wheelie, then drove up, into the sky, where he vanished into the sun as Dale Evans's "Happy Trails" blared from a gigantic boom box made of clouds.

Chills rocked so powerfully through Gatch's body that for a moment he thought he had plunged through the ice and was sinking in the river.

"I'll do it," he muttered, glancing around the confines of his driver's station as he kept a white-knuckled grip on the T-bar. He relaxed, took a huge breath. "I'll get right with you. I promise."

"Hey, Gatch, you all right?" the lieutenant asked.

"Yeah, I'm good. But LT, when we get a chance, can I talk to the chaplain?"

"You don't need to ask."

"Thank you, sir."

"You sure you're all right?"

"Praise God, I am."

Gatch wasn't lying. Life and death were no longer random and meaningless. He had a reason, a purpose. And he couldn't wait to share his revelation with Deac.

ABBOT RUBBED HIS sore eyes for the hundredth time, threw his head back, then groaned. He glanced down at Park, who had been sitting quietly since hearing that Sergeant Lee had been killed. They still didn't know the details of Lee's death, but Abbot was well aware that Park and Lee had been close friends, and Lee's loss was hitting the gunner pretty hard, despite his stoic reaction. Paz was sitting in his chair, eyes closed, singing softly to himself, and Sparrow was keeping watch from his driver's station.

Clearing his throat, Abbot straightened, took another long breath, then spoke softly. "Guys, two things: I'm sorry . . . and I'm proud. I pushed too hard. I know it. It's just . . . this has been the longest couple days of our lives. But we made it. That's what it's all about. And that's all an old fart like me can ask for. You guys are the best crew I've ever had."

"And you're a pretty good TC yourself," Paz said. "But Sergeant, don't apologize. What happened to Keyman's crew? That could've happened to us. It didn't—thanks to you."

Sparrow put in his two cents from the driver's hole: "Paz is right, Sergeant. We're all counting on you to get us home. And you will. Hooah!"

Park echoed just after the driver.

"Thanks, guys." Abbot proffered his hand to Paz.

But the loader extended both arms. "Can I get a hug?"

Abbot winced. "Don't push your luck."

* * *

THE FIRST SERGEANT came in his M113 to pick up Lee's body. Keyman and Hansen carefully handed over the KATUSA, then Hansen felt compelled to further explain what had happened. The first sergeant listened attentively, then simply saluted and rolled off.

"You okay?" Keyman asked as they settled back into the turret.

"It's strange hearing that from you, the most selfish motherfucker I've ever met."

"I'll take that as a compliment. And in case you're wondering, no, I'm not all right. I'm fucked up."

"I wasn't wondering."

"That's 'cause you're fucked up, too."

"Definitely."

Keyman's eyes grew distant before he took a seat at the gunner's station to begin his next scan. "You know, I keep turning around and hearing Webber bitching in my ear. Fuck . . . the way he died . . . on fire . . . burned alive. I can't even—"

Hansen raised a hand. "That's enough."

Keyman gave a deep sigh of exhaustion. "Well, at least you got an upside. You didn't lose your woman."

With a slight nod, Hansen reached into his pocket, withdrew his cell phone. He began thumbing in another text message: I'M OKAY. I LOVE YOU. WILL TRY TO CALL SOON. When he finished, he asked Keyman, "You got a girlfriend?"

"Nope."

"Maybe you should get one."

"Nah. That's a ride no woman'll take. Even the whores hate me—but not as much as I do."

"Hey, we're not the first guys to lose people, and we sure as hell won't be the last. They got through it. So will we."

"Who knows."

"Give it some time."

"Won't matter. I'll never forgive myself. But that's all right. I don't want to. We can't forget these guys . . . what they did here . . . and what I failed to do."

Hansen closed his eyes, watched the faces flash in his mind's eye: Batman, Webber, Smiley, Morbid, and Lee.

The turret fell silent, and neither of them spoke. A few minutes later, Hansen rose into his hatch, and a small miracle occurred: his cell phone rang. The caller ID read KAREN.

"Hello?"

"Oh my God, Jack?"

"Yeah, sweetheart, I'm here. I was going to send you a message. I can't believe you got through."

"Listen, I know you can't talk."

"I have time to say this: *I love you.*"

"I love you, too, Jack. I do. But listen, they're taking me to Pusan. I'll call again from there." She began to sob.

"Baby, don't cry. I'll be okay."

"Me, too."

"I'll talk to you soon."

"Bye, Jack."

Hansen thumbed off the phone, then whispered a prayer that she would be all right.

Keyman rose into the loader's hatch, a puzzled look on his face. "Was that Pizza Hut? Did that fuckin' driver get lost again? I told him to go past all the fires, past that blown-up building, and make a left at the pile of dead guys. What's the problem?" He gave an exaggerated snort. "That punk just lost his tip."

"You're a sick bastard."

"Hungry, too."

"I can't believe you're still wishing for that pizza."

"Give me a big slice and a beer. Best medicine there is. My dad's always saying that."

"Pepperoni?"

"Shit, yeah."

"So when we're done saving the world, I'll hook you up—my treat."

"Thanks, but I'll buy. I'm not trying to kiss your ass. I just need to pay." Keyman slid down into the turret.

Hansen raised his NVGs and surveyed their battle position. The distant booming died down, and for a few moments the "land of the morning calm" became just that. He wished he could appreciate the time to recover, but so many emotions tugged and gnawed at him that he wasn't sure what to feel. He was ecstatic that Karen had made it, but he felt guilty because Abbot's wife had not. Yes, he had saved Keyman's life, but he had been forced to kill a talented and honorable man who had simply experienced too much. No wonder so many combat veterans turned to stone after leaving the battlefield. When pried, some would say, "Maybe after a few beers I'll tell you that story" or "I'm sorry, but I never talk about that."

One thing Hansen knew for sure: what he had seen and done on the battlefield had changed him, and those changes might take a lifetime to fully reveal themselves. Maybe that was okay. That was who he was now—confident and insecure, brave and scared, overjoyed and sad. He vowed to feel it all, live through it all, for the sake of his men. And his country.

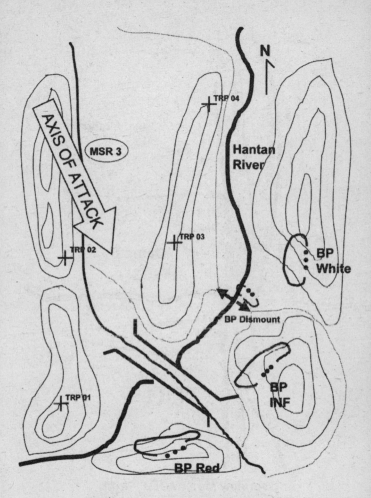

**Map of Low-water Crossing
by Major Mark J. Aitken, US Army**

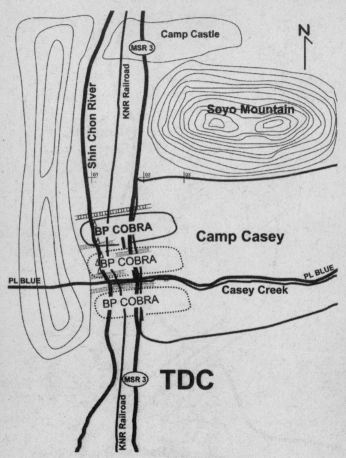

Overview Map (MOUT Fight)
by Major William R. Reeves, US Army

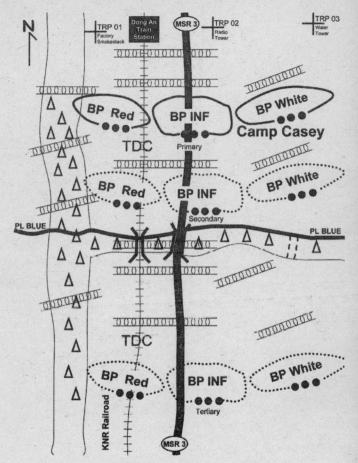

Detailed Map (MOUT Fight)
by Major William R. Reeves, US Army

GLOSSARY

Compiled by Shawn T. O. Priest,
Major William R. Reeves, and Captain Keith Wilson

A

AA avenue of approach; assembly area

AAR after-action review

Abatis an obstacle created by felling trees or poles in an interlocking pattern across a road or path facing towards an approaching enemy; can be reinforced with wire, mines, and direct and indirect fires

ABF attack by fire (position)

ACE armored combat earthmover

ACR armored cavalry regiment

active air defense direct defensive action taken to destroy attacking enemy aircraft or missiles

ADA air defense artillery

adashi Korean: *uncle,* GI slang for any adult male Korean

ajima Korean: *aunt,* GI slang for any adult female Korean

A/L administrative/logistics

ammo ammunition

AO area of operation

AOI area of interest

AOR area of responsibility

AP antipersonnel

APC armored personnel carrier

APFSDS-T armor piercing, fin stabilized, discarding sabot-tracer (ammunition); a high-velocity inert projectile of depleted uranium also known simply as a sabot round

AR armor

ARTEP Army Training and Evaluation Program

ASAP as soon as possible

ASLT POS assault position (abbreviation on overlays)

AT antitank

ATGM antitank guided missile

ATK POS attack position (abbreviation on overlays)

AVLB armored vehicle-launched bridge

AXP ambulance transfer point

B

BAS battalion aid station

BDA battle damage assessment

BDE brigade

BFIST The M7 Bradley Fire Support Team Vehicle is the latest combat vehicle provided to armor, mechanized infantry, and armored cavalry FIST teams. A highly modified Bradley Fighting Vehicle, it contains an assortment of radios, computers, optics, and other accessories for target location and fire support coordination on the modern battlefield.

BFV Bradley (infantry) Fighting Vehicle, equipped with 25-mm cannon and TOW launcher, battle-proven in both Gulf Wars

BHL battle handover line

BII basic issue items

BMNT begin morning nautical twilight; time of day when enough light is available to identify the general outlines of ground objects

BMP Boyeveya Machina Pyekhota; Russian-designed infantry personnel carrier; used by the North Korean People's Army

BN battalion

BP battle position

BRDM Russian-designed four-wheel-drive amphibious light recon vehicle used by NKPA

BSA brigade support area

BSFV Bradley Stinger (missile) Fighting Vehicle, modified to fire the Stinger for antiaircraft defense

BTR Soviet-designed wheeled APC used by NKPA

C

CA civil affairs

cal caliber

CAM chemical agent monitor

CAS close air support

CASEVAC casualty evacuation

CBT combat

CBU cluster bomb unit

CCA close combat attack; attack helicopter aviation in support of ground combat operations

CCIR commander's critical information requirements; composed of EEFI, FFIR, and PIR

CCP casualty collection point; preestablished point to consolidate casualties and prepare for evacuation

CDR commander

CEV combat engineer vehicle

CFC Combined Forces Command

CFL coordinated fire line; a line beyond which conventional fire support may fire at any time within the zone established by higher headquarters without additional coordination

CFV cavalry fighting vehicle

CIP combat identification panel

claymore a command-detonated directional fragmentation mine

CMD command

cml chemical

CMO civil–military operations

CO commanding officer; company

CO TM company team; company-sized combat element that includes attachments such as engineers, aviation, air defense, etc.

coax coaxially mounted (machine gun)

COLT combat observation and lasing team

CP command post; checkpoint

CS combat support

CSM command sergeant major

CSS combat service support

CTCP combat trains command post

CVC combat vehicle crewman

CWS commander's weapon station, from which he can engage targets with the main gun, coax, or the M2HB .50-cal machine gun

D

DA Department of the Army

DD, DoD Department of Defense

DMZ demilitarized zone; space created to neutralize certain areas from military occupation and activity

DOA direction of attack (abbreviation on overlays)

DP decision point

DPICM dual-purpose improved conventional munitions

DPs displaced persons

DS direct support

DS/R direct support/reinforcing

DTG date-time group

E

EA engagement area

ECWS extreme cold weather system

EEFI essential elements of friendly information; critical aspects of a friendly operation that, if known by the enemy, would compromise, lead to failure, or limit success of the operation

EENT end evening nautical twilight; there is no further sunlight visible

ELINT electronic intelligence

EPLRS enhanced position locating and reporting system

EPW enemy prisoner of war

ETAC enlisted terminal attack controller; enlisted Air Force personnel assigned to provide close air support/terminal guidance control for exercise and contingency operations, on a permanent and continuous basis

EW electronic warfare

F

1SG first sergeant

FA field artillery

FAAD forward area air defense

FASCAM family of scatterable mines

FDC fire direction center

FEBA forward edge of the battle area; foremost limits of area in which ground combat units are deployed

FFIR friendly force information requirement; information the commander and his staff need about the forces available for an operation

FIST fire support team

FIST-V fire support team vehicle

FLE forward logistics element

FLIR forward-looking infrared radar

FLOT forward line of own troops; a line that indicates the most forward positions of friendly forces at a specific time

FM frequency modulation (radio); field manual

FO forward observer

FPF final protective fires

FRAGO fragmentary order

FROKA First Republic of Korea Army; mission is to defend the eastern section of the DMZ. The VII ROK Corps defends the eastern coastal invasion route, and the VIII ROK Corps is responsible for the coastal defense of Kangwon Province.

FS fire support

FSCL fire support coordination line

FSE fire support element

FSO fire support officer; special staff officer responsible for helping to integrate all mortar, FA, naval gunfire, and CAS fires into the maneuver commander's combined arms plan

FSSG fire support sergeant
FTCP field trains command post

G

GEMSS ground-emplaced mine scattering system
GPS global positioning system; gunner's primary sight
GS general support
GSR ground surveillance radar; efficient system for tracking enemy troop and vehicle movement in near-zero visibility

H

HE high explosive
HEAT high explosive antitank (ammunition)
HEMTT heavy expanded mobility tactical truck; provides transport capabilities for resupply of combat vehicles and weapons systems
HHC headquarters and headquarters company
HMMWV high-mobility multipurpose wheeled vehicle (Hummvee); the able replacement for the military Jeep.
HPT high-payoff target; a target whose loss to the threat will contribute to the success of an operation
HQ headquarters
HUMINT human intelligence
HVT high-value target; assets that the threat commander requires for the successful completion of a specific action

I

IAW in accordance with
ICM improved conventional munitions
ID identification
IED improvised explosives device
IFF identification, friend or foe
IFV infantry fighting vehicle
IN infantry
IN (M) mechanized infantry
IPB intelligence preparation of the battlefield

IR infrared; intelligence requirements
IVIS intervehicular information system

J

JAAT joint air attack team
Javelin a shoulder-fired, fire and forget antitank weapon capable of killing any modern armored vehicle
JCATF joint civil affairs task force
JDAM Joint Direct Attack Munition; a GPS guidance package attached to conventional bombs giving aircraft a highly accurate, all-weather, autonomous precision bombing capability
JPOTF joint psychological operations task force

K

KATUSA Korean augmentee to the United States Army; a ROK soldier attached to US units to augment manpower and provide cultural and linguistic knowledge to formations; a program that has been in place since the beginning of the Korean War
KIA killed in action
klick one kilometer
KNP Korean National Police; the ROK paramilitary police force
KSG Korean Security Guard; ROK contractors charged with guarding the gates and walls of US Army camps in the ROK

L

LBE load-bearing equipment
LBV load-bearing vest
LD line of departure; a line used to coordinate the departure of attack elements
LNO liaison officer
LOA limit of advance; a terrain feature beyond which attacking forces will not advance
LOC line of communications
LOGPAC logistics package
LOM line of movement
LP/OP listening post/observation post

LRF laser range finder
LRP logistic release point
LT lieutenant (2LT, second lieutenant; 1LT, first lieutenant)
LTC lieutenant colonel
LTG lieutenant general

M

MACOM US Army Major Command
MAJ major
MANPADS man-portable air defense system
MBA main battle area
MECH mechanized
MEDEVAC medical evacuation
METL mission-essential task list
METT-TC mission, enemy, terrain (and weather), troops, time available, and civilian considerations (factors in situational analysis)
MG major general
MI military intelligence
MICLIC mine-clearing line charge
MLRS multiple launch rocket system
Molotov cocktail crude incendiary weapon which consists of a glass bottle filled with flammable liquid
MOPMS Modular Pack Mine System; a man-portable box containing antitank and antipersonnel mines that can be initiated by remote control, scattering the mines in a semicircular pattern
MOPP mission-oriented protective posture; consists of seven levels of preparation for chemical or biological attack, MOPP READY being the least protected and MOPP 4 the most protected
MOUT military operations on urbanized terrain; fighting in cities
MPAT multipurpose antitank (ammunition)
MRE meals, ready to eat; also referred to by troops as meals rejected by everyone, brown bags, or bag nasties
MRS muzzle reference system; a system enabling tank crews to

adjust the gun alignment quickly in combat to compensate for gun tube droop caused by the heat from firing

MSR main supply route

MST maintenance support team

N

N-Hour an unspecified time that commences notification and outload for rapid, no-notice deployment

NAAK nerve agent antidote kit

NAI named area of interest; point or area through which enemy activity is expected to occur

NBC nuclear, biological, chemical

NCO noncommissioned officer

NCOIC noncommissioned officer in charge

NCS net control station

NEO noncombatant evacuation operations

NFA no fire area; an area into which no direct or indirect fires or effects are allowed without specific authorization

NGO nongovernmental organization

NKPA North Korean People's Army; the North Korean Army

NLT not later than

NOD night observation device

NVG night vision goggles

O

OAK-OC obstacles; avenues of approach; key terrain; observation and fields of fire; and cover and concealment (considerations in evaluating terrain as part of METT-TC analysis)

OBJ objective

OIC officer in charge

OP observation post

OPCON operational control

OPD officer professional development; mentoring sessions usually given to junior officers by more experienced middle or senior officers to educate them on subjects not taught at the military school house

OPLAN operation plan
OPORD operation order
OPSEC operations security
OPTEMP operational tempo

P

passive air defense all measures, other than active air defense, taken to minimize the effects of enemy air action
PCC pre-combat check
PCI pre-combat inspection
PEWS platoon early warning system
PFC private first class
PIR priority intelligence requirements
PL phase line; platoon leader
PLL prescribed load list
PLT platoon
PMCS preventive maintenance checks and services
POL petroleum, oils, and lubricants
POS position
POSNAV position navigation (system)
PSG platoon sergeant
PSYOPS psychological operations
PVT private (buck)
PV2 private

R

R3P rearm, refuel, and resupply point
RAAM remote antiarmor mine
recon reconnaissance
REDCON readiness condition
REMBASS remotely emplaced battlefield area sensor system; a set of seismic/acoustic, magnetic, and infrared sensors
REMS remotely employed sensors
retrans retransmission
RFL restrictive fire line; line between two converging friendly

forces that prohibits direct or indirect fires or effects of fires without prior coordination

ROE rules of engagement

ROK Republic of Korea

ROKA Republic of Korea Army

ROM refuel on the move

RP release point

RPG rocket propelled grenade; a Soviet-designed shoulder-fired weapon; deadly to both personnel and armored vehicles

RTE route

S

S1 adjutant (US Army)

S2 intelligence officer (US Army)

S3 operations and training officer (US Army)

S4 supply officer (US Army)

SALUTE size, activity, location, unit identification, time, and equipment (format for report of enemy information); abbreviated format is SALT or size, activity, location, and time

SAM surface-to-air missile

SAW squad automatic weapon

SBF support by fire (position)

SFC sergeant first class

SGM sergeant major

SGT sergeant

SHORAD short-range air defense

SINCGARS single channel ground/airborne radio system

SITREP situation report

SITTEMP situational template

SOFA Status of Force Agreement; an agreement that defines the legal position of a visiting military force deployed in the territory of a friendly state

SOI signal operation instructions, a code book for encrypting and decrypting coded messages

SOP standing operating procedure

SOSR suppression, obscuration, security, and reduction (actions executed during breaching operations)

SP start point

SPC specialist

SPOTREP spot report

SROKA Second Republic of Korea Army; is responsible for defending the rear area extending from the rear of the front area to the coastline, and consists of an army command, several corps commands, divisions, and brigades. The Second Army has operational command over all army reserve units, the Homeland Reserve Force, logistics, and training bases located in the six southernmost provinces.

SSG staff sergeant

STAFF smart target activated fire and forget (ammunition)

T

TAA tactical assembly area

TAC or **TAC CP** tactical command post

tac idle tactical idle (speed), keeping the engine at high RPMs for maximum efficiency of hydraulic systems and electrical output

TACP Tactical Air Control Party; USAF personnel attached to maneuver units to conduct terminal control of Close Air Support (CAS) where friendly and enemy ground units are in close proximity to each other

TC tank commander

TCP traffic control post

TDC Tongduch'on; a city north of Seoul containing several of the US Army's 2nd Infantry Division camps and the majority of the division's ground combat units

TF task force

TIS thermal imaging system

TM team

TOC tactical operations center

TOE table(s) of organization and equipment

TOW tube-launched, optically tracked, wire-guided (missile)

TRADOC US Army Training and Doctrine Command

TROKA Third Republic of Korea Army; South Korea's largest and most diversified combat organization, is responsible for guarding the most likely potential attack routes from North Korea to Seoul—the Munsan, Ch'orwon, and Tongduch'on corridors

TRP target reference point

TSOP tactical standing operating procedure

TTP tactics, techniques, and procedures

U

UAV unmanned aerial vehicle

UMCP unit maintenance collection point

UN United Nations

UNC United Nations Command

USFK United States Forces, Korea

V

VIC 3 vehicle intercommunication

VTT North Korea–designed tracked APC; similar to the BMP-1

W

WARNO warning order

WIA wounded in action

WP white phosphorus, also called "willie pete"

X

X-Hour an unspecified time that commences unit notification for planning and deployment preparation in support of operations not involving rapid, no-notice deployment

XO executive officer

Z

Zulu (time reference) Greenwich Mean Time

ABOUT THE AUTHOR

Pete Callahan is the pseudonym for a popular author of fantasy; science fiction; medical drama; movie, television, and computer game tie-ins; and military action/adventure novels. His heavily researched work has been sold worldwide and translated into Spanish, German, French, and Japanese. He invites readers to contact him at armoredcorps@aol.com.